GETTING THE UPPER HAND

Cas suspected the other Regulators were watching, so he palmed his .44 and walked directly up to the vigilante.

"The hell's scratchin' at you, mister?" the man demanded, taken by surprise.

The surprise, however, had just begun. Cas squared his shoulders, lowered his center of gravity, and raked upward at a forty-five-degree angle with his open right hand, swinging straight from his heels so he put cold will and hard muscle behind the effort. The heel of his palm caught flush under the point of the vigilante's chin and snapped his head back hard. His feet actually lifted up from the boardwalk, and then he slackened and went down flat on his face.

Until Cas made his lightning attack, another vigilante, this one with a goiter on his neck and sporting a .45 caliber Army revolver, had been loitering nearby and paring his fingernails. The moment Cas dropped his comrade, Yancy saw the man start to draw.

"Cas!" Yancy bellowed. "On your left."

Cas spun on his heel as he coiled for the draw, slapping leather and verifying his target. Despite getting a late start, Cas cleared leather while his opponent only had his gun halfway out.

"Might's well finish what you started," Cas told him. "Skin it

D0957050

Ralph Compton

Deadwood Gulch

———

A Ralph Compton Novel
by John Edward Ames

A SIGNET BOOK

SIGNET
Published by New American Library, a division of
Penguin Group (USA) Inc., 375 Hudson Street,
New York, New York 10014, USA
Penguin Group (Canada), 90 Eglinton Avenue East, Suite 700, Toronto,
Ontario M4P 2Y3, Canada (a division of Pearson Penguin Canada Inc.)
Penguin Books Ltd., 80 Strand, London WC2R 0RL, England
Penguin Ireland, 25 St. Stephen's Green, Dublin 2,
Ireland (a division of Penguin Books Ltd.)
Penguin Group (Australia), 250 Camberwell Road, Camberwell, Victoria 3124,
Australia (a division of Pearson Australia Group Pty. Ltd.)
Penguin Books India Pvt. Ltd., 11 Community Centre, Panchsheel Park,
New Delhi - 110 017, India
Penguin Group (NZ), cnr Airborne and Rosedale Roads, Albany,
Auckland 1310, New Zealand (a division of Pearson New Zealand Ltd.)
Penguin Books (South Africa) (Pty.) Ltd., 24 Sturdee Avenue,
Rosebank, Johannesburg 2196, South Africa

Penguin Books Ltd., Registered Offices:
80 Strand, London WC2R 0RL, England

First published by Signet, an imprint of New American Library,
a division of Penguin Group (USA) Inc.

First Printing, November 2006
10 9 8 7 6 5 4 3 2 1

THE IMMORTAL COWBOY

This is respectfully dedicated to the "American Cowboy." His was the saga sparked by the turmoil that followed the Civil War, and the passing of more than a century has by no means diminished the flame.

True, the old days and the old ways are but treasured memories, and the old trails have grown dim with the ravages of time, but the spirit of the cowboy lives on.

In my travels—to Texas, Oklahoma, Kansas, Nebraska, Colorado, Wyoming, New Mexico, and Arizona—I always find something that reminds me of the Old West. While I am walking these plains and mountains for the first time, there is this feeling that a part of me is eternal, that I have known these old trails before. I believe it is the undying spirit of the frontier calling, allowing me, through the mind's eye, to step back into time. What is the appeal of the Old West of the American frontier?

It has been epitomized by some as the dark and bloody period in American history. Its heroes—Crockett, Bowie, Hickok, Earp—have been reviled and criticized. Yet the Old West lives on, larger than life.

It has become a symbol of freedom, when there was always another mountain to climb and another river to cross; when a dispute between two men was settled not with expensive lawyers, but with fists, knives, or guns. Barbaric? Maybe. But some things never change. When the cowboy rode into the pages of American history, he left behind a legacy that lives within the hearts of us all.

—*Ralph Compton*

Chapter 1

A lone horsebacker, astride a chestnut gelding with a white mane and blazed forehead, slowly appeared like a wavering mirage out of the scant-grown hills to the west. He followed County Line Road through the former cotton-plantation country nestled between the Trinity and Sabine rivers of southeastern Texas.

Cas Everett had taken the old Shawnee Trail route south from Kansas City, turning east at Fort Worth. From long habit, his eyes stayed in constant sweeping motion, like those of veteran payroll guards. Despite knowing that Quanah Parker and his Comanches were powerless wards up north on a Fort Sill reservation, Cas still expected to hear their shrill eagle-bone whistles. Until recently the "red raiders of the plains" had virtually owned the Texas Panhandle and raided into the east with impunity. Now only the stubborn Apaches to the southwest still resisted captivity.

Cas switched hands on the reins to rest his arms. Overhead, sparrow hawks circled high in a cloudless sky as blue as a gas flame. He watched a quick-darting prairie falcon swoop down on an unsuspecting squirrel that had wandered from the shelter of an oak grove. The squirrel screeched in fright that

quickly turned to pain. Abruptly Cas felt his good
mood become apprehensive.

"Got me a God fear, Comet," he said aloud, and
the chestnut pricked his ears. "But no good reason
for it. They'll be all right, eh?"

Cas bucked the usual frontier tradition of not nam-
ing horses. By necessity he often went weeks without
talking to a fellow human being, and months between
meetings with friends. As Cas saw it, either a solitary
man talked to his animals now and then or he ended
up not quite right in his upper story.

He noticed new homesteads dotting the areas
where Comanche raids had once thinned them out.
When he was still a shirttail brat, there was no
settlement within a day's ride of the Everett farm.
Now there was Iron Springs three hours east of
their place. True, the same circus tent that served
as a saloon and dance hall turned into a church on
Sunday, and the sidewalks were only rammed
earth, but Cas figured you had to trot before you
could canter.

A gaunt man driving a big manure wagon approached from the opposite direction, yellow-
brown clouds of dust trailing him like a plumed
tail. Cas nudged Comet out of the narrow road.

"Mr. Kitchens," he greeted the older man as the
odiferous wagon jounced and rattled past, "how
are you?"

The farmer drew back on the reins, staring as he
tried to place the young man on the chestnut. Cas
wore new-riveted Levi's and a boiled shirt with a
leather vest, a low-crowned black hat with a flat
brim, soft calfskin boots with plenty of heel for
grabbing stirrups. A nickel-plated, ivory-gripped
Smith & Wesson .44, double action, rode in a hand-
tooled holster.

"How am I? Still poor as a hind-tit calf, that's

how," Josiah Kitchens finally replied. "You must be Cas Everett—nobody else around here needs two rifle scabbards."

Cas ignored the barb. Old man Kitchens had been born with a pinecone lodged up his sitter.

"How's the farm?" Cas asked him.

"I'm still sharecroppin' for the grasshoppers." The old man squinted as if puzzled. "Decided to come home, huh?"

"Just for a visit. Been a while since my folks laid eyes on me. Hope they still recognize me."

Kitchens gave him a searching look. "Well, got to git. You take care, boy."

Without another word, the old farmer clucked to his dray team and the wagon lumbered off. Cas sat his horse for a minute, puzzled. Old man Kitchens had always been a queer fish, but he must be getting worse. Or else Cas' reputation around here was sinking even lower and nobody wanted to be seen with him.

However, a half hour later, he met another traveler, who was more than willing to share human company. Cas overtook a conveyance heading in the same direction he was, a colorful drummer's wagon covered with gold scrollwork and painted screens. A middle-aged man in a straw boater and a baggy sack suit occupied the bench seat. As Cas drew alongside on the left, the drummer removed his straw hat and fanned himself with it, revealing heavily oiled hair parted in the middle to the nape of his neck.

"Howdy, stranger," he called out in a suave baritone. "This heat would peel the hide off a Gila monster, hey? And we're only in late May."

Cas nodded, reining in to keep pace with the wagon. "We got two seasons down here: hot and hotter than hell."

The drummer laughed. "Glad you came by. I'm pure people starved. Neusbaum's the name. Hiram Neusbaum from Shreveport."

"Pleased to meetcha. Call me Cas."

The drummer's studious eye swept over the man on the chestnut. He proffered a bottle from under the seat. "Old Tanglefoot?"

Cas shook his head. "Much obliged, but my ma will smell it on me and raise the dickens. She's got Methodist feet."

"Religion's a fine thing—in other people." Neusbaum tipped the bottle, then wiped his mouth on his sleeve. "Say, Texas *is* mighty big, all right. This is my first trip down here, and I've never seen so much land and sky."

"Room enough to swing a cat in, my pa likes to say."

Cas glanced at the black-handled Remington the drummer wore in a shoulder rig.

"I hear very few men in Texas live to old age," the drummer explained, seeing Cas eye the gun.

"You hear right, I'd say. The Comanches are subdued, but since the war, this state's crawling with curly wolves armed to the teeth."

Again the drummer's curious eyes raked over the tall young man. "I'm not one to nose a man's back-trail, but you don't 'pear to be from these parts."

"Born and bred," Cas assured him. "Nowadays, though, you might call me itinerant."

Cas had come to manhood during the bloody era following the Great Rebellion, a war that created plenty of easy-go killers in Texas. Resolute and defiant, he had been determined not to let himself or his family fall prey to the ruthless murderers—Comanche and white—marauding through postwar Texas. After toiling long hours in the traces to coax crops out of the dry earth, he practiced endlessly behind the barn with his crippled father's old single-action Colt. By dint of sheer will and hard work he honed his aim to lethal perfection and eventually developed a draw one newspaper wag up in Kansas described as "quicker than eyesight."

However, no man could outshoot a drought. When the Everetts' hardscrabble farm eventually went under, only seventeen-year-old Cas could save his family. Forced to leave home in search of wages, he began a ten-year frontier odyssey that, against his will, secured his place in the pantheon of storied Texas gunfighters: teamster, express rider, railroad guard, he, with his Smith & Wesson .44, earned a wider reputation with each hardcase who pulled down on him and got himself planted. However, he truly earned the unwelcome moniker of "gunfighter" as a bounty hunter, running to ground the hardest of the hardcases—the killers of no-church conscience few others would pursue.

"Well, friend," Neusbaum called above the rattling of his tug chains, "have you finally come home to husband the land?"

"I'd rather be caught in ready-to-wear boots."

"Why, tilling the soil is noble work."

"Well, then, guess I'm just a commoner," Cas admitted. "I walked behind a plow for five seasons, and all I saw was the hind end of a nag. Got so I was hoping for a Comanche attack to liven things up."

"Who can blame a young fellow? The world is changing rapidly. First it was the telephone. They say Hayes will be the first president to have one in the Executive Mansion. No doubt his lovely Lemonade Lucy will use it to deliver teetotal lectures."

Neusbaum laughed at his own joke, but Cas only grinned politely. In Texas a gentleman could deride the president, but never his wife.

"And now," Neusbaum prattled on, "they've just invented an electric light although I can't see such a dangerous thing ever catching on."

"I've heard of telephones," Cas said, "never seen one though. Can't see the need of it, what with the telegraph. That electric light might catch on though—no smell."

"Yessir, a rapidly changing world," Neusbaum pontificated as if Cas hadn't spoken. "Only a few years ago the red aboriginals were still terrorizing civilized people. Now Slightly Recumbent Gentleman Cow, known to the vulgar masses as Sitting Bull, is selling his autograph at two bits a pop. Don't it beat the Dutch? Geronimo, meantime, is on the run in Mexico, living on lice and fleas. Custer would be proud of soldier blue."

Neusbaum took the reins in one hand and used the other to rummage through a burlap bag near his feet. "Speaking of Geronimo, could I interest you in some truly unique doorstops? These were Apaches."

He produced two sun-bleached, eerily grinning skulls. Someone had painted satirical messages on them. SAFE ON THE RESERVATION AT LAST, proclaimed one. NOBLE, SAVAGE, AND DEAD, boasted the other.

"They're funny," Cas admitted. "But it's the kind of funny that makes me feel guilty for laughing. More of Ma's influence, I expect."

Undaunted, the drummer reached into the wagon behind him and produced a dark blue bottle. "Sir, you look like a gentleman who's seen the elephant. It's around the eyes, mostly, and the calm air about you. I would not hornswoggle a man of your caliber, not by a jugful."

He handed the bottle up to Cas. "You will hear of many cure-alls, but *this* is the only proven medi-

cal panacea known to man. Mixer's Cancer and
Scrofula Syrup. Only one dollar per bottle. Cures
cancers, tumors, abscesses, ulcers, fever sores, goiter, catarrh, scald head, piles, rheumatism, and all
blood diseases."

"How does it know which one to go after?" Cas
joked, eyeing the bottle from a skeptical face.
"Anyhow, I believe in helping a man earn his living. I'll take it."

Cas paid with an Indian head gold dollar. Neusbaum eyed his clearly bulging chamois money
pouch. "Ah, carrying a pocket full of rocks, I see.
Care to see something in the way of a hernia truss?
Or perhaps Dr. Doyle's new weight system to
straighten the spine? Too much time in the saddle
can curve the backbone permanently."

"Like to help you, Mr. Neusbaum, but I do indeed live in the saddle and have very little room
for frivolous purchases."

Cas was about to bid the drummer good day and
move on. For days he'd been anticipating the plea-
sure of showing up at home unannounced. And not
only did Comet require feed and a rubdown, but
Cas required his mother's hot cornpone and back
ribs. On the trip down from Kansas City, he'd had
little besides hardtack, dried fruit, and canned
beans supplemented by the occasional greasy
rabbit.

However, Neusbaum's next question delayed
him. "I notice your cutaway holster. Are'n'cha
afraid your gun might fall out while you're riding?"

"Never has," Cas replied, hoping he'd buried
the topic.

"Fancy pearl grips, too," the drummer added
quickly.

Cas grinned in spite of his irritation at the man's
nosiness. "Dime novel writers call them pearl-

gripped, but they usually mean ivory-handled like mine. Mother-of-pearl would slip."

Neusbaum seemed to finally achieve enlightenment. "Friend, I'm not very good at grabbing on to a man's handle the first time he gives it to me. Might I ask your name again?"

"Caswell Everett. I answer to Cas."

"Everett," Neusbaum repeated woodenly, sunburned face paling.

"Mean something to you?" Cas demanded.

"Absolutely nothing. Never even been down here before."

Despite the man's denial, Cas noticed a sudden change in his leisurely manner. Neusbaum slipped a watch out of his fob pocket and thumbed back the cover. "By the horn spoons! Here I am jawing away like an auctioneer when I have an appointment to keep."

At first Cas attributed the drummer's behavior to sudden recollection of the notoriety Cas never asked for. A moment later, however, he remembered old man Kitchens and the searching look the cantankerous farmer gave Cas when he mentioned his folks.

Twice now . . .

"Steady, old son," Cas whispered when his hands began trembling. "They're all right."

A little insect prickle of alarm moved up his spine. By now Hiram Neusbaum had grabbed the whip from its socket to gig up his team, but such flight was unnecessary. With a sharp "*Hi*-ya!" Cas touched his spurs to Comet and they were off at a gallop.

Chapter 2

Just south of a low, pine-covered mound called Morgan's Hill, Cas left County Line Road, following twin ruts that led past Yancy Carlson's farm to the Everett place. His mind was a confused riot of thoughts and fears, of guilt and regrets.

He had no solid proof anything was even wrong, just a premonition that turned his stomach into a ball of ice. Cas was too shaken to even spare a glance when Comet tore past Yancy's hardscrabble farm. Instead, his inside eye saw his careworn parents, his plucky kid brother, David, and sweet twin sisters, Janet and Jeanette, on the verge of young womanhood and pretty as four aces.

"They're just fine," Cas told himself, wanting hard to believe it. "Hell, the Comanches are long gone and this area is peopling up. There's electric lights coming soon, cryin' out loud."

The Everett homestead lay in a teacup-shaped hollow, the house blocked from view by a windbreak of dense pines. Cas drew back on the reins, slowing Comet to a trot. His pulse throbbed in his ears, and his armpits broke out in sweat.

"It's too dang quiet," he told his horse.

That was just the beginning of the ominous clues. He spotted no one in the surrounding fields, which had been plowed but were starting to go to weeds. New cattle pens stood empty, and a stray dog was sleeping on the hide flap serving as well cover. No chickens were foraging for corn in front of their coop—his mother sold as many as ten dozen eggs a day to neighbors, though in starving times she gave away more than she sold.

Sudden fear pinched Cas' throat shut. Comet was bridlewise, and Cas had only to lay the reins on whichever side of the neck he needed to go. He flipped them to the left side, and they started up a path that led through the pines.

"God in whirlwinds," Cas whispered when they eased out of the pines. Shock gripped his senses, and he was forced to grip the saddle horn with one hand when the world around him seemed to spin crazily.

The long-familiar home of his youth, the solid plank structure built by his father the same year Cas was born, 1850, was now a heap of charred rubble. Cas gazed at it in numb confusion, praying to wake up from this unspeakable nightmare, praying his people got out.

Comet had been trained to stop when his reins touched the ground so Cas wouldn't need to bother so much with hobbles. He threw them down now and dismounted, walking slowly forward.

The enormity of the loss made Cas dizzy, and he fought down the urge to vomit. Even before the 1862 Homestead Act made the Everett claim legal, his father had cleared and tilled this land. Always a hard and uncomplaining worker, even after a Comanche's sheet-iron-tipped arrow seriously damaged the muscles of his left leg. Cas thought, *Pa protected his family from warpath Indians and raiding Mexicans, and even the Panic of Seventy-three. And by God he protected them from this fire.*

"Ma?" he shouted, gazing around for some temporary shelter they might be using. "Pa? Anybody here?"

No answer except the wind soughing in the pines. The lonesome sound moved up the bumps of Cas' spine like a feather. Suddenly unsure, he slid the riding thong off the hammer of his six-shooter.

Reluctant, yet duty bound, he walked slowly forward to survey the ruins of his past in closer detail. The mud-daubed chimney and flagstone hearth survived, though carpeted with soot. So did the cast-iron cookstove, and a few sections of plank flooring, covered with new linoleum Cas had shipped from Kansas City.

A scorched corner of a magazine page survived, one of the Currier and Ives prints his mother so carefully clipped and collected. But no sign of the walnut sofa with spool-turned legs or the slat-backed rocker of Shaker design, his mother's favorite.

In his agitated state at seeing the ruined dwelling, Cas hadn't even glanced toward the wind-polished knoll about fifty yards behind the house. He did so now, and his blood seemed to stop and flow backward in his veins when he spotted five wooden crosses outlined against the deep blue sky.

"God in heaven," he breathed, "make me strong."

Cas felt his calves go weak as water and a painful clenching in his stomach. With wooden reluctance, he started toward the small, round hill, knowing what five crosses had to mean, yet praying against all odds this was not what it seemed.

He discovered five fresh graves awaiting him, each marked by a simple but well-made wooden cross bearing the name of an Everett: Ansel, Dorothy, David, Janet, Jeanette. There were no years of birth, only the year of death: 1878. His knees came unhinged and Cas sank to the earth. Out of the throbbing center of his physical hurt, a sob jolted his body. It tore at his throat, and hurt him coming out. For a moment, there was a hot trembling in his eyeballs as everything bent and blurred.

But Cas had survived the travails of life through discipline and stoicism. He swiped a sleeve over his eyes.

In his grief he paid no attention to his surroundings. The hearty, basso profundo voice spoke from a respectful distance behind him. "I hope you got my letter, Cas. I sent it to your hotel in Kansas City."

Cas pushed to his feet and turned around to watch his neighbor slide down from a big dobbin, a gentle farm horse.

"Never got it," Cas replied, swallowing to find his voice. "I don't spend much time there."

Cas stood an even six feet without his boots, but Yancy Carlson overtopped him by at least four inches. He wore heavy, ankle-high work brogans stained by mud and manure. The big Swede's weather-rawed face peered out from shaggy blond hair cropped raggedly with tin shears. The emigrant from the Minnesota prairie was ten years older than Cas and spoke with only a slight trace of his parents' old-world accent. When his young bride died in childbirth, cut off from the midwife by a vicious winter blizzard, he swore off cold weather forever and headed to southeast Texas.

"When did it happen?" Cas said, struggling to control his voice.

"Three weeks ago today."

"Right before I headed south from Ellsworth," Cas said quietly, thinking out loud. "If I'd come home before I flushed out those two train robbers for the Missouri-Pacific . . ." He trailed off, unable to bear the thought.

"Cas boy," Yancy said, his tone apologetic, "we got us an undertaker's parlor in Iron Springs now, and you know how your ma's church would expect a Christian burial. But, Cas, the bodies . . . oh, Jerusalem! They just had to be buried here. I made crosses and pine coffins for each one, and before the dirt went in, I prayed my soul out for them. Besides, it seemed right to let them rest here."

"You did everything just right. At least you were *here*," Cas added bitterly. He paused, debated the question, then decided he should know. "You say all of them were burned past recognition?"

Yancy looked down at his work-callused hands. "None of them died in the fire, Cas."

The younger man visibly started. "Didn't die in— Yancy, you're taking the long way around the barn."

"The fire was started a-purpose in the middle of the night," Yancy announced bluntly. "They were shot as they ran out. Shot repeatedly, and then the bodies was terribly mutilated and left for carrion. That's why I buried 'em here. Oh, the butcher's bill was steep! Some sights get stuck on a man's eyelids."

Yancy carried his constant companion, a double-ten express gun with both barrels sawed off to ten inches. The gun could turn solid wall into a window. He raised it up in one hand.

"What good is this smoke pole?" he asked bitterly. "I slept right through all of it."

Cas stared at each cross, unable to believe what he was hearing. "Who?" he demanded. "*Who* did this?"

"That's got me treed, yah shoor. Whoever they was, it was professional killers. You'll catch a weasel asleep before you sneak up on a man like your pa. And young Davey, too."

Professional killers . . . The burden of guilt those words placed on Cas almost sank him to the ground again. The Comanches were gone now, and even in violent Texas, white men did not senselessly butcher women—a crime that usually got a man beaten to death before he reached the gallows. This unspeakable act of slaughter was a vengeance strike—and bounty hunter Cas was the only Everett with enemies sick and hateful enough to do this.

"What about the law?" Cas asked, his attention focused on a little dogwood copse beyond the knoll.

"Shoo! Cas, you know the law around here ain't worth an old underwear button. The prairie rats who done this shoulda danced on air by now. Here it is, thirty years after we whipped the chilipeps and won Texas, and Sabine County still tries cases before a circuit judge in a saloon tent. Our 'constable' is a snot-nosed infant who can't tell gee from haw. He claims it was Mexers who done this."

Cas shook his head, still watching the copse. "Mexicans don't raid this far north of the Rio Bravo, not anymore. And they raid to steal, not to wipe out sleeping families."

"Well, by Godfrey, it's terrible enough when redskins do something like this. But these was white men, Cas. It's soul-rackin' just tryin' to understand it. I can't. Everything I thought I knew and believed was just plowed under by it. Who needs Satan anymore? Nowadays the devil packs a six-gun."

"Soul-racking," Cas repeated. "You struck a lode there."

He reached down and took a pinch of dirt from each grave, carefully depositing it inside his handkerchief and folding it up again. When one of the worst grasshopper plagues in U.S. history wiped out the harvest of 1874, the Everett farm was ruined. But Cas sent home enough money to carry his family through. Things had started to improve dramatically—until this.

"I'll be settling some accounts," Cas said with quiet conviction. "Five of them."

Again he studied the copse as he loosened his .44 in the holster. "Yancy, you got rock salt in your shells?"

"Since this happened, Cas, I carry only heavy buckshot."

"Good. We're going to pay a little visit to that copse."

Yancy, forehead runneled in puzzlement, turned to study it. "Why?"

"See those angry jays circling over it and scolding? I think somebody's hiding in there to watch us. Let's go pay our respects."

Chapter 3

Cas skinned his shooter and led the way down the grass-tufted knoll, spurs chinging. Yancy carried the express gun braced in his hip socket.

"Cas," he said nervously, "anybody hid in the trees has got a clear bead on us."

"They've had a clear bead all along," Cas pointed out. "Just to play it safe, spray some Blue Whistlers right in the middle."

The express gun bellowed and leaves swirled in the air as claws of buckshot stripped bark and ripped small limbs from the trees.

"*Ho*-ly jumpin Jehosaphat!" screeched a reedy voice from within. "Please don't shoot no more! I ain't armed 'cept for a bowie!"

"C'mon out," Cas said. "All of you."

"It's just me by my lonesome, mister."

Cas watched a bearded, rail-thin man in threadbare clothing and a greasy flop hat emerge into the bright afternoon sunlight. He was pale with fright.

"Keep him covered," Cas told Yancy.

He stepped within the shelter of trees. A gaunt mule was hobbled in the middle. No one else was hiding, and a quick search turned up no weapons.

"All right, you listen up, mister," Cas told their captive when he came back out. "This isn't just trespassing. That's my family buried behind us, freshly murdered."

Cas raised the .44's muzzle and planted it snugly in front of the man's ear, thumb cocking it. "I'm in no funning mood, understand? I'm going to ask you some questions, and you're going to answer them—*all* of them—quick and truthfully. The first time you hold back or tell me a lie, I'll leave your brains all over this field. Am I making myself clear?"

"Yessir. Real clear."

"What's your name?"

"Dooley Johnson."

"That a summer name?" Cas demanded.

"No, sir, it's real. I hail from Fort Belknap. Got kin all over up there."

Cas looked at Yancy. "Know him?"

"Don't know him, but I've seen him in Iron Springs. He was a liveryman for a while, but I hear he was cashiered for stealing from saddlebags."

"That's just scuttlebutt," Johnson protested. "See, I—"

"Cinch up," Cas snapped, his eyes as hard as the bunched muscles of his jaw. "I'm making the medicine and you're taking it. Now what were you doing in those trees? And don't short change me— I'm not in a generous mood right now."

The man's Adam's apple bobbed when he swallowed audibly. Cas watched a flea leap from his filthy homespun shirt. "I was watching for you to return home."

"And then what?"

"Well, all I'm spoze to do is pile up some rocks out where your farm lane joins County Line Road."

"What's the point of that?"

"Sir, honest to God, I don't know. I was told nothin', just paid fifty dollars to stay and watch."

"Damned liar," Yancy growled, drawing back his mallet-sized left fist.

Cas caught his arm. "I think he's telling the straight, so far. This is not a road agent, Yancy, just a two-bit dirt worker. All right, Johnson, here's where you better not try to play it foxy or you're standing on your own grave. Who hired you?"

"Oh, Lordy, mister, don't shoot! The fellow never give me his name. Honest to criminy, he never did. I never seen him before."

"If you don't know him, how'd he come to hire you?"

"I got a little shack about five miles from here. He claimed he nosed around Iron Springs asking about fellows that might want to pick up some easy wages, and somehow got my name. Showed up at my door, is all."

"What's he look like?"

"Nothin' too special. Medium height, slim, had long, hangin' sideburns. Mousy hair. Some old scars on his cheeks like maybe he had smallpox when he was young."

"Northern range or southern?" Cas pressed.

"How's 'at?"

Cas swore impatiently. "Northern range men tend to wear low-crowned, flat hats like mine and woolly chaps. Southern range men generally wear high-crowned hats and leather chaps."

"Oh. Well, like you he didn't have no chaps, but his hat was low like yours, only the brim was curled."

Cas glanced at Yancy again. "Rings no bell for me. Seen him around here?"

Yancy shook his shaggy head. "Nope, and I know every soul in this county."

Cas mulled all of it. By now it was clear to him that someone he had brought to justice, in the past four years, had achieved a monstrous revenge, either personally or by hiring it out. Whoever did the actual killing was probably well paid, but knew the risk because of Cas' reputation. So Johnson was paid to give them warning when Cas was coming. Probably so they could dry-gulch him along the road.

"All right, Johnson," Cas said, lowering his weapon. "I think you were straight with me. You're down on your luck, and you needed wages. You'll clear off my property now and never come back."

Cas pulled out his money pouch and plucked out a double eagle gold piece. He dropped it in the man's shirt pocket.

"Mr. Everett," the man protested, "this ain't necess—"

"Sure as the dickens it's not," Yancy protested. "Cas, this mange pot—"

"Never mind," Cas cut him off. "Johnson, when you leave, you're going to pile up the rocks just like you were told, understand?"

The man nodded. "Whatever you want."

"Not a word to anybody about our little talk, eh?"

"Nary a peep," Johnson promised.

"Good. I just gave you twenty dollars. Your other job ends when you pile up the rocks. That means you're working for me now. And it makes it that much easier to kill you if you ever double-cross me."

"Cas, I confess it's a stumper to me," Yancy said as the two men walked slowly toward the charred pile that used to be a home. "The very idea of not only paying that egg-sucking varmint, but you never even split his skull open. He's in cahoots with the same men who—"

"He's small potatoes. The point is to get at the killers, not their petty lick fingers. Besides, if I pistol-whip him just to vent my spleen, I make an enemy out of him. Then Johnson might run to whoever hired him, show his bruises, and warn him that we cut up rough with him for information. I believe in keeping my enemies guessing."

"Huh. If that's so, why announce you're here by having Johnson pile up the rocks?"

Cas watched Johnson ride into the pines ahead of them and disappear in shadows as if he'd been swallowed.

"I'd bet my horse," he replied, "that the actual killers—it had to be more than one to get both Pa and Davey—are long gone. Whoever hired Johnson is likely the one who was ordered to stay back, but not the ramrod of the bunch. And since the signal that I'm here is a pile of rocks, he likely also has the job of riding past here to check for it."

"If he does, what's next? Curl his toes?"

"Right now he's more useful to me alive. A lone rat usually returns to the pack."

Yancy pulled at his chin. "You *have* got used to thinking like owlhoots, huh? The newspapers say you're hell on two sticks."

"I've read that," Cas said dryly. "Ink slingers like to shovel it deep. Hard to tell their bilge from the saloon gossip."

Yancy paused beside the dobbin and pulled a paper sack of gingersnaps from a saddle pannier. The big Swede munched one as he studied Cas carefully. He saw a boy who left home at seventeen but had since grown into an impressive man, quiet in manner but with an air of possessing deep reserves of inner strength. Nothing about his manner suggested the frontier bully, yet most bullies surely

gave him a wide berth, for his confidence in himself
was obvious.

Yancy had read in *Police Gazette* how most of
the fabled gunfighters had blue eyes, and Cas was
no exception. So far those eyes remained as calm
as the rest of the man, but Yancy didn't trust a
thing like this. Severe grief could work on a man
like a cactus spike. It lodged in the sole of his boot
and then gradually worked its way through—so
gradually he was limping long before he realized it.

The weathered sodbuster pointed to a garden
patch that had been plowed but not planted.

"Thanks to you," he told Cas, "things been lookin' better around here. Your ma had plans to sell
spun truck in Iron Springs. She was lookin' forward
to that garden. I even brung her some seeds.
She—"

Yancy fell silent when a shadow moved across
Cas' smooth-shaven, angular face.

"Sorry," Yancy muttered. "You know how I run
off at the mouth."

"Sorry for what? I want to hear about her, about
all of them. I missed plenty. We both know I wasn't
the best son or brother in the world."

"Shoo, your ma would've switched anybody who
said that, you included. You know, your ma was
no mealymouthed psalm singer like me. She *lived*
her religion—you know how she set store by it. She
kept all you Everett whelps on the straight and
narrow. But you were always her favorite, even
after it was plain as bedbugs on a new sheet that
you'd always have your full quota of original sin."

Cas laughed at the truth of this. He stopped beside Comet and stripped him down to the neck
leather, leading him to a rain barrel at one corner
of the ruined house. As he threw the bridle, part

of a scorched newspaper clipping caught his eye. It was tacked to a section of wall that had collapsed without burning completely.

Cas squatted and cocked his head to read. It was from the *Democratic Statesman* out of Austin. He read it aloud:

" 'For most deadly gun throwers, skill at draw-shoot killing is more science than art, more the result of boring, repetitive practice than "fabled luck" or superior reflexes. Steel-nerved Cas Everett is in the mold of Wild Bill Hickok—he has the rare ability to stay calm and aim true even while his opponents toss a wall of lead at him. Getting off the first shot means less than scoring the first knockdown hit. Bill Longley, Ben Thompson, King Fisher, Curly Bill Brocius, even the fearsome John Wesley Hardin, who carved forty-four notches by age twenty-one—none of these Texas gunmen has ever shown any interest in bracing Cas Everett.' "

Cas glanced up at Yancy. "Maybe they will now," he said with dry sarcasm before he resumed reading. " 'This is a professional courtesy, and whether Cas likes it or not, he is a respected member of the walk-and-draw fraternity. Never mind that, unlike most of the rest, he has always honored the fine line between justifiable killing and outright murder. Most of his wanted men are brought back alive—a point of gallantry that may, in this writer's opinion, come back to haunt him.' "

Cas rose and stood motionless, stunned by the grim prescience of the writer's final remarks. He gazed at those five crosses on the knoll, and guilt lanced him deep.

"I met this writer in Austin," he said, "and he's a good fellow. But there's no mold for Wild Bill Hickok. He was the first and best gunfighter, period. Most of Hardin's notches are for outright murders, not gunfights. He guns down unarmed colored men. Anyhow, I'm no gunfighter. I haven't cracked a cap except in self-defense or to prevent the murder of someone I was paid to guard. Not that it matters now to my family."

Cas moved out into the hoof-packed yard and dropped to his hands and knees, studying the area minutely, his face inches away from the ground.

"That won't help much," Yancy told him, walking closer. "Your folks were well liked and had plenty of company. Besides, the attack was three weeks ago. Those prints are old."

"The real old ones have lost their shape as blow sand fills them," Cas replied. "Any that are left can be roughly dated by how much indentation is left. Look here."

Yancy's tall form folded like a jackknife as he bent down.

"Here's a print," Cas said, pointing, "with the last edges crumbling—that makes it maybe three, four weeks old. It's a rear offside shoe. Here's another, and a third, same shoe."

"Same shoe?" Yancy said. "How do you know that?"

"Because it's slightly chipped. You can see where the missing chip of iron has left a tiny mound in each print."

"Yah shoor!"

"Of course," Cas added, "there's no way to know if this was one of the killers. Still, it's good to know about."

He stood up again and returned to Comet, tethering the chestnut in the shade of the pine windbreak and strapping a nose bag of oats on him.

"Come see something," he told Yancy, walking toward the nearby saddle Cas had left in the grass. He reached into a saddlebag and pulled out a soft chamois drawstring pouch. Yancy whistled when Cas slid a beautiful cross out into the dazzling sunlight.

"Hammered silver with gold filigree," he explained. "Made by Weinstein Brothers, famous jewelers in St. Louis. Ma never wanted anything for herself, not even a store-bought dress. But Pa gave me a catalog sent by these Weinstein boys and said Ma was looking at this cross every chance she got. All the way home, I pictured the look on her face when I finally gave it—"

Cas suddenly felt as if a stone had lodged in his throat. Hands trembling slightly, he put the cross away.

"Anyhow, this farm need not tether you," Yancy told him. "You can sell it at a good lay. Knobby Pendergast has been trying to buy it for years."

"Maybe later. Right now it's all I've got left of my family."

Yancy said, "You don't think this thing is going to be settled close to home, do you?"

Cas shook his head. "This is Texas. Law may be scarce as hen's teeth, but no low-crawling sewer rats who murder three women in this state are going to feel safe staying close by. That's why I'm going to be watching that pile of rocks to see who rides by. That'll be the messenger."

"Take me with you, Cas boy," Yancy pleaded.

Cas shook his head. "Much obliged, Yancy, but bird-dogging killers is not what it's cracked up to be in the newspapers. Matter of fact, it's a job for the insane."

"Fine. Cas, I'm hopelessly crazy and always have been. It runs in my family."

"Yancy, I said—"

"Cas, you yourself said law out west ain't yet ready for such hellish monsters as these killers. This is a time when *justice* is required in the absence of law."

"Yancy—"

"No, *don't* you shout me down. I will have my say!"

Like many big men Cas had known, Yancy had no chip on his shoulder. But he possessed a deep well of inner feeling, and he dipped into it now.

"I been stewin' on this for twenty-one god-awful days. It's true I'm no draw-shoot killer like you, but I'll pull my freight. You think I don't have the caliber for the job, don't you?"

"I know you've got enough courage for ten men. You fought in the war. You fought Comanches. But you've got a farm to work. Besides, this is my business."

"*Your* business? If that don't beat all, Caswell Everett. All the years you was gone seeing the elephant, I sided the Everett family: stood with them in Comanche attacks, helped Davey and your pa seed and harvest. And I think you know who it was that found and buried them, blubbering like a dang baby. I stood in for you, Cas, and this was *my* family, too. It's our business, not just yours."

Cas had a defiant streak and didn't like being put in his place. He had just been clobbered hard with the truth, however, and he had to wait until he could trust his voice.

"Straight talk," he finally said, "except that I wasn't gone to see the elephant. I was supporting my—all right, *our*—family the best I could."

"I never thought or said otherwise. A man can't be two places at once. So can I go with you? I'm no great shakes with a short gun, but you know I'm just the lad for a scattergun. Got hard knuckles, too, if it comes to a dustup."

Cas watched his friend, remembering. Before

Davey could stand in for a man, Yancy had indeed been a strong right arm for the Everetts, doing work Cas should have been there to do.

"Honored to have you along, Yancy," Cas finally answered. "This will be a family matter."

Chapter 4

The sun sank lower and the shadows purpled and flattened out. Cas sent Yancy home to prepare for a journey and spent the rest of the afternoon at the edge of the pine windbreak, listening for traffic out on County Line Road. It was light. Each time he heard someone approaching, he raised his brass-framed field glasses for a better view.

An express rider on a large bay loped past heading for Iron Springs, his letter satchel flapping. An hour later a farmer in an old buckboard clattered by in the opposite direction. By sundown two boys carrying fishing poles completed the traffic.

Yancy returned after dark with roast beef sandwiches wrapped in cheesecloth. Both men moved down the lane and closer to the pile of rocks, carrying canvas ground sheets and blankets. They also lugged along their saddles to use as pillows.

"Cas, who mighta done this?" Yancy asked.

Cas was using his boot knife to soften up some sleeping ground. "I've been wonderin' the same thing. I've hauled back thirty owlhoots by now. And I always make it strict policy to stay strangers with prisoners."

"Get too friendly and your guard goes down, huh?"

"It happens. So I don't allow any chin wag, and even though I have to look at 'em to guard 'em, I don't look eyeball to eyeball. They talk to me, I shut 'em up in a puffin' hurry. So it's hard for me to say now which ones nurse the sickest grudge. They *all* hate me."

"You brought back thirty," Yancy reminded him, "but there's some who pulled down on you and didn't get jugged. They got buried. Couldn't one of their friends or kin have done for your family?"

"Anything's possible, I reckon, but the unsavory specimens I run to ground are usually loners even their mothers couldn't love."

Before dark Cas had brushed and curried Comet, even removing the stubborn witch's bridles, tangles in his mane. The chestnut's white blaze and mane were liabilities after dark, so Cas left him tethered in graze behind the pines.

Before he rolled into his blanket, Cas used saddle soap to clean and soften all of his leather riding gear. The insect hum filled his ears, and now and then one of the horses whiffled. An endless explosion of stars marked the blue-black dome of sky. Cas gazed into that glittering profusion and prayed his family was up there somewhere, at peace.

Yancy's rumbling voice broke the stillness. "Cas?"

"Yeah?"

"You should be proud. It's a good farm now, especially on account of the money you sent. New equipment, and there *was* new stock. Your brother even built a new bobwire fence on the south slope to pen beeves. Only twenty-five head of mean Longhorns, but it was a start. Those murdering devils killed all the stock, too, even the chickens."

Cas said nothing to this. The shock of grief was

still too new for him, and the vengeful anger Yancy was starting to feel after three weeks was still only a hard seed within Cas. As his shock wore off, he knew, the vendetta would begin. For now he was numb except when the horror of his own guilt touched him in waves like nausea, forcing him to Herculean efforts of self-control.

He spent a miserable night beside the road, haunted by dreams that inevitably turned to bloody nightmares. Cas welcomed the first salmon pink streak of dawn in the East.

He let Yancy sleep a little longer, rolling up his blanket and canvas sheet. Cas was a light sleeper, and he was sure no one had passed by in the night. He walked back to the knoll and visited his family in silence, alone with his turmoiled thoughts in the morning mist and breeze.

Yancy rolled out while Cas was boiling coffee beans in an open can he always carried with his gear. By now the eastern sky was ablaze.

"I miss my shuck mattress," Yancy admitted to Cas as he pulled on his massive brogans. "You live under the stars, but the last time I slept rough was in the war."

When Cas offered Yancy a strip of jerked beef, the big Swede muttered some choice words unfit for women and children.

"If you're going to side me in a manhunt," Cas rebuked him, "you'll have to eat this and worse. Out in the New Mexico Territory, I once ate my own horse."

"Yah shoor. But at least that was fresh meat," Yancy pointed out. "This embalmed beef chews like old shoe leather. Don't eat any more. I'll be right back."

While Cas moved back up into the pine trees, Yancy caught up the dobbin and rode out after quickly saddling it. Cas spread his ground sheet out under the pines and broke down his weapons to clean and oil them. Now and then his scalp tingled and he gazed all around at the shake-roofed barn and outbuildings, his pulse speeding up.

Yancy returned carrying a cast-iron skillet with its lid tied on. "Ham, eggs, and potatoes," he announced as he slid off the big horse. "I brought two forks. We'll just eat it from the pan."

Smelling the food reminded Cas it had been a long time since he'd shoved his legs under a table and tied into some tasty grub. But he'd had enough trouble last night just forcing down a few bites of sandwich.

When Cas waved off the food, Yancy persisted. "You're hurtin', Cas boy, but you got to eat if you're going to wage battle."

Cas surrendered and sat on the ground beside Yancy, spearing at the occasional chunk of food.

Yancy looked at the weapons laid out on the ground sheet. The farmer had carried a Springfield rifle in the war, but knew little about firearms. "What's that old gun?"

"Assurance. It only comes out when I need it."

Yancy studied it closer. "Why, that's prac'ly an old mountain man relic. Hawken gun?"

Cas laughed. "Old son, you don't know sic 'em, do you? This here's the famous fifty-caliber Sharps—the Big Fifty."

Yancy hefted it and whistled. "Heavy."

"Over twelve pounds, and it's single shot. But it'll stop a freight train, and I've scored hits at almost a mile with that telescopic sight."

"And a Spencer carbine," Yancy said, his face puckering as he studied the seven-shot weapon. "That one I know from all the stories about Custer's unit. Cavalry issue—the same weapon Custer's men were *trying* to fire at the Little Bighorn battle. Why in Sam Hill would you choose that death certificate over the Winchester Seventy-six?"

"A carbine is smaller than a rifle," Cas explained, "but gives me more range than a handgun. I like it out to two hundred yards. The Spencer is light, accurate, the fifty-six-caliber slug deadly. And look here—" Cas pointed to the carbine's butt plate. "In the middle of a cartridge session, you can reload quick right in the saddle. You just cram your rounds through this trap. Custer's men might have survived if they hadn't panicked and fired so fast—the soft copper shells will stick in the breech if the gun gets too hot."

"You're the expert," Yancy said doubtfully. He hefted his express gun. "Me, I like a good riot-control gun. You—"

"Shush it," Cas cut in, grabbing his field glasses. "Somebody's passing by out on the road."

Moments later a one-horse gig flashed past, heading east toward Iron Springs. The driver was a white-haired man wearing a gray duster to protect his clothing.

"It's just Prescott Harrison," Yancy explained. "Owns the hardware."

Cas finished running a wiping patch through the Smith & Wesson's muzzle.

"Cas," Yancy said, peering at the weapon, "why in blazes have you filed off the front notch?"

"If you don't make a clean jerk, it's curtains. A front sight is near worthless on a handgun, anyhow, so why risk having it catch in the holster?"

Yancy shook his head. "This gunfighter business is a grim sort of an affair, I see."

Perhaps forty-five minutes after the gig rolled by, a larger conveyance passed: a Concord coach rocking on its braces and cutting dirt at an ungodly rate.

A driver and a shotgun messenger sat on the box, the driver raising Cain with his six-horse whip.

"See? Look there how they sit," Yancy remarked. "The driver's on the off side. In the ten-cent romances, he's always on the near side. Seems like they could get a piddlin' thing like that right."

"Why? They won't learn single-action from double-action or a pistol from a revolver, neither. And they're forever having a fellow with a six-gun score kills at one hundred yards or better. At thirty yards I switch to the carbine."

Another hour ticked by, and Cas began to wonder if there was any point to this sentry duty. Then a lone rider clopped into view, heading east, and Cas perked up like a hound on point. The man rode an Appaloosa, its spotted rump easy to pick out from the terrain.

"Look," Yancy said, his voice tense. "He's got them long, hanging sideburns Johnson mentioned."

"Dundrearys, I think they're called," Cas supplied, bringing the glasses to his eyes. "The rest of him fits the description, too."

If the rider had any interest in the piled-up rocks, he covered it well. He simply eased by at a trot and didn't bother to speed up.

"He's playing it foxy," Cas said, "but that's our man. C'mon."

They hurried down to the road on foot, and once again Cas dropped down on all fours to study the prints minutely.

Yancy shook his head in admiration. "You always could follow a wood tick across solid rock, even when you were just a tad."

"No chipped shoe," Cas announced, his voice disappointed. "We can't link him directly to . . . to what happened here. But let's hop our horses and raise dust before we lose him. I've got a gut hunch this is one of the gang."

They sprinted back up the lane.

"Blast it!" Cas exclaimed. "The hell am I thinking?"

He pointed at the big dobbin grazing near Comet. "You don't plan to ride that plow nag, do you?"

Yancy shook his head. "Socrates is a going-to-town horse. He was in the traces too long, and I can't push him past an easy trot. I bought a good sorrel gelding last summer from a peeler in Iron Springs. Good horseflesh."

Cas nodded. "That's more like it. That dobbin is at least eighteen hands, and with a giant like you riding on the hurricane deck, you'd need a canyon just to lower your skyline. Get back to your place and get that sorrel tacked. I'm going on ahead, but I'll hold a trot until you catch up."

Yancy's farm horse was already saddled and he left immediately. Cas threw the blanket and pad across Comet's back, then tossed the saddle on him and cinched the girth. He took the bit easily when Cas slipped the bridle on him. Cas bent down to check the latigos and stirrups, then stepped up and over, reining the chestnut toward the road.

Just before he entered the pines, Cas sent a cross-shoulder glance toward the lonely knoll. The sight of those five bright white crosses stabbed at his heart. Nothing he could do would ever bring his family back, nor balance the ledger for what he owed them. Still, Cas was determined to let nothing interfere with the most important mission of his life.

"This won't stand," he promised his family in a choked whisper. "I swear by all things holy, this will not stand."

Chapter 5

Yancy, astride a young sorrel with four white socks, caught up to Cas about two miles down the road. At first they rode full chisel, making up for lost time. Abruptly, Cas reined in and Yancy followed suit.

"What? You see him?" the Swede demanded.

Cas shook his head. "Not yet, but those dust puffs out ahead haven't quite settled, so he can't be too far in front of us. We don't want to get too close. He's seen Johnson's signal and knows I'm back. Let's see what he does with the information."

They continued at a trot, Cas unrelenting in his scrutiny of the road ahead. The terrain hereabouts was a sporadic mix of open fields and cottonwood groves, with stock ponds and portable windmills dotting the area. Cas couldn't shake the feeling they were being watched, the same feeling that gnawed at him back at his place.

Yancy's voice sliced into his thoughts. "Cas?"

"Hmm?"

"Ask you somethin' that's sorta personal?"

Cas glanced at him. "Is it about women?"

Yancy shook his head.

"Well, you're family, right?" Cas shrugged. "Fire away."

"I'm just all-fired curious to know exactly how many men you've sent under? The newspapers claim sixteen."

"It's fewer than that, but more than I like to say."

"They all deserved it, huh?"

Cas hesitated. "I figure *any* man who draws down on me deserves it. Remember, I don't pop them over for being ugly."

"Shoo, I know that. I'm proud as a game rooster to know you. *My* neighbor, showin' up in newspapers from as far away as Kansas City and New Orleans."

" 'Preciate the kind words, Yancy. But someday a bullet will knock me out from under my hat, and I'll have the newspapers to thank for it."

A half hour later, knowing they were near Iron Springs, Cas thumped Comet up to a lope. He wanted to keep the man on the Appaloosa in sight now.

"What in tarnal blazes is he doing?" Cas complained. "I was convinced he plans to send a telegram. But he just rode past the turnoff to Iron Springs. He's headed straight toward the Texas-Louisiana line."

"While you been gone," Yancy explained, crunching on a gingersnap, "Sabine County passed a hog-stupid law taxing telegraph poles. Now the nearest Morse tapper is across the river in Louisiana. A little hamlet called . . . shoo, I disremember."

Nearly an hour later, at an approaching crossroads, Cas spotted a fingerboard, a signboard with a pointing finger indicating the direction to Padgett's Landing.

"*That's* it," Yancy told him. "We're close now."

"This place wasn't here when I was a kid."

" 'Bout five years ago," Yancy told him, "they figured out how you can float on bayous from this

Padgett's Landing to the Red River. Then it's a short spit to the Mississippi. The few local cotton growers still left use it."

"Dang it," Cas said in frustration. "I think he might've spotted us when we came out of that long curve just now. I saw him looking back."

Yancy tapped the stock of the express gun in his saddle sheath. "What now? Snare him before he gets away?"

Cas shook his head. "You grazing loco weed? We want him to send that telegram—then we know whose boots he licks. And where the top kick is."

Padgett's Landing was little more than a wooden dock at the edge of a calm, wide bayou. A work gang of Negroes in pillow-tick caps hauled bales of cotton from a field wagon to a flatboat moored at the dock. A few shanties were scattered about, including one with a Western Union sign. Cas saw the Appaloosa's spotted rump projecting past the corner of the shanty.

"We'll tie off here," he told Yancy, swinging his right leg over the cantle and landing light as a cat. "No point in rushing him."

Yancy was considerably less agile leaving the saddle and thumped heavily in the dusty street. "At least you mean to collar him *after* he sends the telegraph, hanh?"

Cas looped his reins around a tie rail in front of a deserted shack that looked like an old grog shop.

"After? He's ours then," he assured Yancy. "And we *will* turn him religious in a hurry. First, though, we talk to the telegrapher. Our boy on the Appaloosa has nowhere to run, and if he does, Comet scoots along like his pa's name is Going and his ma's name is Fast. That curly wolf is ours."

"There he goes," Yancy said, excitement pitching his voice higher.

Cas watched the man with the Dundrearys ride around the shanty and north along the bayou. If he knew he was being watched, he made no sign.

"Let's go," he told Yancy after loosening his .44 in the holster.

Cas stepped up to the window.

"Hep ya?" asked an obese telegrapher with a folding face.

"That jasper who just left—any chance we could read the telegram he sent?"

The telegrapher slid his green eyeshades higher to study the two men in the window. Yancy crowded in even more, giving the man an eyeful of the sawed-off express gun cradled in the crook of his left arm.

"It's not usually done, gents," he replied, "but I can't see the harm."

He handed Cas a message form the customer had filled out. It was routed to Deadwood, Dakota Territory, a fact that made Cas' armpits break out in sweat. He had barely survived that Black Hills hellhole, winter before last, and was hardly eager to return. The message itself was short and to the point: *Our friends came home. I'm on my way.*

"On his way to Deadwood," Cas mused aloud.

"Deadwood!" Yancy exclaimed. "Moses on the mountain! They say Deadwood has a man for breakfast."

"Every day," Cas assured him. "You'll generally find one or two bodies in the streets each morning. Cattle towns are wide open, but gold-strike camps are the real hellers."

Cas returned his attention to the cooperative telegrapher. "Say, friend, this form doesn't say who it's sent to."

"That part gets torn off." The man pulled a sheet of paper off a long spike. "It's for a Mr. Johnny

Smith, for pickup only, no delivery. That means it's likely a fake name."

Cas nodded. " 'Preciate it."

He led the way, heading for the front corner of the building and the street beyond. Had he not been so preoccupied, he might have thought again about the man on the Appaloosa. "It helps us, Yancy. At least we know—"

The next moment things started humming ten ways a second. Cas rounded the corner and ran headlong into a hammering racket of gunfire. A slug spun his hat off. Another penetrated his vest with a sharp tug and grazed his ribs like a white-hot wire. A third shot in the rapid string chunked into the cottonwood log building only inches from his head.

All this happened in a second or two. Cas willed himself calm and gave Yancy a sharp push back. He dived to escape the fusillade, rolled hard, and came rocking onto his feet, coiled for the draw and jerking steel.

Even now, in the heat of action, Cas would have only wounded this mysterious man who held the key to the slaughter of his family. He needed to interrogate him. However, Yancy ruined that option by leaping around the corner to protect Cas. Cas saw the impetuous farmer would never get his double ten pointed in time before a fatal bullet found him—no wing shots now, or Yancy might be going to glory. Cursing, Cas snapped off a round that drilled the owlhoot through the pump. The would-be killer folded to the ground like an empty sack.

"You all right, Cas boy?" a visibly shaken Yancy asked.

"I'll need some salve on my ribs, is all," Cas

replied as he knelt beside the dead man and searched his pockets. "Nothing to identify him."

"Did you reach kill number sixteen with him?" Yancy demanded. "Cas Everett, that was some fine shooting."

"Nothing special. Anyhow, this one is not the biggest toad in the puddle. That's who we're after, and he's likely up in Deadwood."

Cas headed back toward the window, steering Yancy with him. "Well, as I promised, you've had your first frolic. Our clover was deep this time. But how many of these do you expect to survive?"

"About as many as I expected to survive in the War of Northern Aggression—all of them. You settled his hash, didn't you? That's the main mile."

A grin tugged Cas' lips apart. "You'll do to take along."

The telegrapher, frozen with fright, had not moved from his chair.

"What's the nearest law?" Cas called through the window.

"Parish sheriff."

"Close by?"

The telegrapher shook his head. "I'll have to send a rider to fetch him. Takes him as much as three hours to get here."

"I don't have three hours. That yahoo outside jumped us. It was self-defense."

The telegrapher nodded, wiping his sweaty face with a handkerchief. "That'll be my version, too. The sheriff will be happy with that. He'll hold a sheriff's auction for the guns, tack, and horse. That Appaloosa will sell high, and there'll be plenty left over after the burial is paid for."

If anyone in the decrepit hamlet was curious

about the shooting fray, Cas saw no sign of it as he returned to his horse and swung up into leather.

"The only thing more disheartening than killing a man," he remarked when they rode out, "is seeing how little it matters."

"Sometimes it matters plenty," Yancy reminded him, having buried the proof times five. "Well, at least we know we're going to Deadwood. Been there before?"

"Yes, for my sins. I was on the trail of a killer, and it led to the Black Hills. But I found my hardcase decorating a cottonwood. It's not exactly a place that welcomes bounty hunters, either."

He looked at Yancy. "We can expect plenty of trouble from here on out. That telegram lets somebody know it's time to kill us, the sooner the better. What just happened, that's only a taste of what's coming. Are you *sure* you want this, Yancy?"

"Does a rag doll have a patched ass?"

"You could end up dead as a can of corned beef," Cas warned.

"I'm not used to such things," Yancy admitted. "In the war, the killing was not so close and personal. But it's not my way to get snow in my boots. The old Swede is with you from here to the harvest."

Chapter 6

On the third day of Cas Everett's return to Texas, he and Yancy set out on a northwest course toward Deadwood. Cas had spent another lonely, guilt-ridden night on his property, resting Comet and allowing Yancy enough time to make arrangements with neighbors for his livestock. Anticipating this journey, Yancy had left his fields fallow this spring.

"But there *must* be a railroad between us and Deadwood," Yancy complained for the third time since they'd ridden out a few hours earlier. "You've rode on a train, but I have not. *Never* have I heard the clickety-click and clackety-clack of iron wheels. Besides, it would save us time."

"I wish we could," Cas told him, adjusting his hat for the late-morning sunshine. "But I've looked into it many times, and neither the Northern Pacific nor the Union Pacific are running any north-south lines yet. The only one I know about is the Illinois Central, and I think they only go straight south into Mississippi."

"It's punishment for the war," Yancy complained. "The Yankees wanted to hang us Johnny Rebs after the surrender, but Lincoln nixed it. So they stick the knife in any way they can."

"That's hogwash," Cas said. "Capitalists will

gladly accept any man's dollar. It's just that, until lately, there were hostilities with the Sioux and other hot-tempered tribes to the north. We still have no railroads north of Fort Laramie. It'll happen soon."

Yancy scowled, most of his big, bluff face cast in shadow by his flop hat. "All right. Well, I've never rode in a stagecoach, neither."

"Then thank the God who made you," Cas assured him. "I did that once and swore I'd never do it twice. Rather be scalped. When the damn thing isn't rolling over, it's bouncing you out the windows. And just guess how many tobacco chewers ever bother to spit to the leeward side? No, it's slower but we'll horseback it."

"Wouldn't be so slow," Yancy stubbornly persisted, "if we'd just follow a straight bead north 'steada this crinkum-crankum you got planned out."

Cas sent the big farmer a pitying look. "Old son, we'll have to find a bumpologist to read your skull. I told you. We can't just ride due north because of the Indian Territory. You know dang well it's off-limits to whites."

"Yah shoor, but so what? You tellin' me no whites ever enter the Nations?"

"Not if they're law-abiding, they don't. Owlhoots go there because white lawmen can't arrest them there, and because Indian courts have no jurisdiction over whites."

"So we head northwest," Yancy recited, trying to remember the route Cas planned. "We cover a big chunk of north-central Texas and cross into New Mexico Territory at the Canadian River. Then what?"

"The rest is easy. We ride due north through

Colorado, the Nebraska Panhandle, and into the Dakota Territory and the Black Hills."

"And . . . Doan's Store on the Red River?" Yancy said, seeming to hold his breath. "It's all a man ever hears about from these hot-jawin' cow nurses. It's right here in Texas, too. Any chance it'll be on our trail?"

Cas grinned. Like Yancy he was covered in so much dust he was sweating mud. This was rolling scrubland, hot and humid and devoid of any growth larger than creosote bushes or wind-stunted juniper trees.

"Doan's is definitely on our route," he told Yancy. "Speaking of rivers—can you swim?"

"Cas, I've yet to meet a river I couldn't just walk through."

"I'll take that as a no. Well, we can wind around most of the bigger rivers, but we'll have to ford the Red, the Canadian, the Arkansas, and the South Platte."

"I crossed the Platte when I moved down to Texas in 1859," Yancy said. "A mile wide and an inch deep. That's featherbed work."

Cas nodded. "I've forded all of them except the Canadian. They can all be trouble in the wrong stretches. We'll have to hope we can find safe fords."

A bright flash of light flickered well off to the left. The U.S. Army had no mirror stations this far east, Cas reminded himself, which meant that not all the Indians were answering roll calls on reservations.

"Mirror signals," Yancy said, as if plucking the thought from Cas' head. "I first saw them back in the days when the Comanches was still a free-ranging tribe. Best thing that ever happened for the white homesteaders was when Iron Butt Custer got himself killed."

Cas had to agree. The U.S. Army's postbellum drive against Indians had quelled or seriously weakened most of the tribes. The widespread Army crackdown, following the humiliating shock of Little Bighorn, had ensured that.

"Nobody but some tough old frontiersmen," he said, "ever believed half-naked savages could whip white men who'd sat on the benches at sacred West Point. It can't be tolerated by the old guard in the Army, so now John is doing the hurt dance."

"May he rot in Injin hell," Yancy snarled. "Noble Red Man, my ampersand. Hadn't been for the Texas Rangers, the Comanch woulda killed every white man, woman, and child in Texas."

"We'll be slicing right along the western border of the Indian Territory," Cas warned. "People call them cracker-and-molasses Indians just because they went onto the reservations. But the fact that they're drawing government rations doesn't make them peaceful. Don't underestimate the threat, Yancy."

Cas had talked to soldiers stationed near the Indian Territory. Renegade bands of young bucks routinely jumped the rez to strike hard and fast in one area, then rode like the devil and struck the next day at a place a hundred miles away. They hit military work details, stagecoaches and stations, and mail riders. They'd also been raiding on Texas cattle, trading them down in Old Mexico for tobacco and coffee and liquor.

Cas slid the field glasses from a saddlebag and studied the vast brownish-yellow terrain surrounding them like an unbroken sea.

"Any trouble?" Yancy asked.

"Just some cowboys hazing cattle way off to our

left. Speaking of that—don't be surprised if we get mistook for brand artists," Cas warned. "This area is crawling with rustlers."

"The world is full of yacks and yahoos," Yancy opined. A moment later he added, "Still no idea who attacked your family?"

Cas shook his head. "Every man I hauled in was a puke pail who'd stop at nothing. Same with the ones I killed. We'll get some answers in Deadwood."

Yancy brightened. "Is it true they have naked saloon gals running foot races in Deadwood?"

Cas snorted. "Not while I was there. It *is* true, though, that men are robbed in broad daylight. I saw it happen."

A few minutes later, Yancy exclaimed, "Say! That gal you was sweet on before you left home, Jeremiah Steele's daughter, Kathleen—didn't she move to Deadwood to teach school?"

Cas frowned. "That's what Ma told me. Said Kathleen left about a year ago. I just missed her when I was up there."

"Whatever happened between you two? I thought you had a real case on her?"

"Oh, I did. But she gave me the mitten."

Yancy looked astounded. "You proposed?"

Cas nodded. "She turned me down, but did it so sweet I never once felt like a fool. She even asked me to try again some day. That gal is right out of the top drawer."

"Why the long face, Romeo?" Yancy roweled him. "Still sweet on her?"

"You're big," Cas said, "but how'd you like to wear your hind end for a hat? The problem is, I didn't notice one school in Deadwood Gulch and only a few kids. Nor has anybody I know ever heard from Kathleen."

"She prob'ly married up and moved on," Yancy suggested. "Surely a woman as comely and smart as Kathleen would not be in danger? The code of chivalry is strong on the frontier, they say."

"I've read there's two hundred men for every woman in Deadwood," Cas replied. He added from a deadpan, "My sisters were comely and smart, too, weren't they?"

The two riders continued north-northwest for the rest of the day, walking the horses for ten minutes each hour to cool them out. Just before sundown Cas selected a little covert well off the trail for their camp. It was water-scarce country, but they had filled a gut bag with water before they left.

A fire of gnarled juniper wood crackled and sent sparks floating into the inky fathoms of darkness surrounding them. After a spartan meal of beans in tomato sauce, canned by Van Camp, they boiled up a can of cowboy coffee strong enough to float a horseshoe. They sweetened it with lumps of Mexican brown sugar. Finicky Yancy refused the hardtack Cas offered, calling the crackers "teeth dullers," but Cas crumbled it into his coffee to help soften them up.

"Cas," said Yancy, who had a seemingly endless supply of questions, "that fellow you plugged back in Padgett's Landing—I been thinkin' on it. How in blazes could he have missed you? Criminy, not only did he have the drop on you, but he was close enough to spit on you."

"He shot too soon—that's how. You don't shoot until you *know* you can't miss—that's the big idea. A man panics and jerks the trigger before he's pointed center of mass, and there goes his entire life in a miss or a wing shot."

Beyond the circle of light from the fire, a coyote howled. The ululating cry ended in a series of sharp barks. The mournful sound made Cas touch the watch pocket of his Levi's. He had transferred the grave dirt from his handkerchief to a small tin that once held throat pastilles. Feeling it now gave him some comfort, though precious little.

"Speaking of that fandango in Padgett's Landing," he told Yancy, "we'll need to get you a handgun. That buckshot cannon of yours is mighty handy to have along, but two shots fired and all you have is a club."

Yancy chuckled. "This old plow pusher is ahead of the game. Glom this, you infant who never marched to war."

He reached into a saddle pannier and emerged with an old cap-and-ball dragoon pistol in his fist—the early Civil War model manufactured by the New Haven Arms Company.

"Took it off a dead Yankee, may he rest in peace," Yancy explained. "Fires big, cone-shaped balls that shock a man to death even when they strike an arm or leg."

"Fine hogleg in its day," Cas agreed. "But you have to charge and cap each shot."

"So? You required only one shot at Padgett's Landing. 'You don't shoot until you *know* you can't miss,' " he quoted his younger companion. " 'That's the big idea.' "

Cas surrendered with a laugh. "I teach them too well. All right, but I still think you need a new revolver."

Comet nickered, and Cas snapped his head in the gelding's direction. The horses were picketed close in. Cas had decided, before he and Yancy rode out, to grain the horses each night rather than let them graze on a wide tether. If enemies wanted to kill him on the trail, the best first step was to kill or steal his horse.

Comet was a good bellwether of trouble, and Cas kept a closer eye on him.

"I'm truly sorry we'll be swinging west of Dodge," Yancy remarked, yawning. "Is it true it's the Babylon of the Plains?"

"It's a wide-open heller," Cas conceded. "But so are all the railhead towns in Kansas. Abilene and Ellsworth give it a run, and Newton is so rough that Wild Bill Hickok refused to tote a badge there."

"Did you ever meet Doc Holliday?" Yancy pressed.

"Made a point *not* to. I was there this past July when John Holliday was yanking teeth in his room at the Dodge House. I had a tooth that ached somethin' fierce, but I wouldn't let that lunger cough on me."

Yancy leaned forward excitedly, all ears—he devoured Western lore. "I read how Doc takes advice from no man except Wyatt Earp, and then rarely."

"John Holliday is a good man to let alone, all right. Doesn't cotton to being close herded. And the way he sees it, being so sick, he has nothing to lose in a gunfight."

Comet looked in the direction of the trail and pricked his ears. Cas loosened his gun in the holster.

"And the Long Branch?" Yancy prompted eagerly. "As wild as the dime novels and penny papers make it out to be?"

"Wild? Not so's I noticed. A drunk waddie was arrested for violating the gun ordinance and puked all over Bat Masterson's fine new boots. Bat cane whipped him."

Comet nickered again, and Cas rose quickly from the log he was seated upon.

"What?" Yancy demanded, seizing his scattergun and unfolding his formidable frame to stand up.

"Maybe nothing," Cas said. "Stand back from the fire until I look around."

Cas skinned his .44 and moved slowly down to the trail, bent low to avoid skylining himself. His hearing had been trained by years spent on the open frontier. He sent it out beyond the immediate area and detected the faint rataplan of galloping hooves, fading to the south.

"I heard one rider," he told Yancy when he returned. "There's no proof, but he could have been watching us. Maybe scouting us for a report. We may have to pull foot at any moment."

"Think it's partners of the man you shot in Louisiana?"

"That's my first guess. Could also be a posse intending to arrest us for that killing, though I doubt it. Sleep on your weapons, Swede, and from now on, keep your eyes to all sides."

Chapter 7

Deadwood Gulch,
Dakota Territory

An attractive young woman, wearing a royal blue velvet dress with a frilly bustle and a lace flounce, stared in dismay at Deadwood's lower Main Street, trying to screw up enough courage to cross it. It was a thick gumbo of mud, night slops, and tripes, all of it attracting a shifting black blanket of flies. Freight wagons with their six-foot wheels and one-inch-thick iron tires had left permanent ruts in the street, ruts that could easily trip a person. All around her the fir trees of the Black Hills pointed into the sky like spear tips, offering a little beauty amid the ugliness overwhelming her.

Bonnets had fallen from favor during the seventies, and she wore a beribboned straw hat with a bavolet attached at the back to protect her neck from the sun. Her front hair had been brushed back without a part while in back it cascaded down long and full, a cinnamon profusion.

"Morning, Miss Steele!" shouted a bullwhacker slogging along beside a wagon piled with gold ore. "Laws, do you look pretty this mornin'!"

"Thank you, Jimmy!" she called back above the constant din of money being made.

"See you later at the faro table!" he added, cracking his long blacksnake whip over a team of oxen.

Every man in woman-starved Deadwood was a bull in the hot moons, but Kathleen's beauty and bearing rendered her immune from coarse advances—except in the case of Dakota Boggs, who respected nothing and no one.

Steeling herself with a deep breath, she hiked her skirts and plunged into the disgusting street, aiming for the Gem Theater on the other side. Young men called runners worked right out in the soupy mess, soliciting customers for the businesses that hired them. A street vendor was doing a lively business selling honey popcorn balls, a favorite with underfed prospectors.

"Drat!" Kathleen exclaimed when her left foot sank deep into a mud-filled pothole. Her side-lacing half boots were practically ruined just from crossing the street.

Her face felt strained from all the gracious smiles she flashed as men tipped their hats and greeted her. Some of their deference, she realized in disgust, was because she was widely perceived as the courtesan of Levi Carruthers. Most of these men didn't know that any decent woman in Deadwood was lured there by Al Swearengen's lies—and *kept* there by outright brutality.

She had almost reached the safety of the board-walk when someone shouted, "Look out!"

Kathleen glanced up just in time to witness yet another act of lawless brutality. A prospector in clothing stained red from ore stepped up close behind another man and pulled a gun from under his sack coat. He shot his victim at such close range that the man's shirt caught on fire from the powder burn. The body took two jerky steps while its nervous system tried to deny the fact of death, then dropped hard right in front of the Gem.

The murderer simply strolled away, and no one tried to apprehend him. She knew Sheriff Bullock would not investigate because the killing happened in the Badlands, lower Main Street beyond the deadline. The body would simply be rolled into the street and left for the hogs. Pigs had the run of Deadwood, welcomed because they ate garbage and human waste—sometimes human remains. They'd become so numerous that the town recently hired a hog reeve to shoo them away from dwellings.

Gathering her wits, Kathleen glanced away from the body and hurried onto the boardwalk and inside the dark, nearly empty Gem. A pretty but careworn woman in a green silk dress occupied a table near the stage.

"Ginny!" Kathleen exclaimed, grateful for some friendly companionship. "Did you see what just happened outside?"

"No, thank God, but I heard it," replied Ginny Lofley, a singer at the Montana Saloon. "Just one more reason why we need to—"

Kathleen sent her a high sign, and Ginny caught herself just in time. She held up her glass. "A brandy sour, and not my first of the day. But I'll be discreet."

At the moment, the Gem was empty of customers except for two drunks passed out at the bar. Kathleen considered Crawley Deacon, the bartender, one of the few true gentlemen in Deadwood. Even so, owner Al Swearengen had his minions planted everywhere, and the wrong remark could get even a pretty girl cruelly murdered.

"Say hey, sunshine girl," Crawley greeted her.

"Can't get enough of this roach pit, eh? Al told me not to set up the faro rig for three hours yet."

"Just got lonely," Kathleen lied, for she had been hoping to meet Ginny and talk strategy. "A glass of applejack, please."

Crawley glanced carefully toward the stairs at the rear leading to Swearengen's office and rooms. Al was married for the second time and had a house to go home to, yet rarely left the confines of the Gem.

"You know," Crawley told her as he filled her glass with iced hard cider, "you were never a drinker when you first got here. I guess being lured to Deadwood under false pretenses will do that to a gal."

Kathleen only nodded, afraid to trust anyone who worked for Al with any confidences. But Crawley was right about her drinking. Witnessing murders, savage beatings, and so much suffering by a community of literally captive women was more than she could endure without a little mind numbing now and then. It was even worse for the girls forced to tender their bodies—nearly all of them were addicted to opium, coca-leaf potions, or laudanum. Not a month passed without one or two of them committing suicide.

"Is that a new magazine?" Kathleen asked as she sat down.

"Yes, it's called *Ladies' Home Journal*," Ginny replied. "Home—remember that word? I'm reading it so I don't forget how women are supposed to live."

Kathleen nodded, her pretty, oval face a mask of longing.

"But this magazine," Ginny added, "is also what we're looking at if Al or Levi look us up, all right? Al, especially, is suspicious of us. I think he knows we're trying to get out."

"Never mind trying. We *have* to get out," Kathleen said with quiet passion.

From where she sat, she could see the legs of the murdered man through the wide-open doors. The *Black Hills Pioneer* had a flippant phrase for such ruthless killings: *He got in front of a bullet.* Around here, where men suffered from acute boredom and backbreaking labor, murders were entertainment fare and little else. These men were here to get rich quick and move on, not to establish a decent community for families.

"Oh, you're darn tootin' we're getting out," Ginny vowed, one hand brushing ringlets of blond hair away from her eyes. "Both of us have been prisoners here for almost a year. I'm escaping from this town even if it kills me."

"Town?" A skeptical dimple wrinkled Kathleen's fair cheek. "It's a den of cutthroats," she corrected her friend. "Most of the decent men are killed or leave in disgust."

Ginny nodded emphatically. "Before I fell for that phony advertisement about teaching music to 'proper young ladies,' I had not guessed so much depravity existed in the entire world, much less in one remote gulch."

"Remote" was the very problem, Kathleen told herself. There were simply so few ways out, which meant Al's toadies could watch everyone. This gulch was barely accessible on horses, and even they had to be left outside Deadwood. Railroads were years away from entering the Black Hills, and the Deadwood Coach was owned by Levi Carruthers—just as he supposedly owned her when she wasn't working at the Gem.

"Anyhow," Ginny said, "forget about the new telegrapher who's staying at Wagner's Grand Central. I saw him talking with Al and Levi."

Kathleen felt the sting of tears, but held them back. She and Ginny had been stymied in every attempt to get word out of here to someone who might help. There was no regular mail service yet except Charlie Utter's, and Al's spies worked for him. Kathleen had tried several times, at great risk, to get a letter to the outside world. Once she was even forced to eat the letter—the alternative was death if Levi found it. He and Al had so many spies and boot lickers that even composing and hiding a letter was fraught with risks.

"I still think we should talk to Seth Bullock," Ginny said. "He seems an honorable man."

"Quiet and courageous," Kathleen agreed. "But his family is here, and if he fails to honor the terms of the deadline, their lives are forfeit. Besides, how could we ever meet with him secretly? He always stays on his side of the deadline, and so must we unless Al or Levi escort us past it."

Even an honest sheriff, in Deadwood, must compromise or be killed. Bullock had met with Swearengen and agreed on a deadline across Main Street running from Al's Gem to the Bella Union across the street. To the left of that line was Bullock's zone, and laws were vigorously enforced. To the right were the Badlands and Chinatown, the red-light district where law entered at its own peril.

"Yes, I suppose they'll serve lemonade in Hades before we cross the deadline unobserved," said an irritated Ginny. "But we can't keep backing and filling, hon. We must come up with a plan and act on it. Perhaps—sakes and saints! Here comes Al. Look down at the magazine *quick*."

"Well, what have we here?" Swearengen's gravel-pan voice greeted them, his eyes lingering on Kathleen. "Have my favorite lap kittens come to see me, reeking of alcohol and pretending to be studious? Crawley, wake up the sports. They need to see this inspiring lesson in home and hearth."

He wore a frock coat, dark wool trousers, and a white shirt ruffled at the front. He was freshly barbered, and Kathleen found his bay rum tonic cloying.

"Al," she greeted him demurely, carefully keeping the loathing out of her face.

"Hear that magisterial tone, songbird?" Swearengen asked Ginny. "My little faro dealer, the main attraction in a cathouse, acts like she's an F.F.V. I like an uppity bitch like her. Classes up the place."

Anger pinched Kathleen's throat closed. Al smirked and leaned down so close that she could hear his breath whistling in his nostrils.

"Here's a lulu just for you girls. Upon signing a new treaty, a Quaker Indian agent and a Sioux chief are celebrating by traveling across the country in a Pullman car. They're accompanied by the agent's mother, wife, and daughter. After two days on the train, the shocked matron takes her boy aside. 'Son,' she tells him, 'do you realize that flea-bitten savage has been enjoying carnal knowledge with your wife and daughter?' 'Oh, don't worry, Mother,' the Quaker answers proudly. 'It's a tough treaty—he can't touch *you*.' "

Swearengen shook with mirth, but his face went cold and dangerous when Kathleen refused to react. "Is that joke too vulgar for your refined farm-girl tastes?"

"It's just not funny," Kathleen replied, trying not to antagonize her unstable boss.

"Don't ever forget, my haughty lady," he threatened, "that the difference between you and a crib strumpet is the amount that faro rig brings in. Should business ever slack off, I'll strip you buck and parade you through the streets just to drum up trade. And remember, *I* don't have Levi's dog-in-a-manger problem."

Kathleen flushed and Swearengen headed back upstairs to his office.

"Whew," Ginny said, "isn't he in a fine pucker today? One of these days that man will kill you. What was that about Levi's dog-in-a-manger problem?"

Ginny was Kathleen's only confidante in Deadwood, but if Levi's secret ever got noised about, Kathleen knew he would kill her. So she eluded the question.

"Al's not worried about profits," she told her friend. "Crawley told me this place brings in five thousand dollars a night or better. And the faro game is rigged so that Al never loses more cash than he has in the drawer. The customers know it, too, but they refuse to accuse me. I feel terrible sitting there and swindling them."

"Oh, to be back in the States," Ginny lamented. "*How* could I ever have thought that Illinois is boring? Even if it is, I'll take it."

"Back in the States" . . . the very phrase filled Kathleen with longing. Not only for family and safety, but for real culture. Places like the Gem Theater weren't really "theaters" at all, just immoral cesspools offering crude burlesque and parodies of decent culture. But thank God not all the theaters in Deadwood were coarse. Soon the Deadwood Opera House was presenting *Tristan and Isolt,* one of the world's great love stories. She treasured these productions as proof she, too, had once been in love.

"That look on your face," Ginny cut into her reverie. "It's a fellow, right?"

Kathleen shrugged. "Not exactly, not *my* fellow.

He did propose once, though. I wanted to say yes, but he had that look in his eye—like he had some adventuring to do. When we were young back in Texas, I used to pretend he was my hero who would someday rescue me. I can't help thinking he still will."

Kathleen had never mentioned Cas Everett's name to anyone in Deadwood, and now that the news of his family's massacre was newspaper fodder, she never would. After word of the slaughter reached Deadwood, Dakota Boggs had sent several of his night-riding thugs out of town—more intriguing, Boggs himself had disappeared from Deadwood for some time *before* news of the slaughter, accompanied by three of his most trusted riders. And since returning, he was living like a rajah and producing flash rolls like a professional gambler.

"Just forget about any knight in shining armor," Ginny lectured. "It's men who put us in this mess."

"And we who must get ourselves out," Kathleen agreed.

"My family thinks I'm dead," Ginny remarked. "My boss at the Montana pretended to be a preacher and wrote that I died of cholera. But why have your people done nothing to find out about you?"

"I had a terrible row with my father. He'd been after me for years to get married. I'd had several proposals, but turned them down."

"Because," Ginny put in, "you were waiting for the other fella to ask you again? The one who needed to do some adventuring?"

Kathleen nodded. "Father considered me an old maid at twenty-five. But the final straw was when he found out I was submitting stories to the ladies' press. He told me I was farm stock, not some blasted scribbler. We had a terrible clash, and I didn't feel welcome. In desperation, I answered Al's advertisement for a 'schoolteacher,' and I haven't been free for a moment ever since."

"You must admit," Ginny said, her tone resentful as she studied Kathleen's velvet dress, "Levi's becoming obsessed with you has made your life easier."

"More comfortable, yes. Not easier. You'd understand if you knew him better. Oh, no, get set for more crudity."

Kathleen watched a big, hard-knit man with a long teamster's mustache and a bluff, weather-seamed face step nonchalantly over the body outside and into the Gem. He wore a new white linen suit with a concho belt.

"Good mornin', ladies," Dakota Boggs greeted them, eyes raking over each of them. "You know, I'm feelin' fit as a ruttin' buck. What say the three of us go upstairs and—"

"I'd rather drink lye," Ginny cut in.

"No need to get on the peck."

Boggs trapped Kathleen's eyes with his. His lips pulled back off his teeth in an eerie smile that failed to include the corners of his mouth. His eyes were hard black agates. "You know, sugar britches, you beat the rest of these ten-penny sluts in Deadwood all hollow. No wonder Levi cottons to you. If he wasn't my boss, I'd—"

"I know what you'd do," she snapped, "and I don't care to hear about it."

Boggs laughed, enjoying himself immensely, for bullying came naturally to him. "Hell, next time try the tornado juice instead of that apple pop. Might get you over your prissy peeve."

Standing in an insolent slouch beside their table, Boggs inclined his head toward the sprawled body on the boardwalk. "Looks like another disappointed gambler cashed in his own chips, hey?"

"He was shot in the back," Ginny stated flatly.

"Then he's lucky. Just like that dandy Hickok in the No. 10 Saloon, he never saw it coming. We kill 'em good here in Deadwood."

A mask of pure hatred settled over Ginny's features, and she opened her mouth to speak. Kathleen kicked her ankle under the table and mouthed the word "no."

Of all the threats in Deadwood, Swearengen included, Kathleen most feared Dakota Boggs. He loved to flash the cards in his wallet, printed back in St. Louis on fancy pebbled stock. They cryptically identified him as a "businessman's agent." He was in charge of a Black Hills vigilante group called the Regulators that had gradually come under the authority of Levi Carruthers, a wealthy and powerful speculator. Carruthers pretended to respectability, but in reality chased after gold strikes and forced prospectors to sell him their promising claims. If beatings or killings were required, Boggs and his men eagerly set to work.

Boggs, Kathleen told herself again, was obviously a rich man lately. He was sporting expensive new clothing and gambling in the high-stakes games instead of the joker poker he used to play. *Did he?* she wondered. *Did he have anything to do with killing Cas' family?* There were only a few weak clues, but this soulless reptile was capable of any reprehensible crime.

Boggs' final words to Kathleen left menace hanging in the air. "Levi may not be around forever. Could be you'll have a new bunkie someday."

"*See* how he's dressing lately?" Ginny demanded the moment Boggs left. "He's copying Levi, trying to act like a big man. It's like wrapping a snake in silk. Dakota Boggs would gun down a nun for her gold tooth."

"He may have done even worse," Kathleen said. Ginny sent her a searching glance, but Kathleen stopped herself from telling her friend about Cas Everett's family—or her growing suspicion.

Chapter 8

For another week the two saddle-weary riders dusted their hocks deeper into Texas, skirting the southern boundary of the Indian Territory. They crossed the now defunct Chisholm Trail, and despite being into the third year since the trail's abandonment, flattened grass at Red River Station still marked the passing of earlier herds.

Doan's Store was located where the new Western Trail crossed the Red. Yancy got his first view of Texas cowboys whipping beeves on the butt and churning the river to foam as they forded, driving agency beef to the Indian Territory. He also finally got his chance to visit the famous trail-drive store, a modest frame building with a corral and sheds attached.

"It's not what I pictured it to be," Yancy told Cas as he pocketed a new sack of gingersnaps. "I thought it would be bigger and grander. The fellow behind the counter has a goiter the size of an onion and coughed snot all over me."

"Welcome to the West," Cas joked, "where mean truth gets turned into storybook lies by dough bellies in celluloid collars."

For several more days, they pushed on across the hot, dry base of the Texas Panhandle. Yellow dust plumes spiraled up behind them and died like wraiths in the still air. Cas enforced a rigorous trail discipline: fifty miles a day, noon meals in the saddle. Camp meals were simple, too. After eating, they scoured their few utensils in the sand and moved on.

"It's been ten days since you heard that rider near our camp," Yancy said as the two friends crossed the cracked bed of a dry, ancient lake. "Any trouble since then?"

"No," Cas said, "but I didn't expect it out here."

He waved an arm to indicate the open, parched terrain. "I purposely picked this country because I've come to appreciate it. Good ground cover is scarce, and the mountains are too far distant to darken the approach of an enemy at night. But I think we're being watched, and at the first opportunity, we'll be dry-gulched."

If this pronouncement struck fear into Yancy's heart, the sunburned blond forgot to show it. He liked to rhyme and sing to pass the long hours in the saddle. He winked at Cas and belted one out now.

> Here lies Lester Moore,
> Four slugs from a forty-four,
> No less, no more.

Cas burst out laughing. "Old son, that's a tonic."

The mirth died in his throat, however, when he saw what was coming.

"It really *is* devil wire," he said in dismay. "And this makes the third time now we've found it strung across the dang trail. Some of these ornery ranchers must figure they own every jackrabbit that crosses their range, but very few of 'em even got a legal deed."

Joseph Glidden's recently patented barbed wire, Cas was discovering to his dismay, was now in widespread use and seriously impeding their journey north. The horses could jump it, but Cas was unwilling to risk injuring them.

"I don't like doing this," he said, taking a good squint around. "But a man has a right to move across these ranges without having his horse shredded to wolf bait by bobwire. This is a public road, not a ranch lane."

Cas swung down and stomped out the staples, pulling the strands low enough for the horses to step over them.

"There's bad trouble coming on this score," Cas said as they rode on. "The West wasn't meant to become giant fiefdoms. The open range lets every man travel and every cow graze."

"You were raised a farmer," Yancy reminded him. "Every farmer knows that fenced land is the best way to protect his fields from cattle and those that trample crops a-purpose."

"That rings right," Cas conceded. "But I'm still a free-range man. These ranchers don't string bobwire to protect their land—it's to keep other ranchers from using their water source. Only, it's *not* theirs. This land hasn't been legally owned since the old Spanish land-grant days."

"Cry all you want," Yancy told him. "Devil wire is here to stay."

Cas nodded glumly. "I know. But the old frontiersmen tell me there was a time when you could travel from El Paso to Canada and never even see a fence. I guess the shining times are gone."

Onward the two riders pushed, hoarding their water in this dry expanse of northwest Texas. Most water in the region was still hauled or hand pumped. But Cas spotted a few windmill pumps bringing water into attics of homes, where it was gravity-dispersed.

Cas' mind kept returning to his family like a tongue to a missing tooth. Each time he thought of them on that lonely, wind-swept hill, a knife turned deep in his guts. Yancy, Cas noticed, was holding up like a trouper even though pounding a saddle was foreign to him. Only the monotonous diet seemed to drive him to complaints. Beans and hardtack were the main fare on this trail, with a can of peaches every few days.

"Augh!" Yancy exclaimed two hours after they pulled down the most recent barbed-wire fence. Both men were gnawing their lunch in the saddle. "Beans and 'tack every night, jerked beef in the saddle. No Cincinnati chicken? A man can't live without it." He meant bacon.

Cas shrugged. "Sorry, old son. Guess I've got used to mean grub. In my line the fare gets mighty spartan. Fugitives on the prod generally don't select settled areas. They prefer god-forgotten spots like Robber's Roost or Hole-in-the-Wall. And I'm damned if I'm leading a pack animal—that tempts every hardcase in sight to bushwhack me for my supplies."

Yancy scowled as he chewed. "And you call that a job?"

"Call it a case of the squitters, if you prefer, but I reckon it's what I'm best at."

"You were a good farmer, as I recollect."

"Busting sod is honorable work but always bored me."

Yancy shook his head stubbornly. "Right there's the trouble with you notional young bucks today. Don't *matter* if a man's bored. No law says labor must be fun."

"Fun isn't in the mix, chucklehead. Is this fun

right now, broiling under a sun hotter than the hinges of hell? Was that *fun* back in Louisiana when lead was flying twelve ways a second?"

"I take your point," Yancy said. "So it's the money."

"Sure, but it's more than that. It's a question of . . . well, of doing the thing that *matters*. I don't hunt down debt skippers or rustlers, only the dregs of the criminals. Unfortunately, that's what got my family killed—even the dregs have friends."

For some time Cas had noticed dust boiling up behind them. He turned around in the saddle and studied the situation through field glasses.

"Just like I feared," he told Yancy. "Some cowboys have finally caught up to us for stomping down their bobwire. Stand by for the blast—these Texas waddies are real hotheads."

Yancy speared his express gun from its boot. "*They* can stand by for the blast."

"Drop that weapon, you fool. There's five of them, and if you raise a weapon at these harumscarum cow nurses, they'll give you a bad case of lead colic. Besides, do you want to kill fellow Texicans who are only being loyal to the brand?"

" 'Course not," Yancy replied, "unless it's them or us."

"Most waddies only unlimber to shoot at snakes or train lanterns. If we don't brace them first, they won't likely shoot at us."

By now the galloping riders bore down on them like the devil beating bark. Six-shooters erupted with a sound like whips cracking.

Yancy's words were tipped with scorn. "Must be shooting at snakes, huh? We better shoot back before they find their range and blast us out of our saddles."

"Leave your hand off that gun," Cas snapped.

"They're shooting at clouds, not us, just making noise to scare us. You know cowboys are wild. Just keep your mouth shut and don't antagonize them."

Cas pulled back on the reins, then wheeled Comet to face the oncoming cowboys. He kept his left hand on the reins, his right raised high in the universal range sign that he held no concealed weapon.

Whooping and yipping like Comanches, the cowboys tried to frighten the two riders by racing their horses as close as possible before reining in.

"Both you sons a bitches," said a lean young man with a Deep South accent, "toss down them lead chuckers."

Not one of the cowboys, Cas noticed, looked to be over twenty. Their exaggeratedly hard scowls couldn't eliminate pimples and shaving cuts. Nonetheless, this was at close range now.

"Boys, I know you ride for the brand, but be fair and go by the range rules," Cas cajoled. "You never strip a man of his weapons out here unless you know he's guilty of a crime. See, you're s'posed to ask a few questions, get the lay of the land first."

The speaker looked less sure of himself. "Did you two cut a bobwire fence 'bout eight miles back?"

"Nope," Cas replied immediately.

"He's a chicken-pluckin' liar, Rudy!" shouted a cowboy with freckles and carrot-colored hair. "These two jays are the only ones to leave tracks in the past two days."

"No need to get your bristles up," Cas assured them. "You said the fence was cut. Cutting fences is a crime, right? Because it means you have to lug out a wire roller and repair the wire. But I kicked out the staples. That's a nuisance, granted, but the wire is still intact. It's easy to fix."

Rudy still scowled, but he was thinking about Cas' evident legal talk. In truth, Cas had made it up in hopes the green cowboys might be cowed—after all, the spiel was also common sense.

"I don't give a lick. You still have no right," Carrot Top piped up, "to damage that fence. And right now you two are trespassing on the Lazy S spread."

Cas watched a third cowhand, his leather chaps so new they were hardly cactus-scarred, turn his attention to Yancy. His eyes widened at the sheer size of this horsebacker, but his face hardened with contempt as he realized the second rider was a lowly dirt scratcher.

"Take a gander at the big pig farmer, boys!" he called out. "He's wearin' *shoes* in the saddle! Shoes covered with dried pig crap. And his 'hat' is gra'maw's clothespin bag."

Yancy couldn't suffer such abuse in silence. "Another pup who thinks he's a full-growed dog."

New Chaps flushed and wagged the muzzle of his old single-action Colt Navy. "The last pig farmer who insulted me took a long trip over the range."

Cas nearly botched it by laughing out loud—this little sprout had never cleaned a fish much less killed a man. But these lads were all pointing firearms, and Cas knew how "accidents" happened.

"Look here, fellows," Cas said in a take-charge manner, "since when do Texas men allow the murder of innocent women?"

Rudy was more startled than offended. "The hell you jabbering?"

"Yancy and me," Cas explained, "are on the trail of the men who killed my family, which included my ma and two sisters. Does *that* give us license to pop out a few staples?"

All five youths looked like they'd been slapped

hard. The seriousness of the claim made them stare in motionless shock—either it was horribly true or a brazen lie by desperate men.

"Well, I'll be switched," Rudy suddenly said. "Are we ever blockheads! Fellas, meet Mr. Cas Everett. That's him. It's all true, every word he said."

A change came over the young cowpokes. Word of what happened to the Everett family had spread through the Lone Star State like fire in dead grass.

The cowboys hastily leathered their short irons.

"We know about your family, Mr. Everett," Rudy said. "And we're powerful sorry. Some of us cowboys are even talking about an all-Texas posse to run these killers down."

"Thanks, boys, but I'd nix that idea. I've found that one or two men usually get the job done better. Unleashing a posse is like firing a shotgun into a rain barrel."

New Chaps caught Yancy's eye. "Mister, I apologize all to hell for my mouth. I was raised on a farm myself, in Missouri. It's just, when you become a cowpuncher, you're expected to hot jaw the farmers. Mostly it's talk."

Yancy waved off the offense. "You're all stout lads."

"Touch you for luck, Mr. Everett?" Carrot Top asked.

At this, Yancy sent Cas a puzzled look. Cas groaned inwardly. This "touch you for luck" business had started with Wild Bill Hickok. Now it had spread to any man in the West who was said to be a gunfighter. The reasoning was that any man who survived multiple gunfights must have extraordinary luck—luck that might even rub off. Never mind that "lucky" Wild Bill's brains got sprayed all over a mediocre poker hand in Deadwood.

Cas shook hands with all of them.

"They say you're a gentleman, Mr. Everett," Rudy said as the saddle stiffs prepared to ride off. "I know it's true now. You coulda killed all five of us for waving guns in your face."

"Not all five of you," Cas gainsaid. "Two or three, maybe. I can tell you men know how to take care of yourselves. One of you would've popped me over. You're Texans."

The young cowboys seemed to grow a foot taller in the saddle.

" 'Touch you for luck?' " Yancy repeated as the two men rode on. *"You?"*

"Never mind," Cas said. "We need to start watching for a line of chaparral hills. That's where we turn north again. By late afternoon tomorrow we should cross the Canadian into New Mexico Territory."

"Hills, you said?"

Cas nodded. "I take your drift. Yeah, after we cross a piece of the Jornada, we run smack into plenty of good ambush country. And we're fools if we don't assume somebody will try to curl our toes."

Chapter 9

By Cas' reckoning it was on the fifteenth day of their journey when he and Yancy reached the Canadian. Northeastern New Mexico Territory lay on the other side, through which they must traverse to avoid the western boundary of the Indian Territory.

"River's bank full," Cas remarked, casting a careful eye around them. The terrain here was mostly barren scrub hills with the occasional mesquite tree or jackpine. "It's still catchin' snowmelt from the mountains. But I've crossed worse."

"Not I," Yancy confessed. "It's not so wide, but that current looks brisk."

"I usually try to find a gravel bar," Cas explained as he swung down. "But I don't like the idea of spending much time in these hills. Let's just swim it and get out into the open again, at least for a bit."

Yancy, too, lit down and emulated Cas, who was loosening the saddle girth.

"They'll need extra wind," Cas explained. "You just watch me and do what I do. Wait until I'm on shore again before you cross."

Cas coaxed his reluctant chestnut into the swift-moving river. The moment he felt the bottom fall out from under Comet, Cas stretched out in the cold water and let himself float backward until he had the gelding's tail firmly in his hands. He scissor-kicked to help the effort. Comet was a strong swimmer, and they gained the sandy bank after only a brief ford.

"Easy as pie!" he shouted across to Yancy. "Just ki-yi him into the river!"

Yancy looked nervous but waved his hat gamely. However, when he thumped the sorrel with his heels, trying to head him into the river, the gelding chinned the moon and sent Yancy cartwheeling into the sand.

The moment Cas saw that Yancy wasn't hurt, he doubled up with mirth. "Good plan, Swede—just have that churnhead *toss* you over the river!"

"Shut your fish trap!" Yancy hollered back. "How do I get this stupid glue tub to ford?"

"Back him up and run him in," Cas suggested. "Make sure you hold his head high. He'll have less time to debate it."

That plan worked, at first. Yancy and the sorrel got up a head of steam and were too far into the river for the horse to change its mind. Yancy also did a good job of easing back from the saddle to grab the horse's tail.

However, Cas quickly saw how Yancy's inability to swim made him hang on too tight. And the big man's weight threatened to submerge the sorrel.

Cas already had his rope ready. "Let go and grab hold of this!" he shouted, flipping the coils out and watching the hemp unloop.

The horse's head bobbed desperately as it tried to counter both the current and the weight of its master. Despite the fact that Cas' rope practically smacked him in the head, Yancy was too scared to give up his hold.

"You lunkhead!" Cas roared. "Grab that rope or I'll shoot you!"

He jerked back his .44 and sent a bullet skipping past Yancy. Without a moment's delay, the big farmer let go of his horse and grabbed the rope. Cas led him in like he was a helpless whale.

"Well, sir," Yancy managed, spouting water as he rose to his feet, "I b'lieve I made a good showing at my first river."

A moment later, however, he checked his saddle panniers and scowled. "We've lost our whiskey. And I'll soon be dried to jerky on that desert you talked about."

"For a fact you will," Cas assured him.

They tightened the girth again and headed north across the notorious Jornada del Muerto or Journey of Death. At its full length, it was a ninety-mile stretch of some of the worst desert in America, at times as dry and deadly as the Great Salt Desert of Utah Territory. Cas figured, though, that they would need to cover only about thirty miles of it, sticking to their present course.

Yancy stared, fascinated and a bit cowed by the exotic, barren landscape. The only trees were wind-twisted junipers, stunted and widely scattered. The stately and tall cactus called Spanish Bayonet thrust high into the pure blue sky, with cholla and prickly pear dotting the parched ground. Now and then bleached bones—some of them human—poked up from shallow drifts of sand.

"Expect any trouble here?" Yancy asked.

Cas shook his head. "An ambusher would not only have to hide himself but his horse. Once we cross the Jornada, though, we'll be in hills. Timbered hills."

"Cas? Them young cow nurses yesterday, askin' if they could touch you for luck—does that happen to you every place you go?"

"Nah. Thank God. There's still few likenesses of

me, and usually I give only my front name or just make up a summer name. And I fight shy of cameras—a man's a fool to turn himself into a target."

"Still don't seem real," Yancy mused. "Those cowboys all knew of you. My neighbor, a newspaper darlin'!"

"Oh, hell, stop being a schoolboy. It's easy for any fellow to catch himself a reputation as a gun thrower. You got to remember, back in the Land of Steady Habits, people are death on heroes and bloodcurdlin' tales of pistoleros—can't get enough of it. I see it all over, even out here. Why, half the hombres I've snared call themselves Wild Bill."

"I've pondered it, and it's farming that drives some of 'em to it, Cas boy. Me, being a mite soft between the head handles, I like scratching dirt. Gives me a proud feeling when something I plant and tend lives to yield. Most men ain't like that, though, including you."

Cas nodded, feeling the dry desert air sap the moisture from him. "It's backbreaking labor from can to can't, and only a coin toss separates feast from famine. Boring, monotonous work, whereas a young man is full of vinegar, of wanting and curiosity."

"Yah shoor. Maybe an older outlaw buys him a drink and shows him his notches. And there's another new road agent."

"I guess you *do* employ some gray matter when you're loitering out in your fields," Cas told him. "Partly it is farming, I s'pose. And it doesn't help that the penny press turns every skunk-bit coyote into Robin Hood. Look how the newspapers are treating Frank and Jesse James ever since those harebrained Pinkerton men blew off their ma's arm and killed their stepbrother back in seventy-five."

"Huh!" said Yancy, who stubbornly hewed to honesty and had little tolerance for those who didn't. "She wouldn't be any kind of martyr at all if her boys were just plain dirt farmers. Robin Hood, my sweet aunt."

"I just wish that every knucklehead who admires these cheap, town-fighting murderers had to watch a gutshot woman or child die from wild bullets."

"Or bury a decent and loving family," Yancy added, his face closed now. He didn't have to knuckle the sudden moisture from his eyes—the dry air took it.

"Yeah," Cas agreed quietly, "or that."

The two riders cut north through the Jornada in a little over three hours, entering the timbered hill country. Cas slid his Spencer carbine from its boot and held it straight up with the butt plate riding on his right thigh. Late-afternoon sun blazed on the grassy slopes and threw the menacing shadows of the trees into stark relief.

Behind him, Yancy was again serenading Creation.

> Oh, the moon shone bright
> on the tipples of her nits,
> the tipples of her nits,
> the tipples of her nits.
> Oh—

Yancy abruptly fell silent as he caught up with Cas on a steep ridge. "Gog and Magog!" he exclaimed, gazing into a green valley below them. "Did you know about this place?"

"Nope. There's new towns along every trail. Most won't last."

The narrow valley below them was bright with

wildflowers. Along the banks of a stream, a settlement had sprung up. Some of the buildings had glass windows, and the last of the day's sunlight tinged them copper.

"Well," Yancy said, "my toggery's not so impressive, but my thirst is. Matter fact, I'm dried to jerky just like I predicted. Any objection to us seeing if they got a thirst parlor?"

"Why not?" Cas agreed. "If our killer in Deadwood has plans to dispatch us, I'd rather face him in a saloon than on the trail."

"Place is called Perdido," Yancy said, reading a painted sign on the side of the livery barn as they rode in. "Queer sorta name, huh?"

"It's Spanish. Means 'lost.' "

Despite the pastoral location, Cas saw it was a typical crossroads settlement of the day, more of a naked profit center than a town. No church, no school, no courthouse. Just a saloon with batwing doors, a general store with barrels of crackers and pickles out front, a barbershop, a hotel hardly larger than a packing crate, an undertaker's parlor, a harness shop, and a handful of private dwellings, most made of raw lumber. A few at the very edge of town were made of puddled adobe and had *ristras,* strings of bright red chili peppers, hanging by the doorways.

"Shouldn't we leave our horses at the livery?" Yancy asked. "They could use a rubdown and hay."

Cas looked the place over. At the moment the wagon-seamed main thoroughfare was empty except for a water wagon sprinkling down the dust.

"I think we best skip it," he told Yancy. "Looks peaceful enough right now, but the place will fill up when the heat of day burns off. We'll rub the horses down good when we camp later. I don't want them out of our sight."

They reined in at the Three Sisters Saloon, a big, raw-plank building with a board canopy and a long hitching post out front. They looped their reins around the tie rail. Both men loosed the girth and dropped the bridles so the horses could drink from a narrow wooden water trough behind the rail.

"Can I take my gal Patsy?" Yancy asked, sliding his double ten from the sheath. "I'd feel naked without her."

For the past decade or so, more and more Western towns had passed strictly enforced gun ordinances: check them in when you enter; pick them up when you leave. Cas had no desire, given what he and Yancy were undertaking, to go unheeled. Fortunately, New Mexico Territory and the Arizona Territory were still wide-open and virtually without law in the more remote reaches. Which meant law-abiding men were expected to be armed.

"Take it," Cas said. "I didn't see a sheriff's office. If there's a gun ordinance, we'll just leave."

He followed Yancy up onto the boardwalk. Cas stopped suddenly when his scalp tingled. He glanced up and down the street, eyes searching.

"What is it?" Yancy asked him. "Got the fantods?"

"Must be," Cas admitted. "I don't see anything amiss. But I'd bet my horse we're being watched."

"I know I am," Yancy said. "Look what's waiting to greet us out front, Cas boy. You may be the famous pistolero, but it's a handsome farmer for *this* lass. See how she ogles me?"

Cas saw a painted woman step outside to greet them. She wore a rose taffeta dress with a bustle. The ample-bosomed redhead had draped a feather boa around her plump white shoulders. She had a pretty enough face. But it was a brittle kind of beauty Cas had seen before—those features, he knew, could suddenly go hard and hateful in a heartbeat.

The woman's low-necked bodice had Yancy grinning like a butcher's dog.

"Lord, Cas," he muttered as they thumped along the boardwalk, "she might's well plop 'em on the counter for us. Ladies' fashions have got bold, huh?"

Cas smiled wickedly, realizing a capital show was about to unfold. Yancy had spent very little time in saloons except for the crude tent back in Iron Springs, and he knew next to nothing about sporting girls.

"Land sakes!" the sport greeted them. "You boys need to leave *some* dust in the road."

She quickly brushed both of them off with a whisk broom. Her heavily painted eyes held Yancy's gaze when she added, "The name's Rosy. I've got a tub up in my room in case you'd like a bath later."

Yancy blushed, and Cas bit his lip to keep from laughing. "You've made a conquest," Cas egged Yancy on as he slapped open the slatted batwings.

The interior was dim and reeked of leather and male sweat. A huge, sawdust-covered dance floor filled more than half the structure. A player piano was silent now, but Cas knew men would soon be drifting in for the evening. Many would buy dances from the girls who only gave a man companionship for his money, and thus lorded it over the soiled doves like Rosy, who tendered their bodies.

"Hardly a thriving enterprise," Yancy said. "I hope it's not rotgut they're pouring."

The big building, Cas noted, was nearly deserted.

The girls had not yet come down, and only one customer sat at the bar. At the rear of the saloon, a tinhorn was fleecing two rubes at a green baize poker table.

A bartender with a soup-strainer mustache, a pompadour, and a face as flat as an iron skillet stirred himself to life when they came in. "Name your poison, gents."

"Pop skull," Yancy ordered, planking a quarter.

"You've only paid for half a drink, friend."

Yancy looked scandalized. "Four bits for cheap rotgut? Where's the free-lunch counter? At these prices, a man deserves a steak."

"Friend, where you been grazing? Whiskey went up to four bits almost ten years ago. No offense," he added, recalling how the big Swede had blacked out the sunlight when he entered.

Still muttering, Yancy fished out a large silver half dollar. Cas ordered a beer.

"That'll cost you a short bit," the barkeep told him as he slid a foaming glass along the counter. Cas planked his dime. The beer was warm and a little flat, but it cut the trail dust in his throat.

The bartender produced a packet of Opera Buffs and shook a smoke out. Cas had heard about cigarettes rolled by a new automatic machine, but had never seen one. He studied the one the bartender lit, impressed by the tight, uniform roll. But he couldn't help wondering what was wrong with a fellow building his own smokes by hand. Seemed like there was a machine for everything nowadays, and nobody he knew was being asked if they wanted the blasted things.

Cas led them back to a plank table that commanded a good view of the wide-open front doors and their horses.

"Where's the necessary?" Yancy muttered.

Through a back window, Cas could see the batboard jakes, leaning like a half-felled tree.

"Don't use it," he warned Yancy. "Perfect place to catch lead poisoning. Save it for when we camp."

"Save it? Cas boy, my kidneys are not so young as yours."

Cas nodded. "I know, old son, but I've got a gut hunch about this town. We're both a mite whiffy, and I was thinking we might purchase a bath at the barbershop. But we'll have to settle for the next creek we see."

"I've had a better invitation," Yancy reminded him, "and here she comes now."

Rosy sashayed over to their table, a froufrou of whispering skirts and bustle following her. "Hungry, gents?" she inquired, painted eyes still lingering on Yancy. "The beef supper is only six bits."

"We'll take it," Cas said while a blushing Yancy's eyes played hide-and-seek with Rosy's.

"You know me," Yancy said when Rosy disappeared into the kitchen. "I'm not one for calico fever. But this one seems taken by me, huh?"

Cas had not been in a jovial mood lately, but this godsend was too good to waste. " 'Pears to be," he agreed. "She must like 'em big and dumb."

Yancy's face turned cunning. "No need to take exception, Caswell. Oh, I see the green-eyed monster has you. Who *wouldn't* want a farmer?"

They were served tough Longhorn beef and potatoes swimming in butter, with cherry pie for dessert. Cas had tasted better meals, but this fare put hardtack and beans in the shade.

Cas noticed how the lone drinker at the bar had been knocking back red-eye as fast as the barkeep could pour it. Now he began expounding his wisdom to the barroom in slurred syllables.

"Them weak sisters back in Washington City

passed 'em a law a few years back, says the darkies now got the legal right to drink with us white men. Says they can ride on trains and stagecoaches right alongside whites. Well, chappies, *this* Texan does not favor this damned amalgamation. Race mixing don't go with me."

"Whew," Yancy said, busy forking in potatoes, "he's got a brick in his hat. He best lay off Old Knockumstiff. Why fight the war all over if you're not drawing pay?"

"He's so drunk he thinks he's in Texas," Cas said. "There's always been amalgamation in this territory."

The saloon was filling up now that evening was settling in. Cas closely studied each man who came in, sorting out run-of-the-mill troublemakers from the more dangerous types.

"Back in Texas," Yancy said around a mouthful of pie, "we talked about Kathleen Steele going to Deadwood to teach school. I just recollected— what's queer about it is how her kin ain't heard from her since she left almost a year ago. That doesn't seem like her way, does it?"

Cas set his beer down without finishing it. "First I heard of it. No, that wouldn't be her usual way, except that I'm told she had a sockdollager of a row with her pa. Kathleen is prideful, and if he insulted her bad enough, that firebrand can hold a grudge until it hollers mama."

"Here comes my admirer," Yancy muttered as Rosy swooped down on them. "Watch and learn, infant."

"*Look* at those long, strong legs," she flattered Yancy.

The Swede looked startled and Cas, biting his lower lip, knew why: most decent women of the day primly substituted 'limbs' for 'legs.' When she bent closer, however, and whispered in Yancy's ear, the farmer flushed pink to his earlobes.

She left again and Yancy stared at Cas, aghast. "Cas boy, I could not have heard what I *thought* I heard. How could a woman even know such words? Say . . . she's a dime-a-dance gal, right?"

Cas exploded with pent-up mirth. "She's a dancer, all right, you chucklehead. The giddy dance." Yancy did not appear enlightened, so Cas elaborated, "She's a sport, Yancy."

"Of course, and a good one."

Cas shook his head, laughing again. "Good God, strike a light in this dumb weed warden's head. No, Yancy, a sporting girl, a painted cat, a soiled dove."

Yancy's eyes doubled in size. "You don't mean she's . . . ?"

"An adventuress," Cas supplied. "Yes. She's working her way west, as they say. And believe me, you don't want the French pox on the trail."

"Is this the voice of experience?"

"That's none of your beeswax."

"That sounds like a yes," Yancy said, still embarrassed. "This old sodbuster has a lot to learn."

Cas shook his head in amazement at Yancy. "I'll bet Barnum's Circus could use you. Well, c'mon, Romeo, we need to ride on and find a camp for the night."

They were halfway to the door when a Mexican kid about twelve years old stepped diffidently inside from the circle of oily yellow lamplight outside. He wore a raw wool serape and rope sandals. His eyes settled on Cas.

"Señor," he said when Cas started around him, "I have a *mensaje* for you."

"The heck's a *mensaje*?" Yancy asked.

"I've only picked up a little Spanish," Cas told

him, "but I think it means 'message.' " Looking at the kid, he said, "All right, *chico,* hand it over."

"It is not on paper, *señor.*" The kid pronounced his carefully rehearsed message with exaggerated care. " 'Never step in anything you can't wipe off.' "

Cas and Yancy exchanged a long glance.

"Chico," Cas said urgently, "who paid you to tell me this?"

The kid shook his head, refusing to say. Cas could tell he was scared spitless.

"Señor, he told me . . . he told me"—in his nervousness, the kid's English failed him, so he switched to Spanish—*"punto en boca."*

"Something about 'mouth,' " Cas told Yancy.

The bartender had wandered over, evidently to toss the boy out. *"Punto en boca* means 'keep your mouth shut,' " he translated. "My wife's a Mexer. I hear it all the time."

By now the kid was trembling. Cas slipped him a dollar and sent him packing. He steered Yancy back toward their table. "I got a hunch whoever sent the message will be in here to see if we cut our picket pins and ran."

Both men ordered another drink. Yancy knocked back a jolt glass of whiskey and stood up to get another. Cas stopped him with a grip like an eagle's talon.

"No more whiskey," Cas warned him. "Look what just blew in."

A man with a spade beard and a black flattop sombrero was passing their table. Unlike most of the patrons, he was well turned out. A duster protected his brushed black coat and shirt of fine-spun linen.

"A two-gun rig," Cas muttered, "and those holsters pivot so you don't have to draw. That's a paid killer."

"No shortage of them in the territories," Yancy pointed out. "Maybe he's not the one who sent the message."

"Maybe," Cas agreed, scraping back his chair. "But then why is he eyeballing everybody but us? I've watched him stare down three men already, so why not us?"

Cas did nothing by halves, believing the best way to cure a boil was to lance it. With Yancy hurrying to catch up, he walked straight up to the man lounging against the bar. The new arrival turned to confront him, his eyes heavy with the admission of guilt.

"Let's shuck that artillery," Cas greeted him. With the same blur of speed that drew his own gun, Cas jerked the walnut-gripped Colts and threw them on the bar.

Spade Beard reached for one of them, but hardeyed, jut-jawed Cas rattled him with a hard, openhanded blow to the ear. "You can collect your shooters later," Cas told him, "when you're feeling better."

By now the saloon was quiet as a midnight graveyard. Cas had no hope of getting information from this paid gunny—he'd met the type before on the outlaw trail, and nothing short of Comanche torture could make them talk. Besides, the answers Cas required lay in Deadwood. This gunslick did not kill the Everett family or he wouldn't be sending melodramatic messages through a scared kid— he'd be killing from ambush. Nonetheless, he licked the boots of the killers, and Cas could not abide it.

"Yancy," Cas said solemnly, his eyes drilling into Spade Beard's, "this man called you a stinking pig farmer."

Yancy's double-ten express gun dinted Spade

Beard's midsection. "I admit I know little of the fistic arts, Cas. Being a Texan, naturally I prefer to shoot a man."

This was a lie—Yancy loved to brawl. Cas set both feet hard and lowered his weight. "Then allow me."

Cas punched through, not at, his upper cut, lifting the man off the plank floor before he staggered backward, doing a slow Virginia reel. Cas followed on immediately with a left and right cross, several hard jabs, and an explosive haymaker that sent the man into an unconscious heap in the middle of the floor.

The patrons, no doubt expecting someone to get bucked out in smoke, seemed disappointed.

"If you had a dicker with that hombre," said an aging rancher at a nearby table, "why didn't you slap leather 'steada grabbin' his irons?"

The two men from east Texas ignored the jibes and headed outside.

"Look at him high-hattin' us," taunted another man. "Thinks he's one a the big bugs. Fancy new boots, well, I guess."

"See his cutaway holster?" asked a black-clad youth who looked like a road agent. "He's a specialist in depopulating the West, don'tcha know? A gunologist."

Laughter bubbled through the saloon. Emboldened by this, the same punk snarled at Cas' retreating back, "Don't be swingin' your eggs around here, mister, 'less you plan to use 'em."

"Boys, sheathe your horns and draw it mild," the bartender cut in, "or you'll be adding lead to your diet. Must be dark in here. That younger fellow is Cas Everett."

Cas turned on the threshold to stare at the black-clad mouthpiece. The kid was visibly sweating now.

"Only my friends can insult me," Cas told him. "Are you my friend?"

"I'd be honored, Mr. Everett. And I ain't sayin' that just on account I'm scared. I really mean it."

Cas nodded. He flipped a gold dollar all the way up to the bartender, who caught it neatly. "Good. Bottles, a drink for my friend."

Out in the wide, shadow-mottled street, Cas was silent while both men tightened the girth for the trail. As he slipped the bit in Comet's mouth, he said, "I just figured something out, Yancy. Whoever's waitin' up in Deadwood knows dang well these 'messages' won't scare us off."

"Spell it out," Yancy said. "I'm only a pig farmer, remember?"

"Not much to spell," Cas said, forking leather. "The messages are just to rub it in and show how sick the killer is. They *want* me to come to Deadwood. It's the most lawless spot in the country, and they figure they have their best chance of killing me there. From what I know of the place, I'd say they're right."

Chapter 10

For the next week, Cas and Yancy pounded their saddles north through the rolling foothills of Colorado, finding plenty of waterhole camps. Pastoral valleys and stretches of birch and aspen forest began to break up the monotony of the southern plains. As they advanced, snowcapped mountains etched themselves more prominently to the west, and the surrounding terrain grew steeper and more rugged.

At the beginning, until well north of Pueblo, they had slogged across dry plains, where they had to water their horses from their hats, and then through dunes and spoil banks and deep sand washes that could break a horse's leg. They had to contend with loose shale, miles and miles of slagland, steep and twisting trails. Lightning almost knocked Cas off his horse, and Yancy came within an ace of drowning when a sudden downpour created an instant torrent in the gorge they were crossing.

However, there were diversions to leaven the danger. Once, on the mountainous horizon to their left, a silent electrical storm sent eerie blue fire balls flashing from peak to distant peak. At various points along the trail, they passed motley groups of travelers: a wealthy driver wearing a Prince Albert and a topper, his conveyance a leather-trimmed barouche; lumbering freight wagons with bullwhackers walking alongside, cursing as they cracked their blacksnakes; Concord coaches and mud wagons— a cheaper version of the Concord, their passengers exposed to the elements and at greater risk in rollovers.

It was the hustle and bustle of the railroads, however, that most delighted and impressed Yancy. The two Texans crossed the tracks of the Atchison, Topeka and Santa Fe Railroad, two days later the Kansas Pacific in Twin Turrets, Colorado. They arrived just as a train eased into town along a westbound spur, hissing to a steaming stop when the engineer vented his boilers.

"I'll be dinged," Yancy said, awed by the sight. Two huge steam engines and a coal tender were followed by several fancy new Pullman cars to serve the wealthy. A string of third-class coaches held the less affluent passengers.

Almost immediately after fording the South Platte and crossing into the southern Panhandle of Nebraska, they crossed their third and last set of tracks, the great Union Pacific.

"No more tracks north of here," Cas told his friend. "Indian ranges."

"But I thought the only free-ranging Indians left are the Apaches?"

"Officially, yeah, but there's still plenty of Indians jumping their reservations and starting camps of their own. We feed 'em in the winter and fight 'em in the summer."

Yancy said, "That's why we're seeing so many soldiers."

Cas nodded. "The soldiers destroy the outlaw

camps and herd the bust-outs back onto the rez. It's the main job now for a soldier out west."

The two men were traversing a broad expanse of low sand hills, the westering sun a dull copper orb suspended low in the sky. At times coyotes and wolves trailed at a distance, often in plain view and always more curious than menacing.

Yancy realized he was on the last leg of the journey, and in his dime-novel enthusiasm, he fired off even more of his eager, boy-howdy questions. "Think we'll see cowboys shooting at the moon and hurrahing the town?"

"Swede, we're buying you some maps. You need 'em. Once we left Doan's Store on the Red River, we put the major cattle trails east of us, which means we're skirting to the west of all the railhead towns. You'll see few cowboys cutting up."

Cas reined Comet in and let him blow. "Horses are lathered," he told Yancy. "Let's spell 'em."

He threw the reins forward and swung down to loosen the girth. Yancy watched him carefully survey their surroundings. Cas sent his gaze across the entire vista, studying and reading the shadows. Then he turned sideways and studied it from peripheral vision, looking for the shapes and movements that direct vision sometimes missed.

"You keep watching our backtrail," Yancy said. "Think we're being followed now that we're closer to Deadwood?"

Cas moistened his bandanna with canteen water and swiped out his horse's nostrils, which were caked with dust. He rinsed it again and wiped it quickly over Comet's gums and lips.

"Followed? Not tooth to tail, I don't think," he replied while he worked. "But we are being watched from time to time. Somebody wants me—

might's well make it *us*—in Deadwood. Somebody who figures that's *his* town for the purpose of easy killing. Watching us now is necessary because this man doesn't like surprise arrivals."

"Nobody comes to mind yet, Cas boy?"

"Well, if you mean the man who probably hired it out, I can't land on one name just yet. Far as the man who *did* it, I have a name but no proof yet. Dakota Boggs. I don't accuse him and don't even know if he's in Deadwood—he gets around. But he was plundering the Dakota Territory long before Deadwood became a gold-strike camp. That's how he got his name. He braced me in Rapid City when I was collaring a friend of his."

Yancy frowned. "Braced you? Then shouldn't he be celestial by now?"

Cas weighed the question and felt guilt gnaw at him. "Yeah. He *should* be. But I was feeling generous that day. I meant to blow his shooter from his hand, but I bucked my aim and blew off his hammer thumb instead. Pure accident, and I hear for a spell it ended his career as a gunman. According to saloon gossip, Boggs trained up his left hand, and with a double-action handgun, he's faster than ever."

"If you blew off his hammer thumb," Yancy pointed out, "there's your man with a grudge."

"There's a few out there with bigger grudges against me. Don't stack your conclusions higher than your evidence."

"You thinkin' he's in Deadwood?"

Cas shook his head. "No way to know until we get there. But that grizzly's den would suit him right down to the ground. He might even be one of the heap-big outlaws by now."

Yancy, too, cast a glance at the grass-tufted hills all around, a forlorn and uninspiring landscape.

"Shoo," he said. "Ask me, this Deadwood fellow sounds like all gurgle and no guts. We been better than three weeks on a lonely trail, and nobody has even shot at us unless you count those Texas cowboys, who didn't try to hit us."

"You're way off the bead," Cas assured him. "They thrive on gruesome entertainment in Deadwood, and that's what we're meant to be. Well, let's cinch up. I want us in a safe camp by nightfall."

As they rode north, Yancy's open-air serenading got on Cas' nerves, but he figured it probably kept the rattlesnakes, profuse in this area, at bay. "The Homespun Dress," "Little Annie Roonie," "The Girl I Left Behind Me"—the big farmer trotted out every song he'd ever heard, including field hollers and Yankee marching songs. He added dozens more he made up in the saddle.

So far Yancy was mostly a liability on this journey, but Cas had refrained from saying so. The unaccustomed rigors of the trail showed in the slack weariness of Yancy's face, the soft and sallow pockets under his eyes. For a hoe man who still wore brogans and had never seen the Front Range of the Rocky Mountains before, he was at least holding up and learning some trailcraft.

"Cas boy?"

Cas gave a long, fluming sigh of surrender. By now he recognized that tone. Yancy, a habitual reader who was full of pub lore, had a bottomless well of questions, especially about his Dodge City heroes.

"Do you think Wyatt Earp is honest?" Yancy asked. "I hear he deals for that killer Luke Short at the Long Branch."

"In a new country like this," Cas replied, clear blue eyes in motion, "no man's honest all the time. I never met him, but I'd guess Earp is honest

enough for Dodge. I've met his brother Virgil, and
that man is straight grain clear through."

Comet fought the bit, whiffling at something
ahead, and Cas skinned back his .44.

"What is it?" Yancy asked from behind him.

Yancy's booming voice made Cas flinch. "I don't
know," he whispered back, "but why don't you just
blow a bugle?"

They advanced at a cautious walk. Plenty of daylight remained but the copper sun was barely above
the horizon now. The sand hills had thinned out
to plateaus divided by the clear, peaceful, sand-
bottomed Niobrara River.

"Well, like we were talking about earlier," Cas
said, staring at the destruction ahead, "the soldiers
are stamping out the unauthorized Indian camps.
Either the Sioux ran away or they were hauled
back to their rez."

"Well, raise my rent!" Yancy exclaimed as he
caught his first view beyond Cas. "You sure a cy-
clone didn't do this?"

Tanned buffalo robes, dog skins, antelope and
elk hides, pans and kettles, axes, beadwork, pipes,
old moccasins, oak war clubs bristling with spikes,
stone hammers, grubbing hoes of bone—all lay
strewn as if by a malevolent whirling dervish. The
hide covers of the teepees had all been burned
along with the willow-pole frames.

"I see the Army takes no chances since Custer,"
Yancy remarked.

"True, but Indians didn't cause Old Iron Butt's
downfall. He had only one battle strategy his entire
career: charge full-bore. He was good at it, but
that's what killed his men—lack of tactics."

Yancy slanted a quizzical glance at his friend.
Custer was getting the hero's treatment throughout
the nation, and such casual criticism of him seemed

almost irreverent. "Cas, have you become an Indian lover?"

Cas laughed. "Listen, pudding head, I was sort of in the Army myself once. Four months as a scout with a joint civilian-military posse tracking down a gang in the Bitter Root Mountains. They killed a federal paymaster and his military guard. That was before this new Posse Comitatus Act was passed."

Yancy scowled stubbornly. "Shoo, so what? Plenty of soldiers have gone to the blanket."

"If you ever laid eyes on a young Crow or Cheyenne woman, *you'd* go to the blanket too, I'd wager. No, it's just that the Indian is trapped no matter how you slice it. If we leave him alone, he's cursed as a godless savage. If we teach him how to plow the land and worship the white man's God, he's ridiculed as a dirt scratcher and a praying Indian."

The destroyed camp lay behind them now.

"Don't be galling me with such talk," Yancy fumed. "You can spout that balderdash after losing so many neighbors in Texas to the heathen Comanches?"

"Simmer down. It's mostly Sioux and Cheyenne in these northern ranges," Cas reminded him. "No boys to fool with, but most aren't so torture crazy. Look, if you need to hate Indians, be my guest. You're free, white, and twenty-one. Me, I have other enemies—pale faces as low and vicious as any Comanche who ever brained a baby against a tree."

"Well said, Cas boy," a chastened Yancy replied. "Red killers or white, they *all* come direct from hell."

The western horizon was a rim of ruby red flame, the vast dome of twilight sky aglitter with the first fiery pinpoints as the stars winked to life. They made camp beside a little spring rising up from a clutch of rocks. Trees screened them from wind and sight, and plenty of dead wood made for a smokeless fire.

Before eating, Cas stripped Comet and gave him a thorough rubdown with an old feed sack. As he ran a metal-toothed currycomb over the chestnut's coat, Cas listened carefully to the gathering, starlit Nebraska night.

"Way I see it," a weary Yancy announced over a metal dish of beans, "we're doin' pretty good. It's almost a month since the killers found out we're coming, and they haven't blown our lamps out yet."

"They won't, either," Cas said quietly. "This is *our* fandango."

A coyote barked. Cas spilled the dregs of his coffee out and scoured his cup with a handful of grass. Yancy, who suffered dyspepsia after each meal, munched on a peppermint instead of the usual gingersnap.

"Cas," he said, "after we take care of this business in Deadwood, will you go back to bounty hunting?"

"Can't say right now," Cas replied. "But that trade will thrive now that soldiers can't chase down civilians."

Living in the saddle exhausted even a young man, and Cas rolled into his blankets as soon as he'd cleaned and oiled his weapons. The shape-changing, shadowy darkness beyond the glow of the fire held the potential for violent death at any moment. Cas, however, accepted that risk as the price of earning his living. What dried his mouth to cotton would come later, in the still of night.

He had not suffered one nightmare since discovering his family buried in rustic graves and the only house he knew in charred ruins. For him, the hard times came in the empty, breathing stillness of early morning, lying there wide-awake with dawn still an hour away and no help to be had.

Dreams at least dulled the rough edges, symbolized the pain; waking memories, however, were literal brutes, usually even hostile, and especially in the predawn, they caught him defenseless. It was always the same dominant image: five plain wooden crosses backlit by a heavenly blue sky. Suddenly they were all replaced by the silver-and-gold cross he'd bought for his mother.

Then the faces floated across the screen of his mind, hovering like spirits who died in torment: Mother and Father, Davey, Janet, and Jeanette. They should have comforted him, but the eyes were accusing, pleading, desperate for Cas to save them. Wide-awake, he would feel his body twitch and hear a moan escape his lips, sounding oddly disembodied against Yancy's loud, rhythmic snoring.

Only with the dawn chorus of the birds and the first weak tremble of rising sun would Cas throw off the cold shackles of grief and face the new day.

Kathleen addressed her one-line note to Cas Everett care of the *Daily Journal*, Kansas City: *If you come to Deadwood, I will contact you when it's safe on a matter of great urgency.* She knew that any contact with him must be anonymous and signed it only, *A True Friend.*

She sat at a little French escritoire in her suite of rooms at the Crystal Palace, Deadwood's first and only luxury hotel. Levi Carruthers owned the five-story building and occasionally occupied rooms one floor above her. Even virtual prisoner Kathleen was impressed with her jailhouse. The luxurious rooms showcased ornately carved, lavishly upholstered Belter furniture, alabaster figurines, pillows thick with satin stitch and French knots, gilded mirrors, and velvet drapes.

It *was* a prison, however, and worse—the place where she would soon be killed when Carruthers finally rebelled at her stubborn resistance—or in rage over the talk her behavior was causing.

Only this letter might save her, but would Cas even receive it in time? She wasn't even sure she could get it out of Deadwood, much less to Cas. However, her hunch about Dakota Boggs killing the Everett family was growing almost to a certainty. If Cas did come, she just knew he wouldn't leave her here.

She was tucking the note into a gummed envelope when a key rattled in the hallway door. Kathleen fought down a welling of panic and barely managed to substitute another sheet for the note before a well-dressed man of middle age materialized beside her, his eyes suspicious.

"It's just a shopping list," she told Levi Carruthers, handing it to him for his inspection.

His hair was parted in the middle, and he wore muttonchops with a beard under the chin. A diamond-headed pin adorned his cravat. He carried no weapons openly, but she knew there was always a two-shot ladies' muff gun tucked into his right boot—a gun he often let her see.

He glanced at the list and nodded. "If you'd like, Hop Sing can pick these things up. His English is getting better. I'd rather not have you rubbing elbows with low-bred, woman-starved men."

"In a half hour or so," she reminded him, "I'll be walking over to the Gem to spend most of the night with such men."

"That's Al Swearengen's doing, not mine.

Thanks to me you are not also his concubine. Yet so far you've given me nothing but the little end of the horn, as cattlemen say. Perhaps I should let Al own *all* of you? After all, you've shown me damn little gratitude."

Carruthers was gifted with a sonorous voice, one of the chief reasons he compelled attention whenever he spoke—that and an intense belief in the importance of his own opinions, a belief that defied listeners to ignore him. He stood over Kathleen, eyes dead as two bone chips and probing her like insistent fingers.

She had learned to use her appearance as a defense against brutality. She wore a simple black dress with cream lace cuffs, her thick profusion of cinnamon hair pinned and netted under a snood. Even though the weather was warm, ladies were required to wear outer garments. A paisley shawl was draped over her shoulders.

"I notice Boggs has been gone more lately," she remarked, instantly realizing it was obvious she was fishing.

"And why would you care about a brute like him? Or is he your type?"

Kathleen's nostrils flared, and she answered crisply, "The man positively frightens me. I mentioned him because I breathe easier when he's gone."

"Everybody does, m'love. However, Dakota Boggs is a godsend to the entrepreneur. He clears the profit path of all that encumbers it. But never mind him. I came to tell you something."

His eyes cut to the escritoire again, as if he were thinking about searching it.

"My dear," he told her, a dangerous new tension in his voice, "Swearengen and certain others in this dung pit are starting to engage in . . . innuendos about us. Apparently our little 'secret' is being cried out in the streets."

"I have said noth—"

He raised a peremptory hand to silence her. "Never mind, I am now the growing laughingstock around here. May I remind you, haughty miss, that I gave that uncouth mudsill Swearengen twenty-five thousand dollars to relinquish all claim to you except as a faro dealer?"

And just whom, Kathleen wondered silently, *did your lackey Dakota Boggs murder for that money?*

"Swearengen told me," Carruthers said, droving the point home, "that he intended to strip you naked every night in the Gem and charge the miners to ogle you."

"You have made my life easier here," Kathleen told him. "I never said otherwise."

"That's hardly the point. I'm a businessman," Carruthers reminded her, "and I expect a good return on *any* investment, you included. I won't wait forever. I am indeed enamored of you, but with me love rides postillion behind profit. No, indeed, I won't wait forever."

"I know you won't," she replied in the firm but respectful tone she used with him. "But I must listen to my heart."

From her earliest days as a prisoner in Deadwood, Kathleen had guessed that Carruthers was infatuated with her, also intimidated by her. After he in essence purchased her, he did not try to impose himself on her for weeks. When he finally made some clumsy moves in that direction, she rolled the dice and told him, in no uncertain terms, that she would kill herself if *any* man ever forced himself on her.

Only reluctantly, he had agreed to let things

stand as they were between them. Inevitably, Kathleen knew, Swearengen and a few others had guessed the truth—money tycoon Levi Carruthers lacked the manhood to take a woman for whom he had planked down good money. His next remark confirmed her insight.

"Listen to *your heart*? Don't you understand," he tried to reason with her, "I must protect my authority in this gulch filled with rugged masculinity? If it gets bruited about that I . . . that I lack the purpose of will to bed you, my subordinates will turn on me in contempt. In the rugged West, the cow does not bellow to the bull."

He leaned in closer, so close she smelled his lavender breath mint. "Haven't I given you a good life?" he wheedled. "Most girls Al lures to Deadwood end up sleeping over the Gem in the same beds they—"

"I take your meaning," she cut him off hastily.

"All right then, just look around you. Any furnishings hauled to Deadwood must be lowered on ropes into the gulch. Yet you have the area's only upholstered Sleepy Hollow armchair, not to mention the first built-in bathtub in the Black Hills. Even my own house doesn't have one. You are privileged."

Kathleen bit back a caustic reply and glanced with distaste at a Saratoga trunk filled with dresses of Swiss muslin, pongee, velour. She must be the best-dressed slave in America. Not privileged, but a prisoner of bloodstained money and sick dementia.

"I'm glad I don't live over the Gem," she told him honestly. "But I am not 'privileged.' I am spied upon constantly, denied freedom of movement, and my belongings are regularly searched. I am forced to live in a place so vile and dangerous that men are murdered right before my eyes."

Carruthers gave that a wan smile. "Murder? The word requires a stigma, and there is no such stigma in Deadwood. That's why I'm here making money hand over fist. But never mind. May I plan on visiting tonight—and being here for breakfast?"

The disgusting, unhealthy need was back in his tone, and Kathleen turned her face away to avoid those petrified eyes. Past the parlor's big bay window, she saw the lamplighter making his rounds in teeming Main Street. He also doubled as a night watchman, but rarely made a round unless he'd been drinking—few sober men ever appeared after dark in the Badlands.

"A visit would be fine," she finally replied, "but not the breakfast."

It was yet another refusal, and Carruthers was suddenly so intensely angry that Kathleen could almost smell his rage. Her heart constricted when he raised his right foot and speared the twin-barreled derringer from his boot.

However, after a moment, he thrust it into his coat pocket. His face purpled and his breathing turned ragged. She feared him most when he was like this.

"You can't possibly grasp this," he told her, "but I am a proud and sensitive man who reacts to beauty more acutely than most men. I have needs more refined and rare than those of the 'men' common to your experience. This was God's will, not mine, and I am sure that God does not make mistakes."

His hand dipped into the coat pocket that held the gun, and Kathleen paused on the feather edge of her next breath.

"However," he continued in an ominous tone, "the fact that I must point out my own superiority to you proves only that you have a common mind despite your uncommon beauty. I say again, you are indeed proud—too proud for your own safety."

He drew the muff gun from his pocket, his smile cunning as he watched her. Kathleen was frightened numb and tried to handle the enormity of realizing her life might be about to end. A moment later, he tucked the gun back into his boot and left.

For perhaps two minutes, Kathleen remained at the escritoire, waiting for the trembling weakness to subside. Then she took a sulfur match from a box in the top drawer and crossed to the marble fireplace. She set fire to the note and dropped it onto the hearth, watching it curl into charred remains.

Hot tears welled from her eyes, and the despair of hopelessness filled her like a glass under a tap. Cas was her best hope, a capable, brave man who she prayed still cared about her. But Levi's visit tonight vividly reminded her what lay in store for her if Levi ever got wind of her attempt to reach outside help.

To fortify herself against the coming night, she poured a glass of brandy from a decanter on the mantel. Then she pulled her shawl tighter and left for her forced-labor stint at the Gem, not sure how much longer she could endure all of this.

Chapter 11

The riders from east Texas were only a few hours shy of the Dakota Territory, traversing the massive sandstone formations and steep bluffs of northwestern Nebraska.

"Pretty country," Yancy remarked. "Seems peaceful, too."

"Crazy Horse is dead and Sitting Bull might be eating government pork these days," Cas reminded his friend, "but the Dakota Territory ahead is still plenty dangerous. Look to your left."

Yancy did. "And . . . ?"

"There's somebody hiding behind that spine of rocks in the high rimland," Cas said. "And he's there to watch us."

"How do you know?"

"He's wearing or carrying something that keeps reflecting. It's not quartz or mica in the rocks because the reflections keep pace with us."

Yancy pulled at his chin. "We going after him?"

Cas shook his head. "He might enjoy that. No need to go after him. We're well out of effective rifle range. We'll settle accounts in Deadwood."

Nebraska still enforced blue laws, and it was Sunday morning when they rode through their final Panhandle settlement, aptly named Dry River. Sunday chains were strung across the two side streets to block vehicle and horse traffic.

"I thought these were the great buffalo ranges," Yancy complained when they put the last Nebraska settlement behind them. "We haven't seen a one."

"Prob'ly won't, either," Cas replied, switching his hands on the reins. "They're killed by the millions each year for their hides. Only five years ago, I still spotted entire herds out here."

"But the generals were right—the tribes had to give up when the buff ran out."

Yancy quit talking and watched Cas study the high country on their left. "Our watcher is still out there?"

Cas nodded, face half in shadow under the brim of his hat. "By now I think we're in Dakota Territory. Our enemies are careful—they don't want any surprises. When we hit Deadwood, they plan to know every move we make."

"It's nice to be loved." Yancy took a quick swig from his bull's-eye canteen. "There's *no* honest law there at all?"

"I didn't say that. But one honest man can't control a town chock-full of crazy drunks and cold killers. Deadwood's been an outlaw town from the start. Matter fact, it's been an *illegal* town from its start—the prospectors overran Sioux reservation land. I think they've worked it out so it's legally part of Dakota now, except the Sioux still claim it."

Yancy said, "I read in *Police Gazette* that after Wild Bill was murdered there, Bat Masterson was thinkin' about wearing a badge in Deadwood."

"That's the rumor, all right. But I hear Bat got no farther than Cheyenne, where he went broke at the poker tables and decided to return to Dodge."

"Bat would've tamed Deadwood," Yancy said in a tone of hero worship.

"In a pig's eye," Cas said. "Not him, not Earp, not Hickok. Seth Bullock is doing a good job of policing upper Main Street, but the Badlands and Chinatown are the most dangerous places in the West, along with Cochise County, Arizona Territory. There's a brand-new mining camp called Tombstone."

Cas fell silent, realizing from the boiling yellow dust cloud that they were approaching a conveyance out ahead. "A private coach with two outriders," he told Yancy. "Make sure to swing wide to the flank when you go around it. These private guards are well armed and like to toss lead."

"Why outriders?" Yancy asked. "You said the Indians around here were all whipped into submission."

"And didn't I also say plenty of them jump the rez? Besides, there's no shortage of white cutthroats. Road agents like this area."

As Cas drew nearer he saw a stately black carriage with gold striping and brass horn and running lights. When he swung around to ride past, he glimpsed upholstery of soft gold Moroccan leather. The sumptuously dressed occupants closed the leather curtains to protect their privacy from this commoner on horseback.

Wealthy foreigners, Cas guessed. Touring the American West was all the rage since the son of the Russian tsar, Grand Duke Alexis Romanov, had enthralled the world press with his showy visit.

"Must be royalty," Yancy said sarcastically as he joined up with Cas again ahead of the carriage. "All I did was wave at a pasty-faced woman wearing a turban, and one of the outriders shouted at me to move along."

Yancy twisted around in the saddle for a last

look at the carriage. Cas winced when the big
Swede waved again—this brought both outriders
galloping straight at them.

Cas sighed. "You chucklehead! No, leave Patsy
sheathed. Poke not fire with a sword."

The guards reined in amid swirls of dust, one
aiming a .45 caliber Colt Peacemaker at Cas, the
other a snub Hammond Bulldog pistol at Yancy.
The gunsels had a cheap, store-bought look and
wore stiff felt derbies instead of a plainsman's hat.

"So, b'hoy," one of the guards said in a clipped
New York City accent, "you like to get familiar
with your betters, I see. Who invited you to wave
at that carriage?"

"I require no blasted permission to wave at anyone," Yancy retorted, his deep voice rumbling with
menace. "Nor to break your snot locker, you mou-
thy prison rat."

The thug brought the Hammond Bulldog's muzzle closer to Yancy's face. "Pig nurse, your tongue
swings way too loose. You're already lucky we
haven't sent you and your friend here beyond the
mountains. One more disrespectful word from you,
and I'll irrigate your guts."

Cas had a hard-and-fast rule about confronta-
tions: the moment violence was threatened, he took
charge. Despite the fact that both hardcases already
held shooters on them, Cas' .44 leaped into his fist
and fired twice with lightning rapidity. Both weapons flew off into the dirt, and a heartbeat later the
imported toughs were staring at the unblinking eyes
of Yancy's double ten.

"Now," Cas invited them calmly, "go ahead and
threaten our lives one more time. Under territorial
law, a threat shows intent to kill."

Both men had gone pale as new plaster.

"I don't believe we will," said the one who'd bullied Yancy. "You two aren't road agents, so why should we die over a mistake?"

"Yancy," Cas said, "they've both got shoulder rigs under their coats. Lighten 'em."

Yancy wagged the twin barrels for emphasis. "You heard the man, derby twins. Hand over those guns."

"Hold it," Cas ordered both men. "Yancy, *never* order a man to hand over his weapon. You make him drop it. If he insists on talking about it first, just shoot him. A cornered man who wants to talk means to kill you."

"Now then, boys," Yancy tried it again, "*toss down* those smoke wagons."

Both men complied so quickly that Cas barely suppressed a laugh.

"All right, fellows," he told them, "far as I'm concerned, this is over. But you think very carefully before you lock horns with us again. You've already threatened our lives, and if I even see you *looking* at us again, I'll kill both of you for cause. I'm careful that way."

"You know, Cas boy," Yancy remarked when they were well out ahead of the traveling party, "seeing that fine carriage reminds me I still want to ride in a stagecoach despite all your complaints about them."

"I'm warning you—better to walk. But if you must, the best seat is the one closest to the driver—half the bumps. If a team runs away, and it will, just sit tight and take your chances. I'm told that, most often, you'll hurt yourself if you jump."

Cas spoke only absently, his attention focused on the buttes and pinnacles to the west. Even as he watched, a white flash of light winked at him as if to say, *Welcome to Dakota Territory*.

By the middle of the afternoon, the terrain had grown less spectacular, mostly gentle hills covered with grass and the occasional motte of pine trees. Wildflowers grew everywhere, so profuse a man could lean down from the saddle and pluck a bouquet.

Soldiers on patrol overtook them from behind, and the two riders reined off the trail to let them canter past. Cas counted forty soldiers holding double columns at parade interval. They were led by a captain in a black-brimmed officer's hat, one side smartly snapped up. His high-topped cavalry boots were polished to a high gloss.

The captain glanced at the two civilians and gave them a curt nod.

"Whew. There's a fashion plate," Yancy remarked.

The captain wore a drooping George Armstrong Custer mustache, currently fashionable among younger officers. His blue kersey trousers sported bright yellow piping, and he wore a .44 caliber Smith & Wesson in a stiff leather holster over his right hip. The filigreed gold hilt of his saber sent off heliographs of light.

"He's sure proud of that useless cheese knife," Yancy said, eyeing the saber.

Cas grinned. "And as you can see, dress regulations for enlisted men are far less rigid out here."

Some of the men in formation were experienced campaigners who knew that old clothing should be worn in the field. Not one of them wore Uncle Sam's blue on this warm spring day. A few wore coarse pullover shirts, others the loose four-button

sack coats of Civil War vintage. Several had opted
for straw hats, popular in the unrelenting sun.

"Why, I'm a Dutchman!" Yancy remarked.
"That one white-haired private must be fifty!"

"Your Great War killed too many men. If a man
can walk and still has one functioning trigger finger,
he's fit to soldier out here."

"Wonder where they're headed?" Yancy said as
he and Cas resumed the trail.

"One thing for sure," Cas told him, "it's not
Deadwood. The entire gulch is off-limits to soldiers.
Doesn't take long for men earning thirty dollars a
month to catch get-rich-quick fever."

Yancy perked up. "Perhaps I'll scratch up a little
gold while we're there."

Cas' head swiveled to study this mammoth prod-
igy riding beside him. He chuckled. "Yessir, Swede,
we're getting you to a bumpologist. You definitely
need to have your head examined."

Unlike in DeWitt's Ten-Cent Romances, not
every square inch of the West was dangerous. Cas
and Yancy were passing through a little one-horse
burg called Hiland when a stout, aging lawman
wearing a sheriff's five-pointed star stepped into
the dusty street and flagged them to a halt.

"Boys," he greeted them, "around here we fine
fast riders."

"Fair enough," Cas said. "But we weren't riding fast."

"Didn't say you were, did I?" The old salt studied both of them. "I *could* fine you for violating
the firearms ordinance, I s'pose, except . . ."

"Except what?" Cas prompted.

"We don't have one," the lawman admitted.

Cas and Yancy exchanged puzzle-headed looks.

"Sheriff," Cas said, "if you're trying to raise rev-

enue for the town, 'pears you're doing a mighty
poor job of it."

"I've never been tossed in the hoosegow," Yancy
put in. "Is it a straw mattress or corn shucks?"

"Boys," the sheriff admitted, his face sheepish,
"we got no jail, either. I had no intention to roust
you. I'm just bored and wanted to say howdy."

Yancy looked surprised and a little disappointed.
"A sheriff in the wild and woolly Dakota Territory, bored?"

"Oh, *hell* yes, big feller. I spend most of my time
catching dogs and poisoning coyotes. Where you
boys headed?"

"Deadwood," Cas told him.

The sheriff visibly flinched. "I'd study on that. I
surely would. You look like nice fellows. Even if
you strike a lode, some no-'count trash will kill you
for it."

"Nice enough old duffer," Yancy remarked as
they rode on. "He's a mite corned though. I could
smell it. Matter fact, everybody up here seems
drunk by noon. At least us Texicans wait until sup-
pertime or so."

About an hour of daylight remained when they
rode upon a rustic saloon and eating house in the
middle of nowhere. A tent riddled with bullet holes
served the hungry, and beer and whiskey were
being sold from a canvas-and-plank stall, with
metal drinking cups chained to the counter.

"I could use a nip to wash my teeth," Yancy
said. "How 'bout you?"

"Whiskey makes me sleepy," Cas replied, "but
a beer would cut the dust just fine. Why not eat
here, too? It's bound to beat the chuck we've been
rustling up."

Just before they reined in, Cas spotted several
lines of horses picketed out back. "Our soldiers

stopped here. Now *don't* go picking a fight with them, hear? The war you fought is over."

Both riders swung down, stiff from the saddle, and looped their reins around the snortin' post. Cas made a quick search around. Some bored soldiers were on their knees out front, egging on a battle between red and black ants and laying bets on the outcome. Cas turned his attention to Yancy just in time to watch a claybank stallion behind him suddenly dip its neck and nip the Swede a good one in the sitter.

"*Ouch!* Damnable beast!" the farmer roared, rubbing the seat of his pants.

"Look there, lunkhead," Cas said when he finished laughing. "He's a croppy. You can see where his ears have been cropped to warn folks he's ill-tempered."

"Huh! It's not his *ears* that need snipping. I thought only Indians rode uncut stallions."

Yancy glowered at the croppy, though from a safe distance. "You savage churnhead, I *will* row you up Salt River."

The new arrivals strolled toward the canvas-and-plank stall, which was separated from the tent by a well covered with a dry hide. Several soldiers had congregated around the stall.

"What are them thick leather sashes some of the soldier boys wear round their middles?" Yancy asked. "They look hot."

"I forget what it's called, but on the frontier an abdominal wound is almost always fatal. Indians know that, and they aim for a soldier's belly button."

They stopped at the well. Cas lifted the stiff hide back and lowered a rawhide bucket tied to a horse-hair rope. He raised the bucket, dipped a gourd into it and drank, savoring the cool water on his tongue. His thirst surprised him. He drank the big gourd dry and filled it again, never wanting the drink to stop or his thirst to end.

While Yancy drank, making slurping noises like a fast drain, Cas took another look around. Besides the soldiers scattered in several pockets, perhaps a half dozen civilians were also in view. It didn't bother Cas when strangers took his measure—folks out west weren't shy about their curiosity. But a skinny man, wearing the reach-me-downs produced by America's ready-to-wear industry, watched him from caged eyes with oblique glances.

Yancy wedged his huge frame into the knot of men around the liquor counter and no one challenged him.

"Oil of gladness, old roadster," he told the aged, bearded man behind the counter. "And barley pop for Aunt Nancy here."

Yancy planked two quarters and a dime and tossed back a slug of murky whiskey that made him shudder. As Cas drank his beer, he kept an eye on the skinny man, who was showing a bowie knife to a soldier as if trying to sell it.

Cas spotted the captain who led the soldiers past him earlier. His face glowed from imbibing mash, and his voice rose authoritatively as he spoke to a civilian dressed like a teamster.

"Hell, just because a *dog* returns to its own vomit doesn't mean a nation should," the officer pontificated. "Haven't the boneheads in Congress learned by now that these infernal Indian treaties are written on water? I say exterminate *all* the red vermin. Nits make lice."

"The Indian is mollycoddled, all right," Yancy muttered to Cas. "But this fellow seems a bit bloodthirsty."

"I think he's just lettin' off steam," Cas suggested. "After you've buried enough scalped women and children, you lose your shades of gray."

"Damn parade-ground soldiers," Yancy added, for he was still hostile to Yankee blue. "Stickin' their pants into their boots don't make 'em tough."

"No," Cas agreed, "but their drinking jewelry makes them dangerous."

Yancy wrinkled his face in puzzlement. "How's 'at?"

"Drinking jewelry. See how some of 'em got horseshoe nails bent over their knuckles? Just mind your pints and quarts or you'll be spitting out teeth."

Cas checked to see where the skinny man was, but just then Yancy clamped a giant hand on his shoulder. "Cas boy, I'm so hungry my backbone is scrapin' against my ribs. Let's visit this dubious eatery in the tent."

The inside of the tent was hot and nearly deserted. Two modified Sibley stoves were being used for cooking. The cook was well into his forties, long-jawed and rangy. Purple veins crisscrossed his nose, the legacy of imbibing too many bottles of sour mash.

"Howdy, gents," he called out. "Ten bits will get you a big plate of buckwheat cakes and hot soda biscuits smothered in sausage gravy."

Tightfisted Yancy balked. "Ten bits for *both* of us, you mean?"

The cook shook his head. "Apiece. And no greenbacks accepted."

Greenbacks, or "Eastern money," had been issued for the first time in 1862. But Cas had learned that, out west, paper money was still unpopular. And why not? he figured as he dug out a three-dollar gold piece. A man would rather hold actual worth in his hand, not a paper symbol of that worth. After all, paper was most useful in privies.

Yancy was doing a slow boil. "Mister, judging from the smell in this tent, the food you sell ain't worth a hard-times token much less a three-dollar shiner."

"Friend," the cook said, "case you haven't noticed, nobody around here swills pigs. This is gold country, or near to it, and in gold country, *all* prices go up."

Yancy opened his mouth to retort, but Cas poked him with an elbow. "Shut pan," he warned. "Only a fool argues with a skunk, a mule, or a cook. Just be glad it's something hot."

"Well, I *am* death on sausage gravy," Yancy surrendered. "Why, it's gold country. Of course, a man pays more."

However, Yancy was also one for getting the last word to save face. "I like oleomargarine on my biscuits," he told the cook, "not bacon grease."

"Anything else, your damned highness?"

Both men sat at a crude trestle table while the cook prepared their meals. A minute later Cas recognized the sound of Comet's whiffle. When he sprang to the fly of the tent, however, his chestnut was still tied off with no one around him. There was still no sign of the man who had been furtively watching Cas.

When he returned, two steaming platters sat on the table and Yancy was scowling over his.

"Tarnation!" he exclaimed. "There's too much water in the gravy, and the biscuits are made with saleratus—it's like sucking on rock salt. I'm demanding my money back."

Cas was fed up with Yancy's constant carping. "Just sew your lips and stop acting like some fine-haired princess. It's my money, not yours. Yancy, this is not the back forty on your farm. It's the frontier. Men like you would starve and go naked out here without places like this, so pipe down."

"You can eat that slop?" Yancy demanded, watching with a look of betrayal as Cas tied into his food.

"It's not Delmonico's, but it's better than a poke in the eye with a sharp stick. C'mon, shovel it in. I want us camped by nightfall. Late tomorrow we should reach Deadwood."

Yancy muttered and pouted, but in the end, he finished his food before Cas, even licking watery gravy from his plate.

"Time to cinch up," Cas said, pushing away from the table and leading the way outside.

The soldiers were gone. Cas gazed around, but most of the civilians were gone, too, including the skinny man wearing reach-me-downs.

Not until Cas reached the near side of his horse did he spot the scrap of paper thumbtacked to his saddle fender. Limbs heavy with dread, he stepped closer and read the pencil-scrawled words: *Does your mother know you're out?*

Cas stood riveted in dead, almost painful silence. He felt dizzying heat rise up into his face and tasted bile erupting up his throat. His arms went weak and useless as the rage gripped him. All that passed quickly, a habit of survival, and a cold calm settled into his muscles.

"Are you bolted to the ground?" Yancy demanded. "Hop your horse, gunfighter."

Cas stepped into leather and swung up and over. He unpinned the brief message and handed it to his friend.

Yancy read it and flushed with anger. "Any idea who did it?"

"Think I saw him," Cas said as he reined Comet around toward the trail. "And if I catch him in Deadwood, he's going to answer for this. In spades."

Chapter 12

That night Cas and Yancy made camp on the last stretch of grassy plain before they would reach the Black Hills, an isolated extension of the Rocky Mountains. By noon Cas felt almost lulled by the weight of warm sunshine on his shoulders and the dusty twang of grasshoppers' wings. However, he steeled himself against the temptation to relax his concentration—they were nearing the lion's den now.

"Sheep clouds makin' up," Yancy observed from long habit as a plowman. "There'll be rain in twenty-four hours."

Cas knew his friend was thinking about the few farms they'd encountered out here. They seemed to be doing well, but it was early in the season. One brief drought was enough to ensure that the wheat wouldn't head. They'd both watched scams by "rain makers," back in east Texas, cost many their meager savings.

"Some of these folks," Cas said, "likely came west on the Northwestern Railroad. When I was a guard for them, they bragged how they offered free passage to destitute families, but you oughta heard how they described the Plains. You'd think it was the Garden of Eden out here. They even made up that lie about how rain follows the plow, just to lure folks out."

"Looks more like cattle country," Yancy said. "That's where the money is. Four dollars to raise a cow that sells for forty."

"Cattle will come, but first the gold will have to play out. When color is calling, men can't think of much else. Speaking of that . . ."

Cas glanced across at his companion. Yancy had come through this long journey with badly wind-cracked lips and sunburned skin, his dust-galled eyes swollen and red. His clothes hung more slackly on his frame. Guilt and worry lanced Cas at the sight of Yancy.

"Once we enter the gulch," he warned Yancy, "we'll be trapped like flies in hot tar. Sure you don't want to turn back?"

Yancy's beard-stubbled face formed a scowl. "It's clear *you* want me to. I'm not a gunman like you, and you figure I'll just be in the way until I get myself killed."

Actually that was more or less true, but Cas lacked the courage to say it.

"Easy on that 'gunman' and 'gunfighter' stuff," he protested.

"Give the order"—Yancy forced his hand—"and I'll head back."

"Look, you're green but you're a good man to ride the river with. I wanted to give you one last chance. Just be careful, Yancy—every second of every day that we're in Deadwood."

"Fair enough."

Yancy, in turn, studied his weary trail companion's face. It was Cas who bore the dangers and responsibilities of this mission while also coping on his own with the monstrous savagery inflicted on his family. All of this had left a gaunt, haunted cast to his eyes, which had aged lately and always appeared to focus farther away than they needed to, as if Cas were on a perpetual search for something beyond human ken.

Two hours later they began their ascent into the Black Hills from the southeast. Only a half hour earlier Yancy had seemed disappointed by the terrain. The low, grassy hills and stretches of flat plain seemed remarkably like east Texas, only less humid. Then, almost magically, they suddenly entered a forested, domelike upheaval that was actually mountains, not hills.

Yancy was struck speechless with awe at this high-altitude island of timber surrounded by barren plains. Ancient granite peaks had been wind eroded to spires, and limestone formations and caves dotted the region. These mountains were far less arid than the surrounding plains because some of the peaks rose more than a mile high. They arrested rain clouds that otherwise quickly blew over the dry plains. The resulting forests and streams made the Black Hills a haven for bears and other wildlife.

"God's gutta-percha!" Yancy exclaimed. He pointed to a frothing stream that disappeared as it plunged underground.

Cas nodded. "It'll pop up again miles from here. There's wonders in these hills you won't see anywhere else. I even found a stream that runs uphill."

The riders moved cautiously along a ridge trail, Cas holding his carbine straight up, butt-plate resting on his right thigh. Yancy, however, was too taken with this wondrous place to do more than gaze in awe. Forested slopes were covered with tall ponderosa pine, spruce, and aspen. Here and there, as they moved through, bright flashes of reflected sunlight caught their eye.

"Mirror signals?" a nervous Yancy asked.

"Crystallized gypsum. Giant chunks of it."

"Where's the Argonauts?" Yancy demanded. "I thought this whole area was a gold strike."

"I guess the first prospectors who sneaked in worked along Deadwood and Whitewood Creeks. The town of Deadwood, or maybe it's still a camp, is all the way over on the northern edge of the hills. Once Congress tossed out the Fort Laramie Treaty and got rid of the Sioux, other camps sprang up, like Hill City and French Creek, where Custer found gold and told the world about it."

Even as he spoke, Cas kept his eyes scanning and sweeping the surrounding ridges and high points. This was good ambush country, and hardened killers knew they were coming.

"Up ahead," he said, "is a place I found last time I was here. Follow me."

Cas reined to the right, leaving the trail to follow a nearly grown-over game trace. The narrow path emerged in a small clearing screened by pine trees. Under a traprock shelf, water bubbled up from an underground stream formed into a natural pool by a ring of boulders.

"We just watered the horses," Yancy objected. "I want to get to Deadwood."

"This water's for us, not the horses," Cas explained as he swung down and tossed Comet's reins forward to hold the gelding in place. "One of the favorite spots to kill a man in Deadwood is in the bathtub. So we'll have a bath here."

Yancy dismounted, looking none too happy. "This deep-table water will be colder than a pauper's patooty."

Cas shook his head in genuine amazement. "Old son, you are a caution to screech owls. *Cold* water doesn't bubble up smoking. This is a hot mineral spring—perfect temperature for a bath. Does wonders for saddle sores."

Cas dug two yellowish lumps of lye soap from a saddle pocket. Both men stripped and immersed themselves for a long time in the steaming pool. Cas felt the big muscles of his back, chest, and thighs go slack and heavy and felt pores opening to expel the grit of the hard journey from Texas.

Yancy's mood soon improved in the restorative water. *"Augh!"* he roared. "Blood, guts, deception, and death. Who *wouldn't* go to Deadwood?"

"You may not feel such bravado," Cas warned, "when you actually get there."

"Pee doodles," Yancy scoffed. A few moments later, however, he added in a sober tone, "Cas? I know we didn't come up here to locate Kathleen Steele. But shouldn't we ask around about her?"

"Not one word, hear me? Don't even mention her name. If she's here, we'll find her—Deadwood is a small place. Linking her to me, in an outlaw town, will only get her in trouble."

The moment they returned to the trail, Cas felt his scalp tighten and prickle in warning. But Comet, his best harbinger of trouble, only seemed grateful for the mountain shade and showed no trouble sign. Nor could Cas spot startled birds or even, on this stretch of trail, good ambush points.

"God's trousers!" Yancy suddenly exclaimed a few minutes later. "Look, Cas boy!"

Cas had already seen them—a small group of bangtails, or wild horses, raced across the trail ahead of them and up the slope. Their uncut tails dragged the ground, and their manes were so long they constantly tossed their heads to clear their vision.

"The Sioux captured entire herds from other

tribes," Cas said. "Before Uncle Sam marched the tribe off to their rez, they turned their horses loose. Some hide up here."

"Look at that one," Yancy said, pointing to the high ground above him and a buckskin with a dark eel stripe. "He's watching us."

"That's the ridge runner. He protects the herd. He'll stay up there to keep an eye on us until we're long gone."

The trail opened out as the surrounding trees thinned, and Cas noticed limestone formations above them on the right.

"Swing wide to the left," he told Yancy.

"Trouble?"

Cas opened his mouth to speak, but at that very moment, Comet bridled, whiplashing his head back. A heart skip later came the loud, crisp crack of a large-caliber rifle. The sound multiplied in echoes off the stone faces and basalt turrets of the Black Hills.

Cas saw the slug send up a fountain of dirt just ahead on the trail.

"Head straight left!" he ordered Yancy. "That was a ranging shot to get his bead. Don't stop until you're out of range from that limestone formation just ahead of us."

Cas had no proof yet that the ambusher was up there, but the slug went into the ground at a pene-trating angle typical of high-elevation shots. A sec-ond slug chunked in as Cas was reining off the trail. This one hit close enough to make Comet rear, but Cas punished him into submission with a quick rake of his spurs. He whipped up his mount to a gallop.

However, Cas drew rein sooner than did Yancy. He had already decided, when he learned his trail would lead to Deadwood, that he would not let the notorious thugs of this region intimidate him. He figured he had five good reasons, all recently buried, for his hardened attitude.

"Cas boy, have you nibbled Johnson grass?" Yancy shouted behind him when Cas reined in. "Get clear!"

Cas ignored him, swinging down and tossing the reins forward. First he speared his field glasses out and adjusted the focus to study the limestone. He kept his body behind Comet.

Another whip crack, another divot of earth leaping up in front of his horse. But Cas had spotted his man, tucked into a seam along the limestone face and firing a Winchester rifle.

The same skinny man, he realized with a quickening of his pulse, whom he suspected of leaving the note pinned to his saddle.

"Ah-*huh*, time for your assurance!" Yancy called out when Cas slid the Big Fifty from its boot. From a saddle pocket, he took out a folding bipod and screwed it into the barrel.

The rifle above cracked again and a slug whistled over Cas' saddle fender, so close he felt the wind rip on his right cheek.

"Catch my horse!" he yelled to Yancy, tugging Comet around by the bridle and then slapping his glossy rump hard.

Cas flattened himself and low crawled, looking for a spot. This was a level ridge, but he had learned that even the flattest terrain was never truly flat when studied from ground level. He rolled into a swale and quickly set up the Sharps.

Again the rifle above spoke its piece, the slug thumping in dangerously close to Cas' head. He rolled back the Big Fifty's breech block, thumbed in a long cartridge, closed the breech, and thumb cocked the big hammer.

"Cas!" Yancy's deep voice bellowed. "Damn it boy, pull foot! He's about to find your range!"

Without field glasses Cas could see only a dark speck to aim at. But the telescopic sight gave him a better target.

"At least pre*tend* you got more brains than a rabbit!" a frustrated Yancy shouted. "Damn it, Everett, you're a fish in a barrel right there!"

Cas inhaled a deep breath and expelled it slowly while his finger took up the slack in a slow, patient squeeze to avoid bucking the gun. The Winchester cracked again, and this time Cas felt his hat hop off his head.

"Haul your freight!" Yancy shouted. *"Now!"*

The Big Fifty bucked hard into his shoulder, and Cas watched the ambusher fall, screaming, hundreds of feet to a huge pile of scree below him.

"Does your mother know you're *dead*?" he murmured as he grabbed the heavy Sharps and unfolded to his feet.

Yancy ran forward, leading both horses. "You all right?"

Cas nodded and picked up his hat, slapping the dust off it.

"Well, he sure ain't," Yancy said. "If the bullet didn't kill him, the fall had to."

"It's none of our funeral. He asked for it."

"I was scared pukey when he opened up on us," Yancy admitted. "But you just stayed frosty and set to work—just like the newspapers say you do."

Cas secured the Sharps and bipod, and both men forked leather.

"Going to search the body?" Yancy asked.

"Nah, we'll just leave him for carrion bait. These curly wolves never carry any true identification. I already know he was at the grog shop yesterday just before we found the note on my saddle."

"That's two who've tried to kill you and instead got killed."

"Yeah," Cas said, "but remember, the first try, down in Louisiana, couldn't't've been ordered—he had just sent the telegram reporting I was back. And this attempt here probably wasn't ordered, either."

"How you figure that?"

"So far," Cas told him, "they haven't been hell-bent on peddling lead to us. And why would they leave such an important job to only one man, and at this long range? That's a spy post up there, not a marksman's nest."

Yancy nodded, seeing the point. "You figure they're saving it until we hit the gulch."

"Yep. This jasper today was just feeling frisky. Wanted to test his aim."

"Yours was better," Yancy said proudly.

"That's the problem with going to Deadwood," Cas told him. "Aim never has mattered to backshooters."

Chapter 13

The late-afternoon sun, filtered through the canopy of trees, stippled Cas with golden specks of light as he led Yancy through a stream bed littered with boulders.

"Deadwood Creek?" Yancy asked behind him.

"It's Deadwood or Whitewood," Cas said. "They run close to each other in places and both are showing color."

A glance to their right proved that. A double handful of prospectors worked claims near a long bend in the stream, bends being natural catch basins for gold-bearing placers. A few simply employed flat gravel pans with sloping sides; others had evolved to rockers, and Cas even saw one sluice, or Long Tom, being operated by a team of five men.

Poor man's diggings! That was the early cry that lured many of these desperate men to the Black Hills, said to number at least ten thousand souls in Deadwood Gulch alone. The lure was gold that could be gotten with simple tools and hard work.

"Cas," Yancy said, "I've grown weary of this 'pig farmer' teasing. I'm thinkin', when we get to Deadwood, of buying me a new John B."

"A Stetson is an expensive conk cover even in

an honest town. It's not just the gold strike that drives prices. The Black Hills are hundreds of miles from any source of supplies. I'd hold off. Besides, in a heller like Deadwood, someone may kill you for such a fine hat."

"He'll have to clear it with Patsy first."

Cas laughed. "And get past those ham-sized fists of yours, stout lad. But there's no shortage of gun-handy men swaggering it around the gulch."

Even before Cas cleared the next line of trees, he could hear the din of a lively settlement. The well-beaten trail twisted its way around a cotton-wood thicket and emerged on the south lip of Deadwood Gulch, and suddenly Cas was looking down upon the most dangerous boomtown in America.

Yancy caught up to him and drew rein. "Bleedin' Holy Ghost!" he swore, struck speechless.

The gulch was a dead-end canyon, steep-sided, with smooth rock faces and settlement starting to creep down the sides. The two awed men looked down at the gulch floor and a town well built up while also still building. The street looked more like a muddy buffalo wallow than a thoroughfare and seemed completely blocked by building materi-als. There was an endless collection of rectangular frame buildings, mostly two or three stories, with false fronts. More functional than fancy, as was much of the frontier West.

"I was here a little over a year ago," Cas said. "At that time there were something like seventy-five places calling themselves saloons. That didn't count all the other vice parlors billing themselves as theaters or gambling houses. And I see the town has grown since then."

"That pestilential bog is Main Street?" Yancy asked, his voice skeptical.

"Yep. That's what happens when you don't ditch the streets. One good rain turns it into a hog wallow, and as you can see, I mean that literally. Look at all the pigs. They own the place."

"Where," Yancy asked, excitement spiking his voice, "is the saloon where Wild Bill was sent to glory?"

It took Cas a minute to spot Mann, Lewis, and Nuttall's No. 10 Saloon. He pointed toward the northeast end of town. "That's lower Main, also known as the Badlands. See that simple, rough-sawed structure with the duckboards out front? That's the No. 10."

"I thought Wild Bill preferred easy living," Yancy said, sounding disappointed. "You couldn't prove up government land with that shack."

"I hear he picked it for location, not comfort. He was staying at Charlie Utter's camp to lay low, and he could get to the No. 10 without showing himself to the bustle on Main Street. Don't forget, his eyes were prob'ly going bad and he wasn't eager to face glory seekers."

Cas pointed again. "That big building just up from the No. 10, with the second- and third-floor balconies, is Al Swearengen's Gem Theater. It's the going place in town, but *don't* set foot in it alone. Swearengen and his crew are jackals, and to them killing a man is no more important than kicking mud off your boots."

"The honky-tonks just don't end," Yancy marveled. "Door after door up and down both sides of the . . . street."

Cas nodded, sending a glance over his shoulder. "Deadwood brags it's number one in the hell-raising department—more places to sin than any other town its size."

"I don't notice a church or school," Yancy said.

"Nor, for that matter, a woman or child. Kathleen Steele *can't* be here."

"Hard to imagine she'd even want to be," Cas agreed.

Yancy recovered from his first view of notorious Deadwood and looked at his friend, visibly humbled. "I'm with you till the wheels fall off, Cas boy. But just lookin' at this Sodom and Gomorrah fair gives me the fidgets."

"Same here," Cas admitted.

"Maybe your bein' a famous gunfighter," Yancy suggested, "will keep the curly wolves at bay."

"I'm not famous," Cas corrected him. "Now Wild Bill was famous. That's because a lying ink slinger at *Harper's* sold Bill's mostly made-up story to the entire world."

"You're in plenty of newspapers," Yancy argued.

"That's not fame. It's a reputation. Men admire fame, but they challenge a reputation."

Yancy thought about it and nodded. "I take your drift. Better to just be some anonymous clodpole like me, eh?"

"Clodpole? You're a gentleman farmer from Texas." Cas put a hand on Yancy's shoulder. "Now listen to me, pard. It's impossible to lay low in a snake den like this, all right? They hate any kind of law, bounty hunters like me included, and besides, the killers knew we were coming from the get-go. So go easy, understand? Don't be losing your temper and complaining about prices, food, and whatnot."

Yancy scowled, offended. "Prices? Are you calling me tightfisted?"

Cas gave a fluming sigh. "Never mind, Baron of Gray Matter. There's the livery to our right. Let's get these horses stalled."

Cas immediately recognized the hostler from his last sojourn to Deadwood, an acerbic old Irishman named Cedric O'Flaherty. He sat on a rain barrel just outside the big front doors, swatting at flies with a quirt.

If the liveryman recognized Cas, it didn't show in his bearded, rheumy-eyed face. He showed little interest while Cas carefully studied the hoof-packed dirt in front of the livery barn.

"Lookin' for that chipped shoe?" Yancy asked.

"Yeah, but there's too many overlapping prints. I'll never spot it if it's here."

They led their horses toward the barn. "Heigh-up, old-timer!" Cas hailed Cedric.

"You two lookin' for your own graves out there?" the hostler responded. "That's all you'll find in Deadwood."

"Not me," Cas assured him. "I plan to die in old age with my boots off."

The old man shook with mirth as he took a cigarette paper out of his shirt pocket and shook tobacco into it from a pouch. "Well, you picked one hell of a place, for a man who hankers to die old. I guess 'em two full rifle scabbards, and your friend's sawed-off, are just instruments of peace?"

Yancy scowled. "I don't much appreciate—"

"Cinch your lips," Cas snapped. He turned toward Cedric. "Got room to board two more horses, old campaigner?"

"Fir how long?"

"Oh, figured we'd start with a week."

The old salt nodded. Cas watched him study Comet from calculating eyes. "That can be did. Cost you a V spot, though. Apiece."

"Five dollars!" Yancy exploded. "You said *five dollars*?"

"That's the way of it, Olaf. These are shining times and prices run high. Take it or leave it. No skin off my rump."

"We'll take it," Cas said promptly, heading off Yancy's next outburst. "Matter fact, let's go the whole hog. Grain, rubdown, curry, stalls with fresh straw. What's that tote up to?"

"There *ain't* no 'whole hog' here. For five bucks a week, you can stall your horses, and I provide the grain and water. But I don't take care of 'em. You'll hafta do all the feedin' and curryin' and so forth yourself."

At this outrageous revelation, Yancy was fit to be tied, but Cas silenced him with a homicidal glower.

"All right, I prefer that anyway," the bounty hunter said, handing the old pirate a gold eagle.

Yancy muttered curses under his breath as they led their horses inside past two rows of stalled mounts and stripped the leather from them. They tossed their saddles on wooden racks in the tack room, hung their bridles around old Arbuckle's cans nailed to the wall.

"Cas boy," Yancy complained, "how do we know our horses and tack will even *be* here when we come back? That old gumsucker out front would steal a Camp Rucker mule for a glass of whiskey."

Yancy was right this time, and Cas nodded. "I don't like it either, but there's no room down in the gulch for horses. Half the boardinghouses are built on the sides of the gulch, too steep to keep our horses with us. Things are the way they are, I guess, and we'll have to make a virtue of necessity."

Both men rubbed down their horses, brushed and curried them, then led them to empty stalls and strapped nose bags of oats on them.

"Yessiree, young fella," Cedric said to Cas' back

as he walked out, lugging two rifles, "that chestnut of yours is a huckleberry above a persimmon, all right. Horses sell high around here. You lookin' to sell?"

Cas stopped and turned around. "No, thanks. I'm partial to him."

"A-huh. Well, all I'm sayin' is, sellin' now might be a far sight better than . . . losin' him later."

Cas felt heat under his collar, heat that crept up into his face. So far he had shown remarkable restraint, but the old hostler's last remark was an undisguised threat.

"Yancy," he said in a voice just above a whisper, "I don't like going full bore against an old-timer. But this one is bent, and we *can't* risk our horses. We're just barkin' at a knot when we treat him right, so let's bring that old man to Jesus."

Cas handed the heavy Sharps to Yancy, freeing his right hand. Cedric sat in profile to them on the rain barrel, smoking his perfectly rolled quirly. Cas grabbed leather and shot the cigarette out of his mouth. His next shot sent the old man's stove-lid hat spinning. His third knocked the heel off his left boot.

"God A'mighty!" the hostler roared, petrified with fright. "Don't kill me, son. I didn't mean to offend you!"

Cas moved in closer, blue smoke still curling from the muzzle of his .44. His face set hard as stone, he jammed the muzzle into Cedric's soft belly.

"I generally respect gray hair, but you asked for strong medicine, Methuselah, and now you're gettin' it. My name is Cas Everett, and if I notched my gun, there'd be no grips left. I'm mighty damn fond of my horse. Anything happens to him or that California sorrel, and I come in a-smokin'. Clear?"

"Clear as blood on new snow. Nervy cuss, ain'tcha?"

"When I need to be," Cas replied, spinning his Smith & Wesson back into the holster.

"A-huh. Well, you mistook my meaning, son. *I* don't steal horses. I'm lazy as all get-out, but I'm middling honest."

"I'll believe that," Cas told him. "But who did you mean, then? Who's the horse thief?"

The liveryman glanced nervously around. "There's a fellow in town named Dakota Boggs. Big, mean, raging bull of a man, savage as a meat ax. He makes a good haul by forcin' the small merchants like me to pay him a 'civic tax.' "

Cas and Yancy exchanged a fast glance. Dakota Boggs again.

"Never heard of him," Cas said. "He steals horses, too?"

Cedric nodded. "Sometimes, when he comes to collect from me, he looks over the horses and takes one he likes."

Cas nodded. "I've met the type."

"You'll meet him, too, if you're in camp a week. He's the big he-bear in charge of the Regulators."

"Regulators?" Yancy repeated.

"Vigilantes," Cas supplied. "Every gold camp has them. Problem is, there's an honest sheriff here in Deadwood, and solid structures. That tells me these Regulators are hardcases who refuse to retire gracefully."

The sun was a ruddy afterthought above the Black Hills as the two friends lowered themselves into the gulch with the help of carved footsteps and a knotted rope tied to a tree. Main Street had been busy since they arrived above, and by now the human traffic had thickened to a throng.

Yancy cradled Patsy in the crook of his left arm, his old Civil War hogleg jammed into the waistband of his trousers. Cas looked even more sinister as he lugged the heavy Sharps in his left hand and wore the Spencer in a sling over his right shoulder, stock bumping his revolver. Yet their weapons hardly drew a second glance in Deadwood, where almost everyone carried arms openly.

"I can see the boardinghouse where I stayed last time," Cas said as they joined the crowd on lower Main. "It's on the north face of the gulch, that big, boxy frame house with the timbers bracing it. Let's see if we can get a room."

Cas pulled his hat low and picked the darker side of the street. Yancy didn't know where to look because there was so much going on. A Negro barber wrestled a full bathtub onto the boardwalk and added its murky contents to the witch's brew in the street. A cooper with an open stall for a cooperage was warping staves into a beer barrel. More than one help-wanted sign included the words ORPHANS PREFERRED.

"No calicos?" Yancy inquired.

"Some," Cas told him. "They're in the demi-monde dives like the Gem. After what happened down in New Mexico Territory, think you can tell a sparkling doxie from a preacher's wife?"

"Yah shoor. Just remember, funny lad, I can hit you before you shoot me."

Talking about females got Cas thinking again about Kathleen. What if she *had* been forced, by men or circumstances, to stay here? In a place like this, he supposed many a weak reed developed an iron spine. Others no doubt wilted and perished.

A gun fired somewhere on the opposite side of the street, and received little notice. Yancy looked at Cas. "So it's like the cowtowns? You can discharge firearms right in town?"

"Most of the cowtowns will jug a man for that

now," Cas assured him. "But the mining camps can't stop it, so the rule is, if it's one or two shots, that's just celebrating. Three or more is trouble."

"Speaking of trouble, you called it right on Dakota Boggs. Sounds like he rules the roost around here. But if that's so, why would he take on the job of . . . attacking your family like he did? He oughta be rich by now. 'Course, you did blow off his thumb. Seems a harsh revenge for such a thing."

"You're ahead of the roundup," Cas told him. "I already said there's no proof he did it. But there is his grievance over the thumb, and besides, who's in a better position to order men to watch us and harass us, maybe even kill us?"

However, Yancy wasn't listening. He had become transfixed by a pasteboard sign in the door of a lawyer's office: *Divorces on the Spot.*

" 'Walk in married, walk out happy,' " he read, astounded. "Cas, is that on the square?"

"Yeah, can you b'live it? Dakota Territory has turned into a divorce mill. Utah Territory, too. I hear they run ads back east and do a brisk trade."

Yancy looked mortified. "I can remember when it took an act of the legislature to get a divorce. Why, this way a man could get drunk and lose a real peach."

"Women can get 'em, too," Cas added.

Yancy stared at him as if Cas had announced dogs could walk on their hind legs and preach. "Good God a-gorry! And out in Utah, they can vote. It's petticoat government, Cas, and since we can't shoot them, the future looks bleak."

The strains of harmonicas, banjos, fiddles, and pianos leaked from many of the buildings they passed. Not all the sounds were so entertaining. They passed a cellar where snarling and fighting dogs tore each other apart. Cas glanced inside and saw a man at a table taking wagers on the next match. Despite the crush of passing men, Cas' vigilant gaze settled on an unkempt man in a slouch hat. He wore a vigilante's large tin star, which looked like it was cut from a pie pan.

Each time Cas and Yancy stopped to look at something, the man behind them did, too.

"Here's the No. 10," Yancy said, pausing outside. "Just a nip to cut the dust?"

Cas shook his head. "Maybe later. We need to get a room first."

Yancy lingered, fascinated by the plain, narrow building. "Why in tarnal blazes did this fool town acquit Jack McCall for murdering Hickok—from behind, no less. Granted, Wild Bill was a Yankee in the war, and rode roughshod on Texas cowboys in Abilene. But these are mostly Northern men up here."

"At the time Bill was killed two years ago," Cas explained, "everybody was afraid to even report crimes. Deadwood was an illegal town then on stolen Sioux land, and drawing attention to themselves could've cost some fortunes in gold."

Cas sent a glance behind them. Tin Star, too, had stopped, though he carefully avoided looking at Cas. He slid a cheroot from his pocket, nibbled off the end, and tucked the smoke into his mouth. He struck a sulfur match with his thumb and fired up the cheroot.

The Texans moved on, Yancy still unaware there was any trouble. A minute later he stopped again, whistling sharply.

"Say, that's a fancy saloon," he remarked, staring into a plush interior. "Why, there's velvet all over the walls, and leather chairs."

"I made that mistake, too, when I first went wide upon the world," Cas told him. "That's not a saloon. It's a gambling hall."

"They ain't the same thing?"

"Nah. Saloons're for fellows like me and you. Gambling halls are for high rollers who drive fancy rigs. All the luxury is meant to make 'em bet big and lose calmly without shooting the dealer."

Cas glanced behind them and saw Tin Star had paused yet again, pretending to adjust his slouch hat.

"Be right with you," he told Yancy. "Be ready to bring Patsy up and on the line."

Cas had no way of knowing yet whether these night riders were after him because he was Cas Everett, bounty hunter, or Cas Everett, avenger of his family. But in a place like Deadwood, he knew he'd be worm fodder the moment he showed the white feather to these two-bit tyrants.

He also suspected other Regulators were watching, so Cas palmed his .44 and walked directly up to the vigilante.

"The hell's scratchin' at you, mister?" the man demanded, taken by surprise.

The surprise, however, had just begun. Cas squared his shoulders, lowered his center of gravity, and raked upward at a forty-five-degree angle with his open right hand, swinging straight from his heels so he put cold will and hard muscle behind the effort. The heel of his palm caught flush under the point of the vigilante's chin and snapped his head back hard. His feet actually lifted up from the boardwalk, and then he slackened and went down flat on his face.

Until Cas made this lightning attack, another vigilante, this one with a goiter on his neck and sporting a .45 caliber Army revolver, had been loitering nearby and paring his fingernails. The moment Cas dropped his comrade, Yancy saw the man start to draw.

"Cas!" Yancy bellowed, unable to fire Patsy in this crowd. "On your left!"

Cas spun on his heel as he coiled for the draw, slapping leather and verifying his target. Despite getting a late start, Cas cleared leather while his opponent only had his gun halfway out.

"Might's well finish what you started," Cas told him. "Skin it back."

The vigilante shook his head and let the weapon fall back in the holster before raising his hands. The one on the ground groaned like a deathbed case, trying to sit up.

"Either one of you yellow curs," Cas asked them, "plan to ask me how my family's doing?"

"No, sir," replied the man still standing.

Cas watched them a few moments longer, trying to decide the point of their following him. It seemed most likely, since they were open criminals, that they intended to watch a bounty hunter in their town and kill him if possible. That didn't mean, however, that Dakota Boggs and some of his men couldn't have committed the massacre down in Texas. He resolved to shake that tree and see what fell out.

By now the tin star in the slouch hat had struggled to his feet, looking like hell warmed over.

"Dust," Cas ordered, and both men disappeared into the motley flow.

He and Yancy fell into step again. "Good work," Cas told the Swede. "You saved my bacon with that warning."

Yancy looked more alert now, trusting no one. "You told no stretchers about Deadwood. Why, they were set to murder you in the street!"

"If I could prove that, they'd both be showing their

soles to the world by now. They might only have
been watching me to see who I mean to pinch."

The two friends were walking past the finest
building in Deadwood, a five-story extravaganza
called the Crystal Palace Hotel, when Cas almost
collided with a well-dressed, middle-aged man with
silver muttonchops. The Texan took in the natty
gray herringbone suit, a short gold chain connecting
his watch to a button hole.

"Beg pardon," Cas said in a civil tone.

The man said nothing, watching Cas from eyes
like two flint chips. Evidently he had just left the
hotel. A young Chinese boy in a floppy blue blouse,
his hair a long braid in back, followed him at a
respectful five paces. He carried a folded canvas
camp stool—presumably, Cas guessed, just in case
His Excellency chose to sit somewhere for a spell
and contemplate the pissant drones.

Cas and Yancy continued walking, heading
toward upper Main and a spot where a set of
carved-out steps led up the stone face of the gulch.
Just off Main Street was a solid two-story brick
house that wasn't here last time Cas came to Deadwood. High brick walls surrounded it, jagged cusps
of broken glass protruding from the masonry atop
the walls.

"Three guesses," he told Yancy, "who prob'ly
lives in that fort with the high walls?"

"The snake-eyed clothes dummy with the camp
stool," Yancy replied promptly. "He didn't seem
to cotton to you much, did he? Could be a for-
eigner who expects us to truckle to men of rank."

Cas shrugged. "T'hell with him. He never bought
me a beer. Here's where we turn off and make the
climb up. Let's see if we can get a room. I don't
think I can survive all this warm welcome in the
streets."

Chapter 14

Mrs. Lydia Huckabee was a tall, gaunt widow of indeterminate middle age in a faded print dress. Her false teeth didn't fit and slurred her speech. Cas tried to look decent and presentable as she closely studied these latest arrivals to her boarding-house. So far they hadn't made it past the threshold of the kitchen door.

Her quick inspection of Cas resulted in an emphatic nod of approval. "I recall you. Nice young fellow with clean habits. You caused us no problems."

However, her suspicions quickly focused on Yancy. She took his measure and frowned.

"Mr. Carlson, no offense to you personally, for a man cannot help his size. But I find big men prone to brawling. I have replaced too much furniture because of indoor brawling. You are with Mr. Everett, and I'll take that as a reference. However, you must solemnly promise me that you will take any brawls out front."

Yancy, his disheveled blond hair framing a raw face, looked indignant. "Cas, did I brawl once on the long ride up here?"

"He did not, Mrs. Huckabee," Cas assured her. "He is a dumb galoot, and will not stop carping about everything. And he's so ugly I usually board him in a livery. But he is generally well behaved in a civilized house if you keep a leash on him."

Mrs. Huckabee was hard-worked, but not humorless, and she joined Cas in an easy laugh while Yancy sputtered indignantly. She tugged the door open wider for them.

"I do have one room, boys, on the ground floor at the east side of the house. There's a window that gets a nice breeze."

Cas followed Yancy into a large kitchen smelling of fresh-baked bread.

"Nothing on the second floor?" Cas asked. "We'll pay extra."

Her eyes narrowed. "Why does that matter?"

"Sleep," Cas lied, knowing they'd get the boot if he admitted he feared assassination attempts through the window. "The second floor is always quieter."

Mrs. Huckabee nodded sympathetically. "That's true, but all four rooms upstairs are taken. Would you like to see this one?"

"Yah shoor," Yancy replied, still miffed by the teasing earlier. "Cas, buckle my leash on."

"It's not exactly the Astor House," Mrs. Huckabee apologized as she led them through an almost bare parlor. "Furniture is not easily had in Deadwood Gulch."

The boardinghouse looked clean but reeked of whiskey and onions.

"Drinking spirits is allowed," Mrs. Huckabee said as she crossed a hallway shiny from beeswax. "After all, most of my boarders are prospectors. But no women."

"Where would we get them?" Yancy said. "All I saw below were men."

She snorted as she slipped a skeleton key into a

lock, wiggling it to catch the tumbler. "Mr. Carlson, I'm not talking about mail-order brides. There *are* women in town, of a sort."

She opened the door and let them step inside. Cas saw a narrow room with an uneven floor covered by linoleum. He recognized an icebox in the back corner—a wooden chest with a tin container to hold ice on top and a pan underneath to catch melt water. A crude sawbuck table and a kerosene lamp were the only other furnishings besides two narrow bunks with straw mattresses. The legs of the bunks had been set in bowls of kerosene to keep bedbugs off.

Yancy looked like a disappointed child. "I'll take corn husks over straw any day."

"Fat lot you know," the widow chastised him. "This is barley straw. Everyone knows that's best if you can't get feathers."

"That's good," Yancy agreed reluctantly. "Where's the necessary? I didn't see one outside."

Cas, biting back a grin, elbowed Yancy. "Look at the foot of each bed."

Yancy did as told and suddenly looked horrified. Each tenet would get a chamber set: a basin and large-mouthed pitcher for washing, a cup for brushing the teeth, and a chamber pot for relieving oneself.

"Well, what did you expect?" Mrs. Huckabee demanded. "Built-in tubs and flush privies? You don't exactly look like a palace dweller in those work shoes."

Yancy met Cas' warning eyes and somehow reined in his anger. "And meals?" he inquired almost meekly.

"I provide two meals a day, breakfast and supper. You need to remember that not many foods are easily found in Deadwood. By necessity, break-

fast is usually the same each day: chipped beef on
biscuits."

"One of my favorites," Cas assured her.

"Mine, too," Yancy admitted. "But not every
day. No flapjacks with honey and butter?"

"Caulk up," Cas warned him.

Yancy ignored him. "Well, what about supper?"

"Supper is usually beef dodgers and cold slaw.
We have no vegetables but potatoes and onions,
and those infrequently."

Yancy shook his head solemnly at such human
suffering. "Well, at least, I suppose, the *mean*-ities
keep the rate low?"

"Fifteen dollars a week," she replied. Watching
Yancy with open glee, she tacked on bluntly,
"Apiece."

Yancy looked like he'd been punched but not
quite dropped. Even Cas, who knew the realities
of gold-camp inflation, was set on his heels by the
price. That was at least three times higher than
most places in the West, and he was getting low
on money. But it couldn't be avoided.

"We'll take it, and much obliged," he told the
widow.

"Huh! Judge Moneybags controls this town,"
Yancy pouted, washing his hands of the matter.

Cas paid in United States Notes.

"Gold coins will get you a discount," Mrs. Huckabee said, frowning at the paper money.

"I wish I could oblige you, ma'am," Cas said.
"But I'm low on gold shiners."

"Well, it all spends, I suppose." She started to
leave, then turned back around and addressed herself to Cas. "You strike me quite favorably, but I
confess your name seems familiar in a notorious
way, and it chills my spine to look into your eyes.
You are definitely a man with a mission. No matter

how brave and capable you may be, however, you've met your match in Deadwood Gulch."

Thanks to the presence of Kathleen Steele in the Gem, faro was far and away the most popular game of chance in the house. So long as she sat behind the dealer's box, men lined up all night for a chance to bet against the bank. Swearengen knew most of them really only wanted a chance to inhale her freshly bathed smell and gaze into those translucent green eyes.

Men were lined up now, almost to the door, and Kathleen felt her usual despair. The only person benefiting from all this was Al Swearengen, the ruthless thug from Chicago.

One of the upstairs girls tapped her shoulder. "Break time."

"Oh, *thank* you, Ruby."

Kathleen threaded her way through the early evening crowd, her face strained from so much obligatory smiling. She aimed for her usual small table in the shadow of the stage. Too late she saw who was waiting for her, and she felt her skin crawl.

"Siddown, lap kitten," Swearengen greeted her. "The sports have just put fresh linen on my bed. Care to wrinkle it with me? True, your break is short, but you'll find me very efficient. Indians don't waste time kissing and neither do I."

Heat rose into her face, and Swearengen laughed with delight. "There it is—the fetching blush! Proof that you come from a simpler, more sentimental people for whom church membership is at the center of life."

"That's true for most people—outside of Deadwood," she told him, ignoring the pony glass of whiskey he pushed toward her.

Al swore without heat. "Save it for the dupes.

As you must know by now, provincial morality has no place in Deadwood and is quickly stamped out. Yet you persist in your quaint ways. A liar of your talent *ought* to be starring in great plays."

"My life is not a lie, Al. It is a nightmare."

His eyes watched her with evident hunger. "Bosh! You are an excellent grifter, love. Even the devil can cite Scripture for his own purposes, eh? Levi believes your Maid Purity act although I get the distinct impression he's at the end of his tether."

It was hard to know when poker-face Al was being serious, but his tone now alerted her. Levi's behavior lately did frighten her. She feared that her constant rejection of him had finally met its limit, and that he would soon force her to prove she preferred death over submission to him.

"He was thrilled when he purchased his virginal princess," Swearengen elaborated. "But she has remained so royal and pure that poor Levi is all tied up in carnal knots. And it won't be long now before he carves out your perfumed guts with a boning knife. Then I'll be out an excellent faro dealer."

"Thanks for your concern," she barbed.

"Actually," Swearengen admitted, "I'm quite fond of you and despise Levi. That's why I advise you to kill him first."

Swearengen's leather-knuckled hand slid a thin black dagger in a felt case across the table toward her. "Put that in your handbag."

Kathleen balked. "But what if . . . I mean, he searches—"

"Does he search your underclothing—while you're wearing them?"

She flushed. "Of course not."

Al snorted. "No, *he'd* wait for written permission."

"But—"

"Stick your 'buts' back in your pocket, missy," Swearengen told her. "He's going to kill you— that's obvious. I recommend you get out of the gate first."

"But Dakota Boggs works for him. I'd never go free."

Al laughed. "If you could wait long enough, Dakota would kill him for you. But it appears Mr. Boggs has more pressing problems at the moment."

Kathleen studied his inscrutable face. "Meaning . . . ?"

"Never mind, buttinsky. My advice is to slide that dagger between Levi's fourth and fifth ribs. That way it's straight into the heart. Put it in your handbag before someone sees it."

She did, but her face was a mask of confused impulses. "I've never done such a thing. How . . . Even if I *would* do it, I doubt I could. The opportunity is not there in our daily routine."

Swearengen clucked his tongue. "Murder is nothing. I killed a man last night and slept like a baby."

Ice suddenly encased Kathleen's spine, and Swearengen laughed at her horrified face.

"If you wish to die," he told her, "that's your foolish choice. I've been paid my money for you. As to opportunity . . . the Deadwood Opera House is about to present *Tristan and Isolt*. A theater box like Levi's is a wonderful place for a murder. Ask the ghost of Abe Lincoln. While your rich pansy is transported to the realms of the tragic and epic, stick him fast. And be sure to give it the Roman twist once the blade is in."

Crawley Deacon, the bartender, signaled to Swearengen, who scraped back his chair and strolled up to the bar. Kathleen sat motionless, watching a nearby starling in a wooden cage. She realized she and the bird were in the same predicament—caged. Hers was a gilded cage, but a cage nonetheless.

A brawl erupted near the door, a circumstance so common that Kathleen didn't bother to watch it. Instead, she took advantage of the sudden surge in the crowd to glance at a table near the bar. Dakota Boggs sat there drinking whiskey with three of his most trusted lieutenants. She couldn't remember seeing the four of them together since they all rode out sometime in early April.

Approximately the same time, she reminded herself, that the Everett family was massacred. Was that an additional clue or just one more coincidence? She reminded herself that Texas was a great distance from the Black Hills, and there was no obvious link between the Everetts and Boggs.

"Terrific sensation, Miss Steele!" said a breathless girl in a wine red gown, stopping at Kathleen's table. "A couple newcomers to the gulch just whaled the snot outta two of Dakota's tin stars."

"I hope these newcomers just keep on going, Polly," Kathleen replied, still watching Dakota and his minions.

"Oh, they'll have to be hauled out dead. I saw it. This one fellow—one of them tall, handsome, serious fellows—hit one of the tin stars so hard his feet lifted right off the boards."

"They don't sound like prospectors," Kathleen remarked.

"Not hardly. One's a gunfighter like Wild Bill Hickok. Two of Dakota's lice tried to draw on him, but he had his gun out quicker than a thought."

Kathleen's eyes, usually hopeless, caught sparks at this news. Polly noticed it and gave her a searching glance. A tingling prickle of alarm moved up into Kathleen's nape. She silently rebuked herself and tried to act indifferent—Polly was one of Al's spies.

"The other one," Polly prattled on, "was the biggest farmer I ever seen. He had a shotgun that give me the shakes just lookin' at it. These fellows look mighty consequential, or at least that gunfighter does."

By now Kathleen's heart was racing, and at first she was buoyed by the news. She had felt her hope eroding for so long, had even begun thinking about a trip to the pharmacy to purchase arsenic. For a few moments, however, she felt a wild kind of hope burn inside her. But a year of dangerous captivity had left her a jaded realist. What she was hoping for was too much like a fairy tale to be true. She'd been dreaming about Cas Everett rescuing her, one way or another, since she was twelve.

It was pointless, she forced herself to admit, to place her faith in wishes. Then again, could she really place it in a dagger?

"Boys," Dakota Boggs said, "there's no need to get ice in your boots. We *own* this territory. Besides, this Texas bounty hunter has no proof. He's never seen any of you before, and I hired drifters to haze him on the trail up."

"He's here, ain't he?" Charlie Deets demanded.

"And not to pan for color," Nat Hendry tossed in. "Dakota, just today he killed Ace McGinnis out at Lookout Rock. A damned hard shot to make. That's two men killed and two more beaten so hard their eyes are crossed."

Boggs combed his lush mustache with a finger. "Then I guess it's too bad I can't get men like Everett to back my play. Hell, I could set up Tammany politics in the sagebrush country."

"We ain't in no funnin' mood," steamed Ike

Bass, the fourth vigilante at the table. "Just now he left Bernie stove up for a week. Can't even move his head. And I came within a cat whisker of eatin' lead. Everett might not have all the names yet, but he'll get them. And he made a point of mentioning his family."

"He sure's hell knows you, Dakota," Deets tossed in. "If I blew a man's hammer thumb off, he'd be high on the list of my enemies."

Boggs poured more whiskey into his cup made of black buffalo horn. Nobody had to lower his voice at the Gem. There was a constant din of piano music, voices, and celebration whoops.

"He's got oysters on him. I'll give him that," Dakota said calmly. "But we'll fix his flint. He won't last two days in this gulch. Say, Jack McCall was a spineless half-wit, and he got Hickok, didn't he?"

"Clean your ears," Ike said. "I just faced Everett. He had plenty of reason to be on the scrap, but I never seen a man rile so cool. Never cursed, never scowled, never even raised his voice. That's the dangerous type."

"*No* mother's son scares me," Boggs boasted. "I don't give a continental damn how many newspapers brag him up. Lead ain't partial to fame."

Despite his brave words, Boggs knew what Ike meant. Cas Everett had a dangerous, confident calm about him that would worry any observant man. The money Stone MacGruder paid Dakota was good, but Boggs now realized it wouldn't be the "easy money" it first seemed.

"Boys," he said, "nerve up. If we stick together, Everett will never be able to get names. Without names, he'll do no killing if we don't provoke him. Killing his people was a private job. I wasn't fool enough to tell anybody but you three who went

with me. And Jimbo, of course, who'd still be alive
if he hadn't returned to that telegraph office in
Louisiana to toss lead, the fool. MacGruder danced
on air a week ago in Omaha, so *he* ain't singing."

"Jesus, Dakota, the man blew your cocking
thumb off," Ike argued. "Of course he suspects
you."

"Hogwash. That alone is no reason to wipe out
a man's entire family, includin' three women. Everett has to know that."

Dakota's confident talk had some effect on the
men. They had relaxed, slacking in their chairs and
assuming their insolent, proprietary manner.

"Remember, chappies," he told them, "Levi Carruthers is about to get squoze out. The four of us
will take over his operation, and *then* there'll be no
more hog and hominy on your plates."

"*Hell* yeah!" Charlie Deets burst out. "No need
to go puny, boys. We wasn't born in the woods to
be scared by an owl."

Boggs grinned. "That's the gait. Everett and that
hayrack of a farmer are both gone-up cases. But it
will be a little trickier this time to feed the pigs.
Everett can kill six men before one of them clears
leather and fires. He's faster than Hickok, and I
think he's smarter."

Boggs fell silent, studying his men closer. All of
them were heavy-lidded and appeared to have been
visiting the opium dens in Chinatown.

Boggs said, "Speaking of playin' it smart—I've
told you boys before about hittin' that Chinee pipe.
With Cas Everett around, you'd best stick to tobacco. But it's your funeral."

Boggs topped off his glass, thinking how, sometimes, there *was* honor among thieves. When Everett captured a vicious, vindictive owlhoot from Fort
Worth named Stone MacGruder, he had no idea

what kind of viper he had taken into custody. Seething with rage in prison, Stone bribed a guard to mail a letter to Stone's former partner, Boggs. The deal was simple: kill the entire family of Cas Everett, and Stone would tell Boggs the location of $20,000 in hidden swag.

Boggs, despite his statements just now, had indeed thirsted for revenge against Everett for ruining his gun hand, and Stone had counted on that. Besides, Boggs loved a good gamble, and his former pard was known for keeping his word. Boggs got sick of these newspaper darlings like Cas Everett, who made their reputations rousting criminals. Killing his family had been satisfying enough, but good old Stone came through before he was hanged. His note said simply, *"Devil's,"* and Boggs knew it meant Devil's Mouth, a Black Hills cave where he and Stone used to store loot. The gold was there, all right, $20,000 in double eagles.

"You gathering wool, Dakota?" Nat Hendry demanded.

"Just thinkin', boys. Do you know where Everett and the sodbuster are bunking?"

"The widow Huckabee's place," Ike said.

"And their horses are in O'Flaherty's livery, right?"

Ike nodded, his eyes wandering to the pretty faro dealer.

"All right," Boggs said. "No sense letting grass grow under us. Here's what we need to do. . . ."

Chapter 15

Although Cas feared more trouble during that first
night in Deadwood, it never came. The barley-
straw mattress was a great improvement over hard
ground, but the raucous din from below in the
gulch lasted well after midnight and Cas slept fit-
fully, his gun belt near his fingertips. Both men
were awake and dressed when widow Huckabee
rang the breakfast bell before sunrise.

The four boarders from upstairs were all prospectors in stained boots and clothing, their faces,
necks, and arms burned lobster red. None of them
seemed the chatty type. They wolfed their food,
slurped their coffee from saucers, and left to work
their claims, hauling flat gravel pans, pickaxes, and
rakes. Gold fever had made them single-minded of
purpose, and if they recognized Cas as a "gunologist," they didn't show much interest—a fact that
delighted him.

"Breakfast was tolerable," Yancy conceded as
the two men returned to the room for their weapons. "But it was gone in five tiny bites. My kingdom
for a plate of fried grits and side meat."

"There's vendors all over selling doughnuts,"
Cas told him. "Any place there's prospectors you'll
find tasty bear sign."

Yancy perked up. "Good things from Nazareth! Say," he added as they entered the room, "think the widow will mind about the beds?"

Last night they had moved them so they weren't in the line of fire from the window. Sadly, neither man could now enjoy that nice breeze she'd mentioned.

"She seems a good sort," Cas said as he strapped on his heavy leather gun belt. "It's hurting nothing. We'll push them back when we leave."

"If we leave, you mean."

"*When* we leave," Cas reiterated.

"On that subject . . . Cas boy, you mentioned this fellow Dakota Boggs before we even got here. Now we know he's here, all right, because the old salt at the livery said he runs the vigilantes. You think maybe it was Boggs and some of his lick fingers that rode down to your place?"

Cas knelt to place the heavy Sharps under his bed. "I'm not assuming that yet even though he figures he owes me for his ruined thumb. But what really gets me suspicious isn't the simple fact that Boggs and his Regulators want me dead—that's to be expected in a criminal hellhole like this." Cas stood and brushed off the knees of his denims. "No, it's how *quick* they came down on us like all wrath."

Yancy nodded. "Yah shoor, I take your drift. Just like they were waiting for us to get here."

"Like maybe they were warned in a telegram," Cas said, stretching the point, "by our dead friend down in Texas who watched for the signal we were back."

"We can't prove that."

Cas nodded. "That's the hang fire. I can't prove anything yet, but we're going to take care of that.

And we're going to start by inspecting the offside rear shoe of every horse at the livery."

First, however, they made a quick trip to recover their saddlebags, which they couldn't carry the night before. It wasn't necessary to climb down knotted ropes and cross through town; they simply stayed on the lip of the gulch and rounded it at the point where it abruptly ended, the two sides converging there near the livery.

"Why didn't we follow this path last night?" Yancy complained. "Climbing those steep sides could herniate a man."

Cas kept his palm on his .44 and swept everything with vigilant eyes. "You wanted to see the town, didn't you? Besides, do *not* take this path after dark unless you have to. It's Thieves' Alley."

Cas was impressed by the view from up here. Just beyond the built-up sprawl of town, Deadwood Gulch teemed with sweet clover and wildflowers. The nearest slopes of the Black Hills were golden yellow with arrowroot blossoms, and way up in a bottomless blue sky, a peregrine falcon soared on a wind current.

"All you hear about is the gold and the killing," an awestruck Yancy remarked. "These hills look like paradise."

The scene along Deadwood Creek, however, was less heavenly. Claims were thick here and a strange motley of tar-paper shacks, clapboard shebangs, and tents had sprung up. A Chinese boy carried a water yoke, full pails at each end, to scores of prospectors out in the creek.

The path broke free of tree cover and Cas spotted a lean, stern-faced man wearing a sheriff's badge. He had dismounted in front of the livery and was stripping the leather from a badly lathered ginger.

"That's Seth Bullock," Cas remarked. "I had supper with him last year at the Bodega Café."

"Is he famous?" Yancy asked hopefully, for the sheriff cut a striking profile.

"I doubt it. He prefers to avoid gunplay. But he seems like a good man with iron nerves. Made a name for himself as a straight-arrow lawman in the Montana Territory. I hear he's no scrubbed angel, but he does his best."

Yancy's size had caught the sheriff's attention, followed by Cas' purposeful manner as they strolled closer.

"Cas Everett," Bullock said, remembering. "I read about you now and then."

Cas grinned, taking his hand. "It's a pack of lies, but newspapers are useful in the privy."

Sheriff Bullock's fierce features softened. "Sorry about your family, Cas. I truly am."

" 'Preciate it, Seth." Cas introduced the sheriff to Yancy, then said, "From the looks of your horse, you been earning your pay."

Bullock snorted, smoothing his impressive mustache with two fingers. A soldier's haversack was slung over his left shoulder. "Actually, I just served a simple warrant in Custer City. But I have to ride full-bore each way to dodge the bullets. Swearengen and Boggs have both got men trying to perforate my liver."

Cas nodded, tossing his Spencer across his left shoulder. "Yeah, Boggs kindly sent a welcoming committee for me and Yancy, too."

Bullock frowned. "That doesn't make much sense—unless your being here involves him?"

"It sure does now. Tell me, how long is this hive of killers going to be tolerated? This is U.S. soil now, not Sioux land."

"Sing it, brother," Bullock said. "Their days are

numbered, and only Swearengen knows it. Federal marshals were supposed to've raided by now, but Swearengen and a rich parasite named Levi Carruthers stopped it with bribes. But the reckoning's coming. Meantime . . ."

He shook both their hands and started to lead his horse inside the livery barn. "I recommend you get your business done quick and dust your hocks out of here. Ten percent of our population got themselves murdered this past year, and those were mostly just sourdoughs with no reputation. Think what the odds must be for a fellow with a name?"

"Cheery sort," Yancy muttered, but he cast a wary eye around them.

The two men made a quick trip back to the boardinghouse with their saddle bags and returned to the livery. By now Cedric was back on his barrel out front, reading a greasy copy of Horatio Algers' *Ragged Dick.*

"Mornin', old campaigner," Cas greeted him. "Me 'n' Yancy would like to glance at some horseshoes. We're lookin' for sign of an old friend."

The liveryman shook with silent mirth. "A-huh, and I'm lookin' for John the Baptist."

"No horse will be hurt," Cas assured him. "We just want to look."

Cedric dug at a tick in his beard. "As they say, an empty hand is no lure for a hawk."

Cas was running low on money, but Yancy had pressed forty dollars in silver and gold on him last night. He slapped a three-dollar gold piece in the old man's wrinkled palm.

Cedric winked and slid off the barrel. "Think I'll purchase me some antifogmatic. You boys keep an eye on the place."

Before they went inside, Cas made a complete pass around the livery, spotting nothing worrisome.

"You work up the right side," Cas told his friend. "I'll take the left. Remember, offside rear shoe. You're looking for a small chip at the top of the bend. *Don't* get kicked—it could kill you or addle your brain even more than it already is."

Comet whiffled a greeting when Cas came inside. He checked on his horse and found water and grain. Comet nudged his shoulder, obviously content. Cas quickly set to work, knowing someone could come in at any moment. Any kind of fooling with another man's horse, especially in a wide-open territory, was as dastardly as stealing it.

Yancy swore when a paint gelding almost kicked him head over handcart. "This churnhead is an outlaw himself. These horses are mostly a sorry lot."

Cas carefully positioned himself behind a piebald and bent the right rear leg with no difficulty, seeing a normal shoe.

"Yeah, they're definitely hard up for horseflesh in Deadwood," he told Yancy, moving on to a palomino. "Normal breaking age is three and a half to four years. This buttermilk's not even three."

Cas moved to the third stall just as Comet pricked his ears and whickered.

"Cover down!" Cas barked to Yancy, diving into the dirt and straw right when a racket of gunfire shattered the stillness.

The pandemonium was instant and mind-numbing. The horses reared, sidestepped, or bucked depending on their natures. The shooters were at close range, firing through gaps and holes in the wood. Three or four of them, Cas guessed. For a few seconds, after the hammering racket opened up, he felt fear knotting his insides. Then his survival instincts kicked in, replacing fear with cold determination.

Slugs splintered wood and buzzed past his head

as Cas glanced toward the stall Yancy was in and cursed—the farmer had frozen where he stood, a big and vulnerable target.

Cas tossed a chunk of old board at him, hitting Yancy between the shoulder blades. "Cover *down*!" he roared above the din of gunfire and neighing horses.

Yancy finally gained a purchase on his wits and dived into the stall. All this seemed an eternity but had taken only seconds. Cas drew his Smith & Wesson and distributed six quick shots between two different spots where muzzle fire licked through the walls. Then he tossed the Spencer into his shoulder and sent all seven .56 caliber slugs through the wall. The rate of fire from outside had slowed noticeably because the ambushers were forced to duck to safety.

Yancy's Colt's Dragoon was his closest weapon. It fired with a deafening explosion, the huge projectile blowing out an entire board. That seemed to snap the attack—Cas heard feet pounding away.

He pushed reloads from the loops on his cartridge belt and thumbed them into the wheel of his .44.

"Stay here!" he ordered Yancy, racing toward the front door.

Cas had hoped the attackers would climb down into the gulch so he could eyeball them on the rope. But he spotted several running men disappearing into the thick tree cover east of the livery. Cas wasn't fool enough to chase them into blind cover.

He went back into the livery. The horses were starting to calm down, and Yancy was quickly checking each stall for casualties.

"By the horn spoons!" he exclaimed incredulously. "Not one horse got hit! How can that be,

Cas boy? God's trousers, those shooters emptied an ammo factory on us!"

"Hard to credit," Cas admitted. "Best answer I can see is that whoever opened up on us has friends with horses here, or maybe *they* have horses here. Or else . . ."

"Or else what?" Yancy pressed when Cas trailed off as another possibility occurred to him.

"Maybe they didn't want to hit us."

"Then why bother?"

"Like I said," Cas reminded him, "entertainment. Why just kill us quick? Better to make us worry and suffer first."

Cas glanced at the wide-eyed horses, most of them quiet but still nervous. "One thing for sure, we can't finish checking horseshoes now. Those animals will kick us into Montana."

Suspecting a follow-on attack, Cas watched through the doors.

"Get a peep at 'em?" Yancy asked.

"Nah. They rabbited fast."

"By the lord Harry, I'm shakin' like a rain-soaked kitten," Yancy said. "Even Old Scratch would fight shy of Deadwood."

As Yancy finally realized he was still alive, anger began to edge out his fear. He loosed a string of curses, employing words Cas didn't think Yancy even knew.

"Knock that off," Cas snapped. "I don't mind cussing, but I got no patience for men who can't control their ire. Stay frosty and you last longer."

Yancy simmered down, looking sheepish. "Shoo, don't you *ever* get mad?"

"Sure, but I try not to. Things are the way they are—that's all. You get mad, you get killed."

Yancy shook his head in wonderment while Cas fished copper-jacketed slugs out of his shirt pocket and shoved them through the trap in the Spencer's butt plate.

"I see now," Yancy said, "that it must take a mort of courage to live the bounty hunter's life, Caswell."

"Maybe, but courage isn't nerve," Cas told him. "That's what a man needs most."

"Since when?"

"Since David snuffed Goliath's wick, and earlier. Courage makes you take on a fight, but only cool, steady nerve can win it."

"Or sheer luck, like I had just now."

"Yeah," Cas agreed, mulling a plan. "I was lucky, too. And luck won't last a lifetime unless a man dies young. You feelin' nervy?"

Yancy looked cautious. "Why?"

"Because I think it's time for you and me to send in our cards to Dakota Boggs. Let's go."

"Go where?" Yancy asked as the two men eased cautiously outside.

"The Gem."

"But you told me that place is a death trap. Told me to stay out."

"Why just trim the branches of evil," Cas inquired, "if we can hack at the roots? Al Swearengen's Gem is a meeting place for the vigilantes."

Hand over hand, they started down the side of the gulch, Yancy leading and Cas watching the busy scene below from wary eyes.

"Unscouted country is the most dangerous," he told Yancy, "and that's even truer in towns. Keep your eyes to all sides."

They threaded their way carefully along lower Main. Despite the fact this was prime working time for prospectors, Deadwood drew men from all over the Black Hills, and the Badlands was jumping. A quick glance through open doors proved that, by far, the main pastime was wagering. Roulette, faro, poker, keno, monte, craps—any and every form of gambling flourished here in Deadwood. And when a show was desired to go with the bet, there was bare-knuckles boxing or dog fights.

"This is tame," Cas assured a wide-eyed Yancy. "Last time I was here, Swearengen had a big pit dug west of town. They took bets, then turned a bear and a bull loose on each other. The bull won, but he had to be shot."

Chinese men, Cas noticed, were more numerous than the year before. They scurried through the alleys off lower Main and were hailed by whites as "Johnny" or "John" depending on their age. Mostly, though, he kept his eyes peeled for tin stars.

Just before they reached the wide-open doors of the Gem, Cas halted Yancy with a hand on his arm.

"You proved yesterday how handy you can be," Cas told him. "But stick to me like my shadow when we're in the Gem."

"No man will draw on you," Yancy predicted confidently, "not to your face, anyhow. I've seen how they act when they learn your name."

"*No* man is fast enough against this many guns, especially in a section of town where there's no honest law. Just go easy in there, hear? There'll be Regulators inside, and I know that type. Catch one alone, he'll run like a river when the snow melts. But in a group, they egg each other on."

Cas loosened his .44 in the holster and looked at Yancy. "Let's go. Remember, if they do clear leather on us, they mean to kill us, not arrest us. Give 'em a couple doses of Blue Whistlers, then haul your freight out the doors before the smoke clears."

Chapter 16

Every two weeks or so, Levi Carruthers met with Dakota Boggs in the Gem to discuss the latest claims Boggs considered worth acquiring. The two men occupied a table near the bar, with Boggs' trio of loyal lieutenants seated in a vigilant circle at the next table.

"Right here," Boggs said, his stubby index finger pointing to a spot on a map of the area, "where Deadwood Creek flows closest to Broken Divide. The area's loaded with placers."

Carruthers, whose wardrobe cost nearly as much as a good horse, stared at the table. Dakota realized, however, that he wasn't looking at the map.

"You got some interest in my right hand?" Boggs demanded.

Carruthers frowned at his employee's insubordinate tone. "I was just wondering about that missing thumb of yours, Dakota. Swearengen claims that the man who shot it off is in Deadwood right now. Might that explain why Ike, Nat, and Charlie are mother henning you?"

Boggs' face turned so hard it looked carved from granite. "Case you haven't noticed, *boss,* I wear my gun on the left now. Any man who wants to test it, Cas Everett included, is welcome to dig his own grave. Offer's open to you, too."

Carruthers smiled smugly. "Men as rich as I am don't need to be fast. That's why you work for me. There's also a rumor that Everett has come here because you had a hand in killing his family."

"A rumor, yeah, and the wise wave it aside," Boggs replied casually, though in fact fear licked at his belly. He wasn't aware of any such rumor, but for some time he had feared that one of the men who rode to Texas with him must have told someone.

Carruthers sipped a brandy, suppressing a grin. He knew little about that massacre down in Texas and cared even less. Only later, after spotting the two Texans outside the Crystal Palace last night, had he learned who they were. However, he had disliked them instantly. They had "Don't tread on me" stamped all over them, and Carruthers was a trampler—of men's rights and of men. He hired out the killings and refused to listen to the details. Thus, in his view of it, he was not a criminal, just a speculator.

"You were saying something about possible new sites," he reminded his man. "Who claims them?"

"Three yacks named Justin McKinney, Harney Robinson, and Oliver Dunbar."

"Never heard of any of them," Carruthers said dismissively. "You say they're productive claims?"

"*I'll* tell the world. They're only working placer gold with a rocker, yet they're pulling out four hundred a day in color."

Carruthers used a cutter on his watch chain to clip off the end of a cigar, then lighted it. "That's impressive. But as you know, I'm interested in deep-rock veins, not placer gold. What's beneath the surface?"

"I'm no mining engineer. But there's ore all around there. So high grade you can see the veins in it. You need to buy these claims."

"They'll sell?"

Dakota's strong white teeth flashed under his teamster's mustache. "Don't they always?"

"Why isn't it done yet? I've given you authority in such matters."

"It's not been wrapped up yet," Boggs told him point-blank, "because I'm tired of getting the crappy end of the stick."

Carruthers shook his head. "That's too thin for me. Spell out your grievance."

"Spell it out? M-o-n-e-y. I want more of it."

Carruthers cast an eye over the vigilante's new black suit and octagonal tie. "You left town for quite some time, and you've acquired a new wardrobe since. I also hear you're gambling at the high-stakes tables. How could you possibly require more money?"

"How could you?"

Carruthers speared the cigar from his mouth. He was so angry that, as he ranted, he dotted invisible *i*'s in midair with his cigar. "You insolent mud sill! This is not a partnership. *You* work for me. You've been well compensated for your services, and I'm damned if I'll let you strong-arm me."

"You're the boss," Boggs said, flashing his odd grin, which failed to include the corners of his mouth. "Me, I get what I want, one way or the other." To make his meaning clear, he brought his left hand down to palm the butt of his hair-trigger, double-action Colt.

Carruthers blinked first. "All right," he surrendered. "I'll cut you in for five percent on future earnings for each claim you . . . transfer to me. That could be a fortune."

Boggs chuckled and tossed back another jolt glass of whiskey. "Not interested."

"You don't trust me?"

"Trust everybody, but always cut the cards. '*Could* be a fortune' cuts no ice with me. What good is your promise if, say, something happens to you? I'll take a bird in the hand."

Carruthers seemed torn between rage and growing unease. "Boggs, are you threatening me?"

"Yeah," the leader of the Regulators said with cold finality, "I'm threatening you."

Just then two women in pinch-waisted gowns entered the Gem and headed for the secluded table near the stage. Boggs recognized Kathleen Steele and the singer from the Montana Saloon, Ginny Lofley. Carruthers watched Kathleen, his face a study in conflicting emotions.

"What's chappin' you, boss?" Boggs goaded. "Problems with the little 'lady? Might be I could help you there, too. I got a way with the high-strung fillies."

Carruthers swore and pushed back his chair, walking rapidly to the door. Boggs, still grinning, took the bottle and joined his men.

"How'd it go this morning?" he asked them.

"Coulda been better," Charlie Deets admitted. A Greener twelve gauge leaned against his chair. "It was darker than we figured it would be inside the livery. I never got a chance to use the scattergun."

"Either one of them hit?"

Ike Bass shook his head. "I saw them both come out."

"They see you?"

Again Ike shook his head. "We hightailed it too soon."

Boggs eyed all three men, shaking his head in

disgust. "Well, I guess it ain't no crime to aid and abet idiots."

"Ballocks!" Nat Hendry protested. "I never saw a man recover from an ambush and start rationing lead as quick as Everett did. Even that pig farmer pitched into the game and put a hole through my coat. *These* boys will sell their souls dearly."

Dakota glanced toward the doorway as two tall men suddenly filled it, blocking out much of the light. "Maybe we're about to find out the price of their souls, chappies. Here they come now."

Cas Everett's observant eyes swept over the mostly empty interior of the Gem, searching for the dangerous men he'd need to keep track of. He briefly noted two young women near the stage, but they were no threat and he dismissed them. The real danger sat about twenty feet to his right, three tin stars with the insolent smirks of the lower-caliber criminal types. And the rawhide-tough, killer-mean man with them, the one with the sneer of cold command, was Dakota Boggs. Cas had seen him only once, but that face like a stone slab was hard to forget.

"*There's* a church choir," Yancy muttered as they stood inside the door a minute to let their eyes adjust from the bright morning sunlight. "One of those tin stars has a shotgun."

"Don't let him use it," Cas warned. "I'll be covering Boggs—he figures I owe him a cocking thumb."

Cas took in the big, powerfully built man with bluff features and a drooping mustache. He wore a leather weskit, a black wool hat, and well-polished oxblood boots.

Cas strolled purposefully forward and stopped a few feet from the table. The Spencer depended

from his left hand; the palm of his right was close
to the holster. The tin stars lost their smirks, but
Boggs kept serenely smiling. Oddly, Cas noticed,
the hardcase was avoiding his eyes. Why?

"Say, Olaf," Boggs roweled Yancy, "you must
brush your hair with the rough side of a buffalo
tongue. We *do* have barbers in Deadwood."

Cas noticed they'd all filed down their spurs to
gouge more speed from their mounts—more proof
they were outlaws, for decent men didn't treat
horses that way. The thugs he could see well had
tied down their guns, too, and one had a swivel-
rigged holster.

"Glom Olaf's shoes, boys," the tin star with the
Greener chimed in. "Look like river barges."

"Which one of you outhouse vermin murdered
the Everett family?" Yancy demanded as Patsy's
barrels came up to the ready. "I'd guess all four
of you."

The Gem had gone silent when the Texans
walked in, faces grim with purpose. When Yancy
pulled back the double ten's hammers, the sound
seemed deafening.

"Now lower your hammers," Dakota hastened
to say. "We heard about Everett's family. I got a
grudge against the man, sure, but not against his
family. You're sniffin' the wrong dog's butt,
farmer."

Cas had been as shocked as everyone else when
Yancy simply blurted out the question. He reached
out and raised Yancy's muzzles toward the ceiling.

"Easy, old son. There's rules to these things."

Boggs seemed to fear he might have lost face
with his men by getting too nervous moments ago.
His hard black agate eyes finally met Cas' stare,
and his tone was patronizing.

"I won't lie to you, Everett. I was plannin' to

hunt you down like a dog and kill you for what you done to me. But what was done to your people, that was way out of line. Besides, I oughta thank you. I'm faster than ever."

Cas ignored this, placing a scrap of paper on the table in front of Boggs. "One of your . . . men tacked that to my saddle south of here."

" 'Does your mother know you're out?' " Boggs read aloud, struggling to keep a straight face. One of his men lost the struggle and snickered. Boggs shook his head. "You're mistaken. My men are all alive and well."

"You're ahead of the roundup," Cas told him. "Who said he was dead?"

"I just figured the big, bad Cas Everett would plant a man for a trick like this."

Cas had learned to ignore goading and remain calm in dangerous situations like this. The tin stars, however, attributed his silence to their intimidation.

"A true-blue, blown-in-the-bottle gunfighter," said a bearded man with his Colts tucked butts first into a red sash. "Why, we're honored, Mr. Everett. 'Course, the last *famous* gunfighter in Deadwood lost his head in the No. 10. Now he's gone to hunt the white buffalo."

"But you won't have to worry about anything, Texas," said a stocky vigilante with smallpox scars pitting his face. "They say bullets shot at Cas Everett fly wide."

"Don't push it, Nat," Boggs advised, more serious than jesting. "He can pop both your eyes out before you even jerk your shooter."

"Say, let's see that lightning border shift of yours," said the vigilante with the Greener. "The one the newspapers like to brag up."

Cas said nothing, showed no emotions. He just

studied each man's face and manner intently, as if memorizing them. Boggs got nervous again.

"Save it, boys," he said. "Evidently Mr. Everett is not on the scrap today."

"That's all right," Cas told all of them. "Say what you want to. It's air pudding to me. Some of it's even funny. But you say the wrong thing, and I'll curl your toes."

"What's the wrong thing?" the bearded toady demanded.

"You'll find out when you say it. Go ahead. You know what it is. You just had a good laugh over it."

The tough sneered and looked uncertainly at his companions.

"Go ahead," Cas urged in a slithering whisper. "I'm listening. Let's open the ball."

He flexed the fingers of his right hand. The entire barroom was quiet as a crypt.

"Say, Everett," Boggs protested. "This is mighty high-handed. We're just peace officers. Sure, we cut up rough now and again—hell, no plaster saints in Deadwood. But we know nothing about who killed your people."

"That's a lie," Cas told him flat out. "I don't have proof yet, but I will. Then I'm going to shoot you low in the guts, Boggs, so it takes hours to die. And I'll kill every yellow cur who rode down there with you."

Cas' stare moved around the table, daring any man to fill his hand. None seemed so inclined.

"All these cowardly ambushes and notes," he resumed, looking at Boggs again, "are being ordered by somebody, and you seem like the head hound around here."

Boggs sat up straighter, hatred stamped into his hard features. "You son of a bitch, Everett, I'm ordering you out of Deadwood Gulch right now."

Cas gave him a tight-lipped grin. "Order a cat's

tail, you woman-killing coward. I'm on the feather edge of putting a bullet in your brain right now. This is Deadwood, remember? I won't swing."

"This is *my* town, you sanctimonious mouth-piece. Go ahead and kill me—you'll have ten bullet holes in you before you reach the door."

Cas held the taunting grin. "So what? You'll still be dead, won't you? Dead as a Paiute grave."

He stood there, inviting their best effort, yet real-izing they wouldn't likely bite. Cas and Yancy backed carefully toward the door, eyes leveled on the Regulators. Just after they'd crossed the thresh-old onto the boardwalk, Yancy loosed a whistle.

"Whew! That gal in the straw hat is some pump-kins! What's she doin' here?"

Cas' eyes cut to the far back table. He saw a slender, tall beauty whose face was saved from grave severity by a slightly upturned nose. She wore her lustrous cinnamon hair over the shoulder, a style popularized by women of the American West.

"Can't be," Cas muttered. "Not in here."

He hadn't seen Kathleen Steele in several years, and certainly he'd never seen her dressed like this. This woman wore a balmoral petticoat, red with black stripes, under a long plum skirt, and sandals with ribbon straps. Even from here he could see an exciting plunge of cleavage where tight stays thrust her breasts up.

Her eyes, timid and ashamed but also pleading, met his. And then Cas *knew* she was Kathleen—knew in a pulse-quickening, throat-tightening way he'd always felt around her.

"Why, she 'pears partial to you, Cas boy," Yancy remarked, still failing to recognize her in the plush clothing and stingy lighting. "She hasn't taken those big, pretty peepers off you yet."

Cas barely heard this, his gaze still locked with Kathleen's. Time ticked out a long, dangerous silence between them, and he abruptly turned away when he realized how stupid he was being. Whatever Kathleen was doing in this outlaw town, the last thing she needed was to be linked with Cas Everett.

Chapter 17

"Don't tug me around like a naked brat," Yancy protested as Cas dragged him outside of the Gem.

"Shut pan and keep your eyes moving. Don't let anybody brush close to you. Head west. We're taking the long way back to the livery."

"What in blazes for?"

"To finish the job we started."

Eyes vigilant for the ever-expected attack, Cas tried to rein in his stampeding thoughts. Most important, Kathleen was still alive and certainly looking well. But why in the Gem? Cas didn't consider himself a prude, but there were unwritten codes for both sexes. It shocked him to his core to find Kathleen in Al Swearengen's nefarious den of vice—a saloon with sporting gals who took men to private rooms in the back.

"You look like you been mule kicked," Yancy opined, noticing how Cas compressed his lips in nervous concentration.

"I have, old son. That was Kathleen we just stared at."

"Well . . . by the lord Harry!" Yancy pulled up, flabbergasted. "You're right. I didn't recognize her at all . . . dressed up like that. She was plain style at home. Pretty, but plain dress."

Cas wasn't listening, busy berating himself. "Oh, that's just jim dandy, Everett. *Stare* at her like you're seeing a ghost. I did everything 'cept shoot her."

"Balderdash," Yancy scoffed. "Plenty of men must stare at that beauty."

"Thanks for the comforting thought."

"Cas boy, you don't think . . . I mean, that she could be one of the saloon gals?"

"She didn't seem dressed that way. Those clothes cost more than a sport could afford."

Yancy didn't look so sure. "Well, she's sittin' in a saloon unescorted. Could it be she's . . . Al Swearengen's private stock?"

Cas kept up his guard even though they'd crossed the deadline and were heading up Main toward the more law-abiding part of town. His bootheels thumped on the boardwalk. A water cart creaked by and a few actresses in ruffled satin dresses left McDaniel's Theater. They lifted their skirts and crossed the street to an eating house that stayed open night and day.

"Yancy, you're almost kin," he finally replied, "so I take no insult. But Kathleen Steele is right out of the top drawer, for a fact."

"Shoo! Cas Everett, are you telling me *you* have no curiosity to—"

" 'Course I do. And it bothers me just thinkin' about what she might've done in this wicked place. But she's a defenseless woman in an outlaw place that honors nothing."

"Perhaps, but—no offense—what if she *chooses* to be here?"

"That's a stumper. I'd lose my respect for her, I s'pose, but not my regard. I'd still want her to be safe."

"I accuse the woman of nothing," Yancy said

piously. "But appearances can be mighty damming."

"And mighty wrong. Since when does a Texan," Cas demanded, "fail to give a lady every benefit of the doubt? From what I've heard of Al Swearengen, he'd turn his own mother into a chimney sweep."

"I saw no guards around her."

"You turnip head. Look around you—you yourself mentioned how there's no school in Deadwood. So why'd Swearengen place a notice of employment for schoolteachers? Far as guards, why bother? A man can come and go, but not a woman like Kathleen."

Realizing he'd overstepped, Yancy looked contrite. "Yah shoor. Good points, and I'm caught upon them. She was prob'ly shanghaied, so to speak."

"Seems likely."

"You know saloons better than I, Caswell. What *would* a woman of her quality be doing at the Gem?"

"Well . . . you'll often find pretty gals running the faro rig. Or working as singers and actresses."

Yancy said, "No offense intended, but you don't think that, just maybe, Swearengen has forced her to be his—"

"I hope not. But even if he has, the main question is, does she choose to stay here in Deadwood or does she want the heck out?"

"Are'n'cha forgetting," Yancy said in an irritable tone, "how we're stretched thin already? I'm a farmer, not a knight."

Cas nodded. "That's why we're going to let her make the first contact, if she wants to. She knows this place, who to trust and all that."

"And if she doesn't?" Yancy prompted.

"Lady's choice, I s'pose. Like you said, our plate

is full. I hope we hear from her, though. She can't last long here."

By now they'd left the built-up section of the gulch behind. Smaller conveyances could enter the gulch by following a laborious trail alongside Deadwood Creek. A rattletrap buckboard approached them. Sideboards and a tar-paper roof had been added, forming a crude sleeping shelter. Bottles clinked from inside the shelter. Whitewash letters on the sideboards advertised DOYLE'S HOP BITTERS, "THE INVALID'S FRIEND AND HOPE."

Cas knew Doyle's as one of the most popular patent medicines in the West. As a curative, he'd discovered, it was worthless, but its heavy dose of alcohol left the patient too drunk to notice.

"Satan, get behind me," Yancy muttered, getting a good glance at the woman behind the dashboard as she pulled up beside them. She wore frayed men's trousers, an Indian-made beaded leather jerkin, and men's hob-nail boots. She had a homely, careworn face and wore her greasy hair tied in a heavy knot that dangled under an immaculate gray Stetson—the only clean item she had on.

"Be careful with your mouth," Cas muttered. "That's Martha Jane Canary."

"Never heard of the ugly hell hag."

Cas grinned. "I'll tell her you called her that. You fool, that's Calamity Jane."

Clearly three sheets to the wind, Jane called out in a gravel-pan voice, "Boys, don't be followin' that damned creek. I've crossed 'er forty-eight times in three mother-lovin' miles! That's enough turns to make a cow cross-eyed."

Her eyes raked over both husky, well-knit men. "Say! Either of you boys like to go off into the brush with me?"

Yancy flushed beet red and stared at his shoes.

"Jane," Cas replied, "you're too much woman for us."

She belched and took another swig of Doyle's. "And how. Well, boys, you 'pear to be nice fellers. Be mighty careful in that camp behind you. Every Injin I know swears the white man is one of the Creator's few mistakes. I called that hogwash until I came to Deadwood. That pig wallow would fright all the devils out of Hades. Took my handsome Wild Bill, too. . . ."

Jane clucked to her team and the dilapidated conveyance jerk rattled into motion.

Yancy kept his voice low. "Whew! Her breath would fire a steamboat boiler."

"She's gruff, but a good sort," Cas said. "Tells lies for drinks, but the newspapers are starting to peddle her blarney for truth."

"She didn't lie about Deadwood," Yancy said. "Cas, back in the States, Swearengen and Boggs would swing in the breeze."

"Depends which state," Cas replied absently as the two men ascended the north face where it was lower and less steep. His inner eye kept seeing Kathleen, so demurely pretty as she locked startled gazes with him.

"Calamity is too bold and ugly for me, but I've thought of tripping the primrose path of dalliance," Yancy confessed. "But I've talked to men who took the mercury cure, and I'll have none of that."

"Smart choice."

"Voice of experience?" Yancy pounced.

"Tell you the straight, some topics don't qualify for jawboning. I learned that from dealings with newspaper scribblers."

Yancy gloated. "I'll take all that as a yes."

"Take it as a cat's tail, you gossipy schoolgirl. Stop nosing my backtrail and pay attention right now. There's killers lookin' to snuff our wicks."

Cas filled his hand with nickel-plated steel and hurled himself over the lip of the gulch onto the brim, ready to fight but glad he didn't have to. He gave Yancy a hand and the big man's weight almost pulled them both over.

"Cas," Yancy said, "this Dakota Boggs—you had him in mind almost from the start. And looks like he's had us watched since before we left home. Why not just call him out and kill him? The rabid cur deserves a bellyful of lead."

"I agree, but it doesn't matter what I *know* is true, only what I can prove. I've never killed a man on a hunch, and putting the noose before the proof wouldn't be justice for my family."

They moved east through partially denuded timber, and soon they were again overlooking the camp turned hardscrabble town. Everything was wood, canvas, flockboard—no bricks or stones.

"This entire gulch is a tinderbox," Cas remarked. "It's gonna go up before too long—has to."

"If God keeps accounts," Yancy agreed.

Cas forced himself to place Kathleen from his thoughts. "Swede, we have a good clue in that chipped shoe. If it was Boggs and his lick spittles, that horse is almost sure to be in the livery. Just hope the shoe wasn't replaced."

What was Cas thinking, Kathleen fretted silently only moments after he left, *when he saw me here?*

She couldn't read his face, not with his hat pulled so low it covered his eyes. But any decent man—and she was sure he'd always been decent—would be sorely tested to respect any woman found here.

The drinking, the coarse language, the fights and killings, the little rooms at the back of the building—how could he even remember the innocent farm girl of his youth?

"Did you hear what that man said to Boggs and his weasels?" Ginny Lofley asked, keeping her voice carefully low. "I could *kiss* him. He's a killer, though, don't you think? He had that look— fearless and confident."

"Yes," Kathleen agreed, "the look of a killer, but not a murderer like the men who control Deadwood."

"Anyhow," Ginny said, "it's so rare to see a man with spine in here. Do you know him?"

"No," Kathleen lied. "Or if I do, I couldn't recognize him in the dim light."

"Land sakes, he sure stared at you. And not in the usual way men stare—like maybe you had come back from the dead."

Now Kathleen was sure of it—it was Boggs and some of his men, probably Hendry, Bass, and Deets, who had carried out the reprehensible massacre of the Everetts. No other reason for Cas to come strolling in here with Boggs clearly in his sights.

"The fiend-begotten wretch," she muttered, watching Boggs speak in low, urgent tones with his men.

In a case of very unfortunate timing, Boggs looked at her just then. He scraped his chair back, and her fear returned, itching like a new scab.

"God in heaven, have mercy on us both," Ginny prayed in a whisper.

"So, Little Miss Pink Cheeks," Boggs greeted Kathleen, straddling an empty chair backward. Those hard black eyes pinned her in place. "Did you enjoy the show? You worked too hard at pretending not to notice. You've never been a very good liar, have you?"

She raised her chin defiantly. "There's nothing I can say to that."

Those big, strong teeth flashed at her. "Oh, I think maybe there is. Al tells me you're from east Texas?"

She nodded, resenting his invasive eyes.

"Do tell? So is Cas Everett. I find that a tad coincidental, especially after watching you two stare at each other for so long. Don't happen to know him, do you?"

"Texas is a big place."

"Yeah," he snarled, "and water is wet. I s'pose you've never heard of him?"

"Of course I've read about him."

"Got you a big Texas hero in camp now, huh? Like the heroes at the Alamo. And that's exactly how these two do-gooders are going to end up— so shot full of holes the buzzards will be spitting out lead."

He stared until she finally replied in fright, "I certainly hope not. He's a fellow Texan."

"Good." Boggs stood up, adjusting his gun belt to emphasize his point. "You and Ginny can both sew him a Lone Star shroud, if you take my meaning. But you better be quick."

"Dakota!" Nat Hendry called over. "Strip 'em buck! We all been wonderin' about them two gals."

Boggs laughed and took one last, lingering look at Kathleen. "Won't be long before I give you a full report, boys," he promised. "Won't be long at all."

It was late morning by the time Cas and Yancy made their cautious way back to the livery. Cedric

O'Flaherty occupied his usual throne, the rain barrel outside the big double doors. He was braiding hemp strands into rope as the two men walked up.

"Dash it all! Didn't take you two young bucks long to start spraying lead," he groused. "Hell 'n' furies, I heard the shootin' fray from down below, thought the dad-blamed Sioux was back to lift our dander."

"You've got it bass ackward, Dad," Cas assured him. "The Regulators ambushed us."

However, the old salt was livid over the strike. "All I know is, there's two water troughs ruint and hunks the size of Kansas blowed outta the wall."

"You're steamed at the wrong jaspers," Cas assured him. "What's a man to do when bloodthirsty assassins open fire on him? Beg for mercy?"

"Far as that wall," Yancy chimed in, "it's already moth-eaten. What's a few more holes?"

"It's always Texans," Cedric grumped. "You could at least wipe them grins off your maps. Go shoot up a cowtown, why'n'cha?"

"We've got as much right to be here as you," Cas told him. "I'm going back inside to finish what I started. You might's well just pipe down and save it for your memoirs."

"How long you plan to roost in the gulch?"

"Long as it takes," Cas told him.

"You two draw lead the way syrup draws flies," Cedric opined, rocking his weight off the barrel. "Think I'll fade."

Cas and Yancy fed and watered their horses and turned them out into a little paddock near the livery.

"You and Patsy stand guard outside," Cas told his friend. "Don't stop anybody from coming inside, but give me the hail."

Cas counted about a dozen horses in the stalls.

He set to work methodically, inspecting each rear offside shoe. About halfway down the first line of stalls, he reached a coyote dun with badly scarred shoulders and deep girth galls. *An outlaw's horse,* he told himself. Suddenly he felt a tingling premonition of the lower nerves, not the brain.

The sore-used dun acted nervous, so Cas spoke in a low, soothing voice as he reached for the right rear leg. "Short, strong legs—good snow pony, huh? Good kicker, too, I'd wager."

Cas pulled the leg up, and even in the dim lighting, he spotted a crescent-shaped chip at the top of the bend in the iron horseshoe.

A trembling weakness in his legs made Cas stand straight and brace himself against one side of the stall. When the trembling passed, he kicked aside some dirty straw and exposed bare earth, nudging the dun until it placed its rear offside hoof in the dirt. Cas glanced at the mark and knew, beyond any doubt, he'd found one of the murderers of his family.

He whistled Yancy in and showed him the print.

"By Godfrey, we've put the net around one of them," the farmer exalted before he went back outside. "Let's give him Jesse, the murderin' snake."

Cas waited for the old proprietor to return, keeping a wary eye on a well-armed man who came for his horse. Cedric ambled back a half hour later, munching on an apple. Yancy followed him inside.

"Where's the bodies?" the hostler greeted Cas.

"Who owns the coyote dun with the scarred shoulders?" Cas demanded.

Cedric spat out a seed. "Le'me see. . . . That would be Nat Hendry. One of Dakota Boggs' favorite skunks."

"What's he look like?"

"Heavyset fella with his face pitted by the pox."

Cas and Yancy exchanged triumphant glances. "He was in the Gem today," Cas told his friend. "I'll bet my horse it was the four of them who did it."

"I hope you kill him," the liveryman confessed. "He's a backshootin' murderer. I saw him cut down an unarmed preacher just for callin' him a sinner."

Cas ignored this. "When does he generally come for his horse?"

"Well, most often he's a night rider," Cedric replied. "Sometimes he'll ride out after dark with a few of the Regulators to terrorize prospectors that won't sell their claims. Other times he rides over to Lead by himself to consort with a painted cat he favors."

Cas said, "You've been a lot of help, Cedric. You sleep in the loft?"

The old man nodded.

"Might be a good idea to turn in early and make sure you don't come down till morning," Cas advised.

"Far as Hendry, good riddance to bad rubbish," the liveryman replied. "But *don't* kill no horses, or else I'm forced to replace 'em."

As the two men strolled back to Widow Huckabee's place, Yancy asked, "We'll be waiting tonight?"

"He'll need his horse sometime," Cas said. "Right now we need to be in our room."

"In case Kathleen contacts you?"

Cas nodded.

"She might not want to, Cas boy."

"She wants to," he gainsaid, trying hard to believe it himself. "It just might be too dangerous, is all."

Just after the dull orange sun slid below the horizon, Cas and Yancy took cover in lodgepole pines near the livery. Before long a full moon and an explosion of stars gave a ghostly illumination to the blue-black shadows enveloping the livery.

"What if they all show up?" Yancy asked.

"More the merrier," Cas said tersely. "Four against two is not bad odds."

"I'll take your word for it, neighbor. But one of those curly wolves had a Greener."

"Then he's the first one we shoot."

Below them, in the gulch, dim lights glowed inside the sourdoughs' tents and cast dream-distorted shadows as the occupants moved around inside them. Occasionally, they heard muffled laughter, voices raised in argument, heated curses. Shadowy figures glided here and there on footpaths leading to Main Street, as sinister and obscure as Deadwood Gulch itself.

"Is this the worst hellhole you've been to?" Yancy asked.

"So far it is. But I hear that Hays City, back in the late sixties, made your precious Dodge look like a church social. Especially Tommy Drum's saloon and Paddy Welsh's place. And I'll bet that brand-new mining camp called Tombstone will catch up to Deadwood. I tracked a killer into that tarantula hole."

"Was he there?"

"No, but he had been. He had a run-in with a hard twist named Curly Bill Brocius. I found my man in Cochise County's boot hill, at peace with the world."

"This Curly Bill," Yancy pressed eagerly, "I've read his name. He's a rough one?"

"Looked rough to me," Cas said.

"You *saw* him?"

"Met him, actually."

Even in the darkness under the trees Cas could

see the incredulous look on Yancy's face. "You two didn't chuck lead at each other?"

"Why would we? Neither one of us had any cause to."

"I'll bet you a dollar to a doughnut," Yancy boasted, "that he had no desire to test you."

"I hope so," Cas assured him, "because the feeling was mutual."

Yancy started to speak, but fell silent when Cas cleared leather. A dim figure let himself into the livery. Minutes later he emerged on a blood bay and rode due east.

"Not our boy," Cas said patiently, leathering his .44.

So far Yancy had failed to find his beloved gingersnaps in Deadwood and instead bought a bag of hard sassafras candy. Now he irritated Cas by quickly grinding them with his molars rather than letting them dissolve. The sound scraped across Cas' spine like a rusty knife blade.

"Either suck on that candy," he snapped, "or move away from my ear."

A sudden explosion below, from upper Main Street, made both men jump like butt-shot dogs. When no fire erupted, Cas guessed the source.

"Sounded like a hot-water boiler exploding," he said. "They get shoddy workmanship in these grubstake camps. I'll bet they send more people under than gunfighters do."

Another thirty minutes ticked slowly by, the butter-colored moon arcing higher into the sky. The livery remained dark and quiet within except for the occasional snort or whiffle. Cas tried to concentrate on the present moment but couldn't shake the image of Kathleen, her face a war of emotions as she watched him in the Gem.

A figure rounded a corner of the livery and headed for the big doors.

"Look sharp now," Cas whispered to Yancy. "I got a hunch we're about to have us a frolic."

The man emerged leading the coyote dun, and Cas sprinted forward to challenge him before he could fork leather.

"Hold it right there, Hendry," Cas snapped in a cold, authoritative voice. "Hold your arms out *wide*. Make a play for your shooter, before I tell you to, and you'll eat a double load of buckshot. Yancy, bury Patsy's muzzles in his gut. If he so much as twitches, send him across the River Jordan."

"Do you two fools realize who I am?" a familiar voice from earlier demanded. "I'm one o' the big bugs around here."

"Bugs are for squashing," Yancy reminded him.

Cas just ignored him as he moved inside the livery barn and reached up for a lantern hanging from the crosstrees of the ceiling. His fingers trembling as if from cold, he turned up the wick and pulled a sulfur match from his shirt pocket, striking it to life with his thumb. He opened the lantern, fired up the wick, and went back outside.

"Go around on the path and watch for the others," he told Yancy. Then, right hand palming the butt of his belt gun, Cas lifted the lamp to study the killer.

"Everett, you'll pay a hunderdfold for anything you do tonight," Nat Hendry said, his voice reedy with nervousness.

"What do you care, woman killer?" Cas replied. "You won't be around to enjoy it."

Cas took in his dirty and stained hat, the rattlesnake-skin necktie, corduroy trousers shiny at the knees, and midcalf boots with cruelly modified spurs. He recognized the stubby handgun as a .32 rimfire Sharps, favored by outlaws for its easy concealment. The pox craters made Hendry's pasty face look brutal and ugly.

"I guess a fish always looks bigger underwater," Cas finally said. "Seen close on dry land, you don't even rate as a tadpole. It's gonna be boring killing you."

"Say, Everett," Hendry said, his tone changing as reality sank in, "can't we dicker a little?"

Cas set the lantern down and backed away a few paces, squaring off—all quiet, deadly business.

"Like you and your fellow roaches dickered with my family?" he asked with quiet menace. "Jerk it. That's more chance than they got."

Panic gripped him, and Hendry made as if to turn around. "You're a Texan, Everett. You won't shoot a man in the back."

"No, but I'd shoot him in the leg until he turns around."

"Mr. Everett, I swear on a stack of Bibles—it was the others that done it. Dakota left me here to run the rest of the Regulators."

"I know better. You need to inspect your horseshoes now and then. They got you killed."

"I won't draw against you! You can't force me."

Cas felt almost weary—murdering cowards were all alike. "That's your choice, Hendry. Like I said, I'm giving you more of a chance than you gave my people. If I have to pull first, I'll shoot out your eyes and leave you screaming in the dirt. The third bullet will geld you. So skin it back and die fast."

In the oily yellow lamplight Cas didn't bother watching Hendry's eyes—eyes had never once pulled a trigger on him. He watched his gun hand, which the hardcase held well out from his holster.

"I won't," Hendry practically blubbered. "You won't gun me down in cold blood."

"You're sadly misinformed. Now shut your filthy sewer and *pull*."

"Damn it, I won't! You'll have to murder me!"

Yancy had moved to a front corner of the building so he could watch justice being meted out. He almost choked when he heard Cas' next words.

"All right, then, I'll take you to law in Yankton. Hand over your gun."

"Hand over?" Yancy blurted. "But you told me to always—"

"Swede, you talk too much," Cas snapped.

"Sure, Mr. Everett, sure," Hendry truckled, "here it comes, muzzle down."

Cas had deliberately violated his own toss-'em-down rule, knowing what was coming from a scum this desperate. Hendry slid the rimfire from its chamois holster and held it muzzle down as he stepped closer to Cas. Then he suddenly cocked it and, screaming, brought the muzzle up to fire. Cas cleared leather and buried two slugs in his heart before Hendry ever got his Sharps pointed.

In the novels with orange covers, fatally shot men usually tossed out their arms dramatically and fell on their backs. But almost every man Cas killed or saw killed simply folded forward onto his face. Just like Hendry dropped to the trampled dirt in a sloppy heap, his toes scratching twice.

"Well done, Caswell," Yancy congratulated him.

Cas knelt over the body. "Don't be tacking up bunting just yet, old son. This is only one down and at least three more to go."

He rolled the body over. Nat Hendry had died with fear starched deep into his homely features.

"I'm glad I did it," Cas told Yancy. "It's justice, that's all. It won't bring my family back from the grave, and I didn't enjoy it. But it's an eye for an eye, and where my family's concerned, Old Testament justice is good enough for me."

"Amen, Reverend Everett. What about the body?"

"What about it. Did *he* bury my dead?"

Yancy nodded vigorously, liking the point. "He did not. Let his friends plant him. Old Cedric will have a conniption fit, though."

Cas rose and looked carefully around them. "Cedric? Don't waste a hanky over that cunning old grifter. It's only fear of lead poisoning that keeps him from stealing our horses. We need to expect retaliation from Boggs and his men for this."

"So what?" Yancy countered. "They're trying to kill us anyway."

Cas gave him a grim smile. "Yep, you're definitely learning."

Chapter 18

That night Cas and Yancy slept with their weapons, ready to repel invaders from window or door. But although gunshots could be heard down in Deadwood Gulch until nearly dawn, the night passed without major incident for the Texans.

"Thanks for leaving me the compost heap out front," Cedric greeted Cas in a sarcastic tone when Cas and Yancy arrived to feed their horses after breakfast.

"Where's the body?" Cas asked.

"Pigs. Ike Boggs and Charlie Deets just swung it over the side. And both of 'em was all horns and rattles. I was you, I'd skedaddle for Mexico."

"And if I was you," Cas told him politely but firmly, "I'd be mighty darn careful just who I chose to make medicine with around here. Law is coming, courts and prosecutors with it. There'll be warrants, indictments, depositions—and hangings. Legal hangings, not lynchings."

Cedric leaned sideways on his barrel and spat. "You talk like a Philadelphia lawyer."

Cas thought again of Kathleen—would more law help her, or was she here by choice? "Nope," he told the liveryman, "just a lowly bounty hunter who works within the law . . . mostly."

Cas and Yancy moved cautiously through the hay-and-manure fragrant interior of the building, weapons at the ready. Cas stopped at the last stall on the right. Comet nickered in greeting and nuzzled his shoulder.

"Shouldn't we be worried about our horses?" Yancy asked from the opposite stall.

"I am, but this being the only livery in town, maybe it's a battlefield compromise. You know—since any man's horse can be killed, leave the horses out of it. It's risky, but I don't see any way around it."

Comet was sleek from plenty of graining lately, his muscle definition strong from the long ride north. Cas scratched his withers fondly.

"Let's tack up and hop our horses," he told Yancy. "That way we can get the lay of the land around here and explore the gulch from its open end. Our fight is coming and we're fools not to reconnoiter."

They crossed to the slope-off partition serving as tack room, and Cas took his bridle and bit from the cans on the wall. He threw his saddle, pad, and blanket over his shoulder and returned to Comet's stall. The chestnut took the bit eagerly, ready to run, then snorted impatiently while Cas saddled him, cinched the girth, and double-checked the latigos.

Cas had intended to return by noon, but the astounding progress in Black Hills mining and prospecting meant there was much more to observe. Pay dirt was being struck along creeks throughout the hills. Shantytowns, most without names, had sprung up almost everywhere a man looked.

"I feel safer out here," Yancy remarked as they walked their horses past a Long Tom operation in nearby Lead, "but not much."

"Too many trees and brushy ridges," Cas agreed. "This is an ambusher's paradise. That's why we're not riding in the open."

By late afternoon they returned to Deadwood, rubbed down and stalled their horses, and made it back to the widow's place in time for supper.

"They found Nat Hendry's body over to the livery this mornin'," a stolid-faced prospector remarked to his comrade, eyes carefully avoiding Cas at the table.

"Glad to hear it," the other man said. "Whoever did it deserves a medal."

"Boys, that's not fit talk for the supper table," Widow Huckabee scolded. "Launder your speech."

"Were them two sending you a signal?" Yancy asked while Cas keyed their lock after supper.

"Could be. Word gets around quick in this close-packed gulch."

Cas' saddlebags lay across the foot of his bed. For a moment he pulled out the cross he had bought for his mother, its hammered silver and gold filigree glistening in the light of a kerosene lamp.

"What will you do with it, Cas boy?" Yancy asked.

Cas shifted his gaze to the little lozenge tin he pulled from his watch pocket. Silly sentiment, maybe, but not only was it Texas soil in that tin, but dirt from his family's farm and from their graves. It was a physical link, not much but the only one he had—and enough to keep this struggle in Deadwood real, tangible.

"Oh, I got plans for it," he finally replied.

"When I think of them, Cas, layin' there all alone on—"

"No need to slop over," Cas cut in, his voice suddenly harsh. "Stay mean for this fight, hear? A soft spot is just one more place for these yellow-bellied murderers to kill you."

Cas put the cross away and pulled the blanket from his bed, folding it into a narrow strip.

"What in Sam Hill are you up to now?" Yancy demanded when Cas began wrapping it around his head.

"Mountain man trick. I'm hoping we can convince the local dirt workers that outside our window is not a safe place to be. Douse that lamp."

"Why, we'll be in the dark!"

"So what? You need a sugar tit after dark? Douse it."

Muttering, Yancy turned down the wick. "This is just about the—"

"One more thing," Cas added as he stretched out on his bed, "hush up. You need to learn when to shut up."

For some time, as Cas lay in total darkness within the blanket, Yancy obeyed. Then his nature took over.

"Cas?" he whispered. "Still think Kathleen will contact you?"

"Yes," Cas told him, not really as sure as he sounded.

"I don't know. She looked like somebody's been takin' good care of her."

"Pipe down and listen," Cas snapped. "I'd wager there'll be killers outside our window tonight. They saw the light go out, and they won't wait long."

Those words persuaded Yancy. Silence again, and Cas could hear the wooden joists of the house groaning in the fitful gusts of wind. Somewhere upstairs a man with a banjo plucked out the notes to "Woodticks in My Johnny." Outside, the evening wind started kicking up a real fuss. It sent sand stinging against the windows and made a low, moaning sound inside the stovepipe—a lonely groan that filled Cas with instant dread, the kind of hollow, stomach-tickling dread he felt when he woke up just before dawn, naked and defenseless and so damn scared he couldn't even spit. A man without a family, a man . . . .

Outside, a stick snapped, and Cas pulled the blanket off his head, steeling his muscles for action.

"Stay on your bed," he whispered to Yancy, vaulting off his own.

Cas ignored his firearms and tugged the knife from his boot. The ten-inch steel blade was narrow and balanced for throwing. Cas crept to the open window, amazed at how keeping his eyes in total darkness had increased his night vision. The difference was remarkable, as if he had peeled a couple hours off the night.

Where before he had only seen the general shape of trees, now he could make out even the smaller branches at the tips of limbs. He could differentiate bushes, detect movements he couldn't spot before. So of course he easily spotted the crouching shape of a man nearing the window, a gun in each hand.

Cas always tried to avoid a ruckus anywhere near where he was staying. When the would-be assassin was about ten feet out, Cas threw the knife in a hard overhand throw. There was a satisfying sound of solid impact, a choked cry of pain from the startled intruder. The guns dropped thunking to the ground, and a moment later, the injured man staggered through the bushes toward the trees at the brim of the gulch.

"What happened?" demanded Yancy, who had seen nothing in the dark.

"Follow me outside and cover me," Cas whispered, stepping over the windowsill.

After a brief search he found his knife, still dripping blood, and two old Colt Navy revolvers. He wiped the blade of his knife off in the grass and returned to the room.

"Think you killed the son of a buck?" Yancy demanded while Cas lit a stub of candle in a dish, still not trusting the lantern.

"No, but it's even better for us if he's only wounded. Now this cockroach will return to the nest and noise it around how Cas Everett can see in the dark."

Yancy picked up one of the Colt revolvers. "Why all these tacks in the handgrips? The screws seem fine."

"He's copying Jesse James. Jesse uses tacks instead of notches."

Yancy whistled. "I count twelve."

"Yeah, but with outlaws," Cas reminded him, "a notch is every man you murdered, not every one you defeated fair and square in a draw-shoot contest."

Cas sat on the bed and wrestled with his boots, wishing he had a bootjack. "Well, this visitor tonight makes the third try on us since we got here. I bet—"

Three raps on the door silenced him. His .44 jumped into his fist, and Yancy leveled Patsy at the door.

"Mr. Everett?" called a hesitant voice from the hallway. "My name is Harney Robinson. Kathleen Steele asked me to stop by."

Cas and Yancy glanced at each other. "You were right, Cas boy," Yancy whispered.

"You alone?" Cas called.

"Yessir."

"Hang on."

His short iron filling his right hand, Cas stepped to the door and turned the skeleton key. When he eased the door open, he saw a man in his early forties, built stocky, with heavy burnsides and a mustache, his chin smooth-shaven. He had the same haggard look of stoic agony Cas had seen on many around here. He carried an old Henry breechloader.

"The rifle is for self-defense," he insisted nervously as he eyed the revolver in Cas' hand.

"Around here," the bounty hunter greeted him, "a man needs a Gatling gun. C'mon in, Harney. This big galoot is Yancy Carlson, my neighbor back in Texas."

Cas closed and locked the door, leathering his shooter. He waved the prospector toward the sawbuck table. "Sorry for the poor light. So Kathleen sent you?"

"She sure did, Mr. Everett. We've become sorta friends over the past few months."

"Where do you know her from?"

"She's the faro dealer at the Gem."

Cas frowned. "By free choice?"

"No offense, but that's a hoot. The only . . . woman with free choice around here is Calamity Jane. Kathleen despises Al Swearengen. I don't think anybody in Deadwood hates it here more than she does."

Cas felt a great weight lift from his chest. "So she's a prisoner?"

Harney Robinson nodded. "Most of the women in Deadwood are, one way or another."

Earlier today the widow had brought them a block of ice. Yancy took several cork-sealed bottles of beer from the icebox and handed them around.

"I don't think it's Swearengen she's most worried about," Robinson volunteered.

"Let me guess," Cas said. "Dakota Boggs."

Harney nodded. "Boggs is the boy to watch. I've

seen that man lose his temper and fight like all possessed. Tore a man's eyeballs out for starin' at him. Any prospector who bucks him ends up cold as a basement floor."

Cas recognized the bitter, deeply resentful tone. "And you've bucked him?"

Robinson took a swig of beer and nodded. "Me and my two partners, Justin McKinney and Ollie Dunbar. We got adjoinin' claims and they're all showin' good color."

"And Boggs is jumping your claims?"

"Nah, not exactly. Boggs works for Levi Carruthers, the most well-to-do man in the Black Hills. He owns the Crystal Palace and the only comfortable house in this part of the Dakota Territory. Carruthers uses money like a bludgeon to knock little stiffs like me off our claims. It's Boggs' job to make sure we sell. If we don't . . ."

"Yeah," Cas said, "I've noticed the pigs are well fed this year. What does Carruthers look like?"

The prospector described him, and Cas looked at Yancy, both men nodding. They'd seen the man outside his hotel.

"It's got so a duly filed claim ain't worth a shin-plaster," Robinson complained. "The first time a man crosses Boggs and his Regulators, it's a beating with a six-horse whip. The second time, it's the knot for sure."

"Have you boys tried to buck them?" Cas asked. "There's plenty of prospectors."

"To our shame, no. They keep an eagle eye on all of us, and a man who complains too loud is publicly executed. In Deadwood, all you have to do is prop up a wagon tongue and you're ready for a hanging. Once I seen Boggs drag-hang a Chinaman behind a horse. The killers around here don't stand on ceremony."

"You say you crossed Boggs once?" Cas reminded their visitor.

Robinson stood up and raised his coarse pullover shirt. Fresh lacerations, still angry red and scabbed, slashed across his muscular back.

"Justin and Ollie got the same treatment," he said. "We all refused to deed our claims over to Carruthers. The next time we say no, he'll have Boggs kill us."

"And you say Dakota Boggs is Kathleen's greatest threat," Cas said. "How, exactly?"

Robinson squirmed uncomfortably and turned his hat around in his fingers. "He's not the only threat to her. Levi Carruthers considers Kathleen his woman."

"Is she?" Cas asked, more casually than he felt.

Robinson expelled a long breath. "Near as I can tell she *might* be—you see, Kathleen never talks about such things. And Carruthers has got her all set up fancy fine in rooms at his hotel, where he visits almost every day."

"Seems like, if she's his woman, she'd be at the house," Cas remarked.

"Yeah, that's curious. Anyhow, Boggs has been spouting off lately how he plans to kill Carruthers and take *every*thing he owns."

Cas looked physically sick. "Does Carruthers live at the house or the hotel?"

"Seems like he's mostly at the house. You've seen it by now, the walled-in place off Main Street. But like I said, he does seem to visit the Crystal Palace lots at night. Still, it's Boggs you have to watch. Word's out, Mr. Everett—you're a marked man. To most in the gulch, you're already dead."

Cas yawned, suddenly sick *and* tired. "I know. Nobody's talking to me, and everybody avoids me like a smallpox blanket. Well, was there a message from Kathleen?''

Robinson smacked his forehead with the heel of his palm. "Jayzoo, I whined so much about myself that I forgot. If she can sneak away, she'd like to meet with you tomorrow in the old assay shack behind the Bella Union. Around noon. I can't get your answer to her in time, so she'll just go there and hope you come."

Robinson left a short time later. Cas, his face troubled, locked the door and looked at Yancy. "Harney Robinson is made of whipcord stuff. But he and his fellow sourdoughs are not gunslicks, and there's too many curly wolves in this town. Still, he'll do to take along."

"Take along where?" Yancy demanded.

Cas blew out the candle. "Wherever this trail leads us," he replied.

Charles Wagner's Grand Central, Deadwood's first hotel, was actually just a flophouse of the crudest type. For one dollar a night, a man got either a plank bunk or just floor space to spread his blankets. Dakota Boggs, however, lived rent free in a large, furnished room on the ground floor, his reward for steering so many of the Regulators to the Grand Central.

Boggs waited until well after dark, peeved that gunfire hadn't erupted up on the brim of the gulch. Black Hills weather was volatile, thanks to cloud-arresting peaks, and it changed rapidly. The clear, calm night outside his fly-specked window erupted in a low whip crack of thunder, followed by stuttering rumbles as it echoed through the hills.

Boggs hated to get wet, so he corked his whiskey bottle and pushed out of his chair, crossing to a

wooden gun rack on the back wall and raising his
kerosene lantern to look at it. A weapon for every
purpose: a scattergun for nighttime fights; a Winchester '76 for distance shots; his double-action .44
for close-in daylight fighting; a .38 derringer hideout gun to tuck up his sleeve. There was even a
single-edged bowie for when silence was desired.

He wasn't sure about this job tonight, so he took
his sidearm and the bowie. He headed down Main
into the Badlands, passing Jack Shoudy's butcher
shop, where many claimed Jack McCall was captured, and Farnam and Brown's log cabin grocery
store. In the 600 block of Main, he veered left at
the No. 10 and cut down toward the creek.

"Marcus!" he called, stopping in front of a crude
she-bang made of wood and flattened vegetable
tins. "Got a minute?"

Lantern light spilled out when Marcus Bodmer
pushed aside a horse blanket serving as his door.
He was a small, hard-knit man with a scruffy beard
and peeling nose. Once sturdy ankle boots had
been ruined by immersion in water, and now burlap
strips held the soles to the uppers.

"Mr. Boggs," he greeted his visitor in a guarded
tone. "Somethin' I can do for ya?"

Boggs gave a snorting laugh. "We been round
and round on this, Marcus. You been offered a
thousand dollars for your claim."

Bodmer groaned in frustration. "Hell, that's
chicken fixens! I was poor as a hind-tit calf until I
hit pay dirt. Now I got money to toss at the birds.
Why, I pull out three hundred on a *bad* day."

"All good things must end," Dakota said piously.
"You can still file a new claim or grub through ore
tailings with the celestials."

Bodmer had a mercurial personality and his

breathing grew ragged. "But *this* is my diggings, Dakota, claim duly filed."

"A claim is only paper, but *this* is cold, hard steel."

Boggs drew his hair-trigger Colt in a whisper of friction. "You bend with the breeze or you break, Marcus. Let's step inside and transfer a deed."

The scared but stubborn prospector shook his head. "I don't crawfish to nobody."

"But you'll crawfish to *some*body, you red-headed runt."

Boggs had discovered long ago that if you twisted a man's ear hard enough, it took all the fight out of him. He used the technique to drag Bodmer inside and seat him at a packing-crate table.

Boggs pulled a folded paper, a steel nib, and an ink pot from his shirt pocket. He shoved the Colt's muzzle into the prospector's left ear.

"The discussion part is over. Now sign that transfer paper, or I'll leave your brains all over it."

"I don't live in your pocket," Bodmer protested weakly even as he reached for the nib. He glanced at the sheet, then twisted around on his nail-keg chair. "You said Carruthers was buying it. This has got *your* name on it!"

"So what? Either way you're bought out."

Bodmer slowly read a few more lines, then exploded in rage and jumped to his feet. "A *hunnert* dollars? It was a thousand before!"

Snarling, Boggs slammed him down hard and clipped him in the neck with the muzzle of his gun. "You had a chance to nail your colors to my mast. Now you can sink. Sign or die."

The vigilante's left thumb cocked the .44 with a metallic *snick* that sounded dangerously final. Tears of rage and frustration welling from his eyes, Bodmer signed.

"Satisfied now?" he asked in a bitter, broken voice.

"Not quite." Bodmer whisked the paper away and slid it into his pocket. "There's a little matter of a letter."

Bodmer stiffened where he sat, afraid to look up at his tormentor. "What letter?"

Boggs enjoyed a good laugh. "Playin' it foxy, huh? I'm talking about your flowery, speechifying letter to the territorial governor, telling him what's happening to you and others in the gulch. And mentioning me by name."

Bodmer began to tremble as his body realized what his mind still refused to admit. "I wrote no such letter, Mr. Boggs."

"No? Care to read it?"

"Please, Mr. Boggs, don't kill me!"

"Shush," Boggs said soothingly, clapping a giant hand over the prospector's mouth. He holstered his revolver, tugged the bowie from his boot, and jerked Bodmer's chin back hard to expose the throat. With his victim screaming into his hand, Boggs sliced his throat deep. Blood fountained out, making an obscene slapping noise as it hit the rammed-earth floor.

Boggs bent down to confront the dying man face-to-face. "*Look* at me, Marcus," he commanded. "This is the face you're going to see forever in hell!"

The eyes turned to dull glass, and the body slumped forward onto the little table, knocking it over. As Boggs emerged from the shack, however, he felt less omnipotent. He cast another glance up toward the widow Huckabee's place and wondered what in blue blazes went wrong.

Chapter 19

At eleven forty-five the next morning, a freshly spruced-up Cas Everett set out to keep a secret rendezvous with Kathleen Steele.

"I don't like it," Yancy fumed to his back as Cas unlocked their door. "She's been here a year, Cas boy, and she dresses like them Fifth Avenue ladies. How do you know this isn't a trap?"

Cas paused and turned around. "You're paring the cheese mighty close to the rind, old son," he warned. "She's my friend, and until I know otherwise, that's how I'm treating her. I'd do the same for you, and *you're* ugly."

"Shoo! If you're wrong—"

Cas waved him quiet. "Never mind her for now. You stay here and let no one but Mrs. Huckabee in. Keep an eye on that window and Patsy in your lap."

"You keep your eyes peeled, too. Might be a thousand more Jack McCalls out there."

Cas let himself down the face of the gulch, using crude steps hacked into the stone and the knotted rope to move quickly—he knew he was being watched, and a man's back was a tempting target in Deadwood.

The boardwalk was busy, but not crowded,

allowing him to survey the men approaching and passing him. Once a man passed him, Cas kept watching to deter "spin-arounds," a favorite way to murder in crowded, lawless places.

When pedestrian traffic was light, he ducked between buildings and spotted a dilapidated shack in a grassy lot behind the Bella Union. He waited in shadows to make sure no one saw him going in. Then he sprinted up to the only door and knocked.

No answer, no noise from within. *Well, she said if she could make it,* he reminded himself as disappointment welled within him. So much that it surprised him to realize how much he had hoped to see her—even though that hope was laced with misgiving about how she might have changed.

Cas fisted his hand to knock again when suddenly the door opened inward and Kathleen stood before him so close he felt the physical force of her beauty. She wore a dress of dark Swiss muslin and a light cape with an attached hood. The midday sun slanted into her face the moment she opened the door, igniting gold flecks in her sea green eyes. The thick cinnamon hair was swept up under a gold-and-amethyst comb.

"Kath, you always took my breath away," Cas finally greeted her as he stepped inside and closed the door. "This gulch is the last place you should be. It doesn't deserve you."

"Oh, Cas, but it's *got* me."

Overwrought with emotion, her voice climbed an octave and nearly broke as a sob rose in her throat like a tight bubble. Cas encircled her with his long arms and pulled her close, smelling hyacinth in her sun-warmed hair. She was still sniffling, and her words tickled his shoulder when she spoke.

"Cas, what happened to Nat Hendry makes it

clear what you came here to do, and I pray to God you succeed. Deadwood is not your problem, but, oh, it's monstrous what goes on in this territory. Outright crimes are turned into acts of patriotism. Young girls whose only sin is poverty are . . . are outraged over and over until it destroys their will to live."

The anger and despair in her voice struck an answering chord in Cas. But a question nagged at him—one he couldn't quell. The widow Huckabee's words from earlier kept pricking at his memory: *There are women in town, of a sort.*

"You haven't said anything about yourself," he reminded her. "I know you're a faro dealer at the Gem. But what about this Levi Carruthers Harney told me about?"

Kathleen pulled back a little to search his face. He, in turn, studied hers in the generous light slanting through a rotting roof. Youth was still quite evident in the slight puffiness of her lips, the taut and smooth flesh of the neck, the baby down on her cheeks. But there were faint lines forming at the corners of her eyes, etched by constant fear and the weight of a hopeless situation.

"Do you mean," she asked him bluntly, "am I his woman? Yes, I am—to all appearances. But he won't accept mere appearances much longer. And he's sick enough to kill me when I refuse his demands."

"I've looked into his eyes," Cas told her, "and he's sick enough for anything. It's him you had to avoid so you could meet me?"

"Yes. I chose noon because that's when he has a long lunch at the Bodega. For some time I couldn't decide who's the archvillain in this murderers' den, Al Swearengen or Levi. But it's neither."

"It's Dakota Boggs," Cas supplied, feeling her hands tighten on his shoulders at mention of the name.

"Yes, Boggs, the savage. The other two occasionally reveal sentiment, but Boggs is a soulless monster in human shape. Before, he was just a vicious killer for hire. But now he's watched Levi and decided to become a man of large-scale ambitions."

"You won't need to worry about Boggs," Cas promised. "He'll soon join his ancestors. What do those two actually do around here? I never see the Regulators enforcing any laws."

"As near as I can tell," Kathleen's musical voice replied, "Carruthers and Boggs are . . ."

"Shakedown artists?" Cas suggested when she hesitated.

"Yes. Harney tells me they aren't actually claim jumpers, but they force men to sell. Levi finances it. Dakota and his men do the killing and beating."

"Those three roughs who were at the table with him in the Gem," Cas said. "I'm thinking those are his chosen rats. Would those be the men he took south with him when he massacred my family?"

At the mention of this tragedy, Kathleen's eyes glistened with the threat of tears. "Absolutely. All four men disappeared for almost two months—and the timing corresponds exactly."

Cas' jaw muscles bunched. "Nat Hendry got his. Last night I forgot to ask Harney the other two's names."

"Ike Bass and Charlie Deets. They'd both steal dead flies from a blind spider."

Kathleen felt self-conscious under Cas' close scrutiny. She pulled gently out of his arms and paced the empty shack, hugging her elbows even though the day was warm.

"I can imagine what you must be thinking, and

who can blame you? But I'm a prisoner and a slave, Cas. Yes, unlike all but a few of the women and girls here, I eat from silver dinner plates and sleep on satin sheets—by myself, I might add. No matter what happens, Cas, if I can get away, I *will* help the rest of the women trapped here."

Cas nodded, his gaze fixed on the symmetrical beauty of her face. "I came to balance the scales for my family, and they come first. But I hope you'll be leaving with me and Yancy. A woman can't expect to survive here, not yet."

A tear spurted from her left eye and zigzagged down her pale cheek. "Cas, just knowing you're here—I haven't felt hope since the moment I arrived. Now I do."

"Good, hang on to it."

"There's spies everywhere," Kathleen warned. "Swearengen's, Levi's, even Boggs has them. Meetings between us are going to be difficult and dangerous."

"Yeah. I'd just ride you out of Deadwood today, but there's too many guns. At least now you're still alive."

"Yes, thank God. But Levi Carruthers . . . it's hard to shape into proof, Cas, but I think he's on the verge of killing me."

Cas nodded. "I trust your instincts. I'm going to help you, Kath, but until I can, do *nothing* to make him suspicious. That means we meet no more until he's . . . taken care of. Have you got a gun?"

She shook her head. "It goes awfully hard on women in Deadwood who are caught with guns. The men mistreat them so badly they have to be ruthless to avoid revenge. My rooms and all my things are searched. I do have this—excuse me. . . ."

Kathleen turned modestly away and hiked her

skirt. When she turned around, she slid a thin black dagger from its felt sheath and laid it across the palm of her hand.

"Swearengen gave me this," she explained. "He urged me to kill Carruthers with it."

"Prob'ly wants you to do his dirty work for him. Still, it might not be a bad idea to have something for self-defense. Men don't expect a woman to fight back."

Kathleen frowned. "I'm not sure I could use it."

"Sure you can, but you have to understand, it's not easy to stab a man, especially for a woman. It'll take all your strength to sink the blade deep into vitals. If you ever have to use it, drive it in like you mean to come out the other side."

"Sounds like you've done it," she said, glancing at the knife in his boot.

"Once, and I hope I never have to again."

A long silence wedged itself between them, each aware of the other's breathing.

"Cas?"

"Hmm?"

"It's been so much time since we were young and saw each other regularly. I said no when you proposed, and now this horrible camp . . . Do you still feel the way you once did?"

She could see in his eyes what Cas felt in his heart, and for a moment, he watched the vitality inside her quicken, felt her feminine life force in all its power and vulnerability.

He stepped closer to her. "You want proof?"

He framed her face in both hands and pulled her gently into the kiss. Her lips parted for his, surprised but readily yielding, warm and soft and moist. He kissed her mouth, her cheeks, bussed the tissue-thin skin of her eyelids, and tasted the clean tang of her hair. She shuddered under his touch, the need for this gentle, passionate warmth roiling her insides as it did his. Afterward they stood quietly for a full minute, not trusting their voices.

"I should ask the same question," he told her. "I left Texas a farm boy. Now the scribblers call me a gunfighter. Let's face it. I have killed men—in fact, two more just getting to Deadwood, not to mention Nat Hendry. I confess I don't feel like the same Cas Everett you knew."

Kathleen flashed him a warm smile. "Same tall, lean-hipped, blue-eyed Texan who used to steal kisses when we were kids. I've thought about your question plenty. Most men I've ever known are content to lead an unchronicled existence. I've never imagined being with one who wasn't."

"Lady, you've got it hindside foremost," Cas assured her. "I don't go to the ink slingers. They come to me. But never mind all that for right now—we better break this up before one of those spies catches you."

He kissed her again, a peck on the forehead this time, and eased open the door to make sure it was clear outside.

"You go first," he said. "Be careful around Carruthers and Boggs. If you need to get a message to me, use Harney."

She nodded, gazing at his face as if memorizing it.

"Remember," he told her, squeezing her hand, "it's past peace piping now. No halfway measures. The fight is here, and one side or the other will have to win. Let's make sure it's ours."

Chapter 20

The meeting with Kathleen ignited a war of emotions within Cas. However, immediate survival came first and he kept his attention on his surroundings as he made the climb up the north face of the gulch to the widow Huckabee's.

He stood for some time in the shade of a few spruce trees, studying the big frame house and the mostly open ground around it. Lumber to build the town had been cut down all along the brim of the gulch and visibility was good. Reasonably certain he wasn't being watched by tin stars, he went inside and found Yancy seated at the sawbuck table, cracking walnuts with the heel of his shoe.

"Cas boy," the irritated Swede greeted him, "at the prices we pay, a body would expect that miserly widow to toss in a lunch. She—"

"Turn off the tap," Cas ordered brusquely, starting to pace in the portion of the room that was safe from a window shot.

Yancy spat out a piece of shell. "That's your trouble scowl, all right. What's the news from Kathleen?"

Cas ignored the question and flipped his hat onto his bed, still pacing. "Yancy, we've got to stop doing this thing slapdash. Best to take it by the horns."

"This sudden hurry," Yancy said, "is it about avenging your family or saving Kathleen?"

"To me, it's all one. When you stir the water, you stir up the mud. Besides, she's your neighbor, too. A Texan is bound to help any woman who's in a tight fix."

"Even a saloon gal?" Yancy pushed it.

Cas stared until Yancy's eyes fled from his. "You'll be *needin'* your hero Doc Holliday when I get done with your teeth, old son."

"No offense intended."

"But plenty taken."

Cas, however, had bigger fish to fry. He resumed his pacing, bootheels loud on the worn linoleum.

"We've got two choices: we can stick or we can quit. Quitting is out of the question, especially now that I've given my word to Kathleen. So we stick like burrs."

"I never figured to do anything *but* stick," Yancy said. "But stick to what? What's the plan?"

"Kathleen makes our row longer to hoe," Cas admitted. "I plan to take her with us, but the way things look now, I may have to rescue her before we finish what we need to do. Where, how could I keep her safe in a place filled with killers and woman-hungry men?"

"A *plan*," Yancy repeated. "Can't you just call out Boggs and the other two?"

Cas shook his head. "Pointless. Boggs fancies himself a shootist, and I hear he's faster with his left hand than his right. Good chance he's faster than me. But as his ilk see it, why give any man a fair chance to kill them if they can backshoot him instead?"

"Cripes, let's just murder them," Yancy suggested. "They're the dregs of humanity, anyhow. It's execution, Cas boy, and sorely needed."

"I agree, but I haven't got the heart in me to do that. So we'll have to bring things to a head. We'll have to provoke them into a fight."

"Shoo! Killing Nat Hendry should've done that."

"Oh, it can be done," Cas gainsaid. "And I know how to do it."

Yancy stood up, brushed his hands off on his trousers, and picked up Patsy from the table. "Let's get thrashing. The sooner we get it done, the quicker I stop starvin' on the widow's bug-sized portions."

Cas burst out laughing. "Swede, you got the courage of five men. But you were coiling your lariat with both hands when they passed out brains. We can't just rush out there and call down the thunder. They'll shoot us to stew meat."

"Didn't you just now say—"

"The more I study on our situation here, the more I realize we've got no fallback position. We're trapped here in this room like cooties in a bucket. They could torch the place and cut us down when we come out. We need a last bastion—a good position where we can hold out once the showdown starts. And we won't find it in town."

"How 'bout Little Bighorn?" Yancy barbed. "It's close by."

"That'd be fine with me. A battle out on the open plains, may the best shooters win. But these prairie rats won't play it that way. They like their fish in a barrel. If we're going to lure them into an attack, we'll have to fort up in a place where they think we're trapped."

Cas scooped up his hat and knelt to retrieve his

carbine from beneath the bed. "Let's fork leather, pard, and go scout out the gulch some more."

Cas felt unseen eyes watching them as he and Yancy followed the lip of the gulch southwest until it finally sloped more gradually and allowed them to ride down onto the floor. Just as they reined off to head down, a velocipede with a huge front wheel appeared from nowhere and frightened the horses.

"Gog and Magog!" Yancy roared out as his sorrel nearly bucked him. "Get a horse!" he told the rider, who honked his tin horn in derision.

"Yancy," Cas chided him, "why are you so wrathy? A man can't fight everything he sees."

"No, but he can sure cuss it out."

The afternoon was still young, the day warm and breezy. They moved at a trot among the scattered claims, watching men working bends and holes in the creek bed, anywhere the current might slacken and deposit color.

"It's still too early for the annual summer shrink," Cas observed. "That exposes bars loaded with deposits of gold-bearing gravel."

"Pickaxes, rakes, and pans are all most of them are using," Yancy said. "Look, that fellow in the red shirt is prying out nuggets with a butcher knife! Compared to farming, it's featherbed work. I'd try it myself if I didn't have a target painted on my hinder."

"You're ornery enough to take it," Cas agreed. "But it's no featherbed. I panned for a few weeks out in Pikes Peak country. After one day bent over, your back feels like it's been hammered hard. All day long your feet and legs are in ice-cold water while a sun hotter than damnation bakes your exposed skin to jerky. Few prospectors can get extra shoes, which means the ones you're wearing are soggy and ruined. Pretty quick you get scald feet so painful it makes grown men cry. Say . . . there's Harney Robinson."

Robinson was working a rocker with two other prospectors at the edge of the creek. He spotted the two riders and gave them a hail. Cas and Yancy gigged their horses forward.

"Struck a lode yet?" Cas greeted them, swinging down.

"Not yet," Robinson told him, "but the nuggets alone will put us in mansions."

When Cas tossed his reins forward to hold Comet in place, Harney shook his head in warning.

"Best be careful, Mr. Everett. There's plenty of roving bands of mustangs in these hills that like to liberate saddle horses."

"Thanks for reminding me," Cas said, digging into a saddlebag. "I was only looking for two-legged outlaws."

He stamped his picket pin into the ground with his heel. Then he knotted the end of the reins, buried it deeper with the pin, and stomped the earth all around it. Yancy had to settle for hobbles.

"Gents," Harney said, "these are my partners, Justin McKinney and Oliver Dunbar. Boys, this is Mr. Cas Everett and his Texas neighbor, Mr. Yancy Carlson."

Cas was embarrassed by the way Dunbar and McKinney stared at him with open wonderment.

Yancy, too, stared in wonder—at the slanted wooden cradle on rockers. It was equipped with a perforated metal sheet that served to screen out the bigger chunks of waste material when the device was rocked.

"Heard the news?" Harney asked. "A prospector named Marcus Bodmer was found at his shack this morning with his head barely attached to his body."

"Let me guess," Cas said. "He's another sour-dough who refused to sell to Levi Carruthers."

"You bet, just like the three of us," Ollie Dunbar bit off angrily. "And we'll be next 'less we sign them papers."

Cas looked him over. Dunbar was tall, thin, and slope-shouldered, with the brusque, impatient manner of one whose kind heart was perpetually at war with his short temper.

"I can't tell you three what to do," Cas said, "but I do know this much—*all* of us have some common enemies around here even though we're waging separate battles. You do what you think is best for you. But if you should choose to fight, let me know. Just don't take too long deciding."

"We'd be beholden," Robinson assured him. "We ain't pistoleros like you, but we have good repeating rifles."

Justin McKinney, who had a long Irish upper lip and thinning red hair, said bashfully, "Touch you for luck, Mr. Everett?"

Yancy snorted and muttered, "Why not walk on Deadwood Creek for 'em?"

Cas shook McKinney's hand while Ollie Dunbar ducked into a nearby tent. He returned with an inked nib and a dog-eared, orange-covered DeWitt Ten-Cent Romance.

"Would you sign the cover?" he asked Cas. "I'd be pure-dee proud."

"What's this?" Yancy demanded, looking at the book over Cas' shoulder. "*Cas Everett, Texas Tornado.* Why, Cas boy, this is you," the stunned farmer stammered out.

"Not even close," Cas assured him. "No man alive could side *this* Texas Tornado."

"It's lies?"

"More like a harmless fairy tale. If I ever meet the author, a Mr. Hiram P. Snodgrass of Philadelphia, I mean to ask him why in hell a man would fan the hammer of a double-action six-gun."

The prospectors laughed as one man, but Cas saw Yancy suddenly turn green as old brass. "You all right, Yancy?"

"It's the widow's cooking," he apologized. "It has given me the Virginia quickstep."

Yancy raced for the nearest line of trees. He was only halfway there when Cas, eyes searching the lip of the gulch above them, felt blood drain from his face.

Dakota Boggs sat a grulla, a fine-looking horse with a bluish-gray coat. At least a half dozen men sided him, watching Yancy race closer and closer into their range.

"Yancy!" Cas shouted, sprinting toward Comet. "Yancy, get back here now!"

"Can't, Cas boy! Nature calls, and man must—"

A crackling volley of gunfire opened up, bullets pockmarking the ground at Yancy's feet.

"Moses on the mountain!" he roared, reversing fast and nimbly for such a big man.

The unarmed miners, too, quickly took cover. Cas cursed himself for leaving his carbine sheathed. He slid it out now and threw it into his shoulder socket, returning fire to protect Yancy. Cas sank to one knee, making up in accuracy for what the seven-shot Spencer lacked in magazine capacity. His first shot punched into Boggs' saddle fender, and all the men backed hastily away.

"Faster!" Cas urged his friend. "They're coming down!"

Boggs and his pack of killers hit the slope fullbore, and Cas snapped off two quick rounds. He

was unable to fire again before withering shots
from the riders made the air all around him hum
with bullets. Cas jerked the knife from his boot,
cut his picket pin, and turned Comet into a nar-
rower profile to the shooters. As he stirruped and
swung up into leather, he turned around in the saddle and sent two more slugs into the charging
horde.

His timing, though accidental, was perfect. Cas
shot just as the slope narrowed into a near bottle-
neck. After his second shot, the horse beside
Boggs' grulla collapsed and rolled hard, bringing
down nearly every rider except Boggs. Losing his
safety without numbers, Boggs was forced to draw
rein hard.

"Any old time, sweetheart," Cas snapped while
Yancy fumbled with the leather hobbles. "They're
slowed for a minute, but they won't give up on
flushing us."

The two men sank steel to their mounts, Cas
leading them southwest. His plan was to scale the
south wall of the gulch, then double back around
toward Bear Butte northeast of the Black Hills. It
was a Sioux meeting place at one time and an excellent vantage point from which to pick off riders
on the surrounding plains. In fact, Cas doubted that
Boggs would pursue them that far.

Yancy's sorrel pulled even. "Still think law's
coming to Deadwood?" he shouted.

"Can't be stopped."

Yancy shook his head and hooked a thumb back
toward the pileup. "Yeah? Well, then the law better not arrive one at a time or they'll just end up
in the bone orchard with Wild Bill."

Whenever he could, Cas liked to take the vinegar
out of his opponents fast. He and Yancy were

about to emerge from the forested dome of the hills when Cas reined in and stood up in the stirrups to look behind them.

"Three minutes behind us," Cas estimated, grabbing the rope from his saddlehorn and lighting down.

"Has your brain gone soft?" Yancy demanded.

"Pipe down, you jay," Cas replied, busy tying one end of the rope to a dogwood tree beside the trail. Little sun penetrated here, and the trail was dark. "These yacks just took a hard tumble. They won't be looking for another one."

Cas tied a taut, low rope across the trail between two trees. "All right, let's raise dust."

They broke out on the plains, Bear Butte a massive shape against the sky ahead.

"Here they come," Yancy shouted, "with a bone in their teeth!"

This time Dakota Boggs was the first to go down, hurtling out of the saddle and crashing into a tree so hard that he landed motionless.

"*That* loosened his hinges for him," Cas exalted, enjoying a grin.

The last two men were able to pull rein in time, but the rest either flew into the trees or ended up crushed by their horses.

"That caps the climax, Cas Boy!" Yancy praised. "And we didn't need tickets to see the show."

"This is no time to recite our coups," Cas reminded him, touching Comet with his spurs. "Let's see how much fight these bully boys got in 'em."

Comet lived up to his name, the fastest horse Cas had ever ridden. Eager to stretch himself out, the chestnut fairly flew over the barren plains, a rapid three-beat gallop that Cas could barely restrain from becoming a headlong run. Yancy's sorrel made a good showing, never dropping far behind.

The gunshots Cas expected to hear never came. He looked over his shoulder and saw empty plain behind them.

Cas reined in and let Comet blow while he waited for Yancy to catch up. "Looks like they gave it up as a bad job. They know we're headed toward Bear Butte."

"If it gives them the fantods, shouldn't that butte be our last bastion?" Yancy asked, studying the dark formation.

"I thought about it," Cas replied, busy thumbing reloads into his carbine. "Problem is, it's too far away from the gulch. If they burn us out of our room, we'll need to fort up quick. Besides, Harney and his pals might join us, and they don't have mounts. The spot we pick can't be too far from their claims."

Cas stabbed his Spencer into its saddle boot. "You're also forgetting that we *want* to have a cartridge session with them. If we get forced into a wait out on Bear Butte, they could starve us. We need a place that gives us some protection but also lures Boggs and his maggots to attack."

"I'm just a farmer," Yancy said on a weary sigh. "Just show me where to plow. That blasted Dakota Boggs! Did you see his face when he came flyin' down into the gulch after us? I'll be dinged if he didn't look like the devil casting a net for fresh souls."

Cas nodded, his face clouding with unwelcome memories. "He does the devil's work, all right."

"You still don't think it was Boggs that came up with the idea about your family as revenge for you blowing off his thumb?"

Cas shook his head. "Nah. Boggs wouldn't risk the dire consequences just to settle a grudge over a mangled hand. Too much time and effort, too. Boggs is just a jobber. Somebody sweetened the deal with gold, plenty of it, or he wouldn't take the risk."

"So there's your missing link," Yancy said, mulling it. "Who paid Dakota Boggs?"

"I'll find out," Cas vowed. "Harney told me where Boggs lives. I'll be having a look there."

Cas glanced back toward the distant trees. "We shook 'em, all right, but we're fools if we return to the livery at this end. It's a long ride, but let's circle around the gulch."

Out on the plains, both men were safe from attack, but not from disturbing omens. Overhead, vultures wheeled like merchants of death, ever vigilant for their next meal. As the two friends watched, a dark thunderhead boiled up on the horizon.

Comet whiffled nervously when they reached a spot where the ground had been chewed up by many unshod hooves.

"Rustlers," Cas said after a dismissive glance. "You can tell the cattle were hazed at night, which cowboys never do. See all those rocks that got turned over? They would've missed them by day."

"Didn't you fight rustlers for a spell? I thought your pa mentioned it to me once."

"Almost. I was offered good money by the Cattleman's Association in Weld County, Colorado. But, being a one-man outfit, I didn't much cotton to the idea of ganging up with a bunch of hired guns."

Yancy snorted. "*You're* a hired gun."

Cas laughed. "Can't a man ever be a hypocrite around you? Anyhow, stealing cattle is a piker's game up north. Where rustlers truly thrive is out

in the Arizona Territory. Six men can ki-yi an entire herd over the border in one hour and live for
five years off the profit. Law rarely pokes into it—
you see a starpacker south of the Dragoon Mountains, he's collecting his cut."

They entered the Black Hills again and were
tracking along the northern face of Deadwood
Gulch, the town about two miles behind and below
them. Tall ponderosa pines threw deep pockets of
shadow, giving the hills their name. Everywhere
Cas looked, streams were foaming over rocks and
splashing down staircase ledges.

Despite the natural beauty, Cas kept his eyes
skinned for signs of night riders. Vigilantes, especially the purely criminal breed like the Regulators,
were creatures of habit. It might be useful to know
where they were meeting and what trails they preferred, when they were out terrorizing and robbing
prospectors. He found ample evidence that many
riders had recently spent time around a lick, a sa-
line spring surrounded by salt-impregnated earth—
once a good spot for Sioux to lurk for deer, elk,
buffalo, and other game as they came to the salt.

Cas made a mind map of the place and they
moved on. Yancy had learned some hard lessons
since leaving Texas and now appreciated the value
of silence. Like Cas, he kept his eyes in constant
motion.

"Hold it," Cas said, drawing rein. "Look just
below us."

A waterfall churned down the face of the gulch,
turning a rocky pool below into foam.

"Pretty," Yancy remarked absently.

"This isn't a nature hike, numskull. Look at it.
The water pours down on both sides, but there's a
dry ledge in the middle. All it requires is a knotted
rope hidden in the growth above it, and we could

drop right in. And see that rock staircase leading up to the ledge from the gulch? Plus, this spot is close to town and most of the miners."

"Our last bastion!" Yancy exclaimed, catching on.

"Could be. The gulch below us has plenty of cover, and that's where we'd finish the fight, with luck."

"Then why care about the waterfall?"

"*That's* the last bastion, you dumb Swede. Sure, I'd rather finish this business without forting up like that, but the numbers are against us and we may need to fight back to back before it's over. I'd say we have Harney and his partners with us, but that's still only five of us. Still, look what a handful of buff hunters were able to do at Adobe Wells."

"And Kathleen? Will she be there?"

A trouble light glinted in Cas' blue eyes. For him the talking part was almost over. Soon would come the hard doing.

"Lord, I hope not," he said. "But she faces almost as much danger as we do. And considering what a comely woman like her would suffer in a hellhole like Deadwood, she'd be better off on that ledge no matter what."

Kathleen stood in the parlor's big bay window, watching the flow of humanity, and inhumanity, down on Main Street. She had watched it many times before, but this afternoon was different—Cas was somewhere in the gulch now, and hope burned within her. He had given his word and shown his feelings, and now her prayers seemed to have sprouted wings.

With hope, however, came greater fear. In less than an hour, she would be setting up the faro rig and smiling her way through an agonizingly long night at the Gem. Normally polite men would get madly drunk on Swearengen's strychnine-laced whiskey and stare at her from lust-crazed faces. And how many more nights would stray bullets continue to miss her? The threats were more frightening now that freedom might be at hand.

Thanks to Cas, a brave and skillful man—the "gentleman unafraid" all women secretly dreamed of but rarely met. Kathleen had inwardly cringed, during their meeting today, at his probing questions. However, she couldn't resent him for them. He had not accused, and he had accepted her answers even though his troubled eyes told her doubts lingered. How could they not?

The familiar sound of a key in the hallway door made her heart turn over. She pulled the velvet drapes shut and turned to watch Levi Carruthers stroll into the parlor. Watching him approach, she realized she would never again be able to look at a man in muttonchops without a shudder.

His proprietary gaze swept her from satin slippers to gold-and-amethyst comb. "You look incomparably beautiful, as usual."

Kathleen tasted the bile of disgust in her throat. "Thank you."

"Did you venture out today?" he asked a bit too casually.

A warning tingled Kathleen's scalp. But then, he often asked that.

"No. I stayed here and read."

Instantly his bone-chip eyes went livid with betrayal, and Kathleen cried out at the stinging slap he gave her.

"You're a liar and a harlot! You met with this Texas troublemaker, Cas Everett. The two of you— *alone*. Polly! Get in here!"

Kathleen, reeling under the weight of impending doom, watched Swearengen's favorite spy cross the parlor, gawking at everything. Polly avoided her eyes and kept her painted face blank as wind-scoured stone.

"She won't be necessary," Kathleen said. "Yes, I met Cas Everett today, but only briefly. After all, we were neighbors once."

"I don't care if he baptized you. You're *mine* now, bought and paid for. Hop Sing!"

The Chinese boy hurried in from the hallway.

"Search everything," Carruthers told him, "especially all the clothing. When you've finished, haul her things to my house."

Kathleen's legs went so weak she had to hold the back of a chair. His house was a virtual prison, and once she went inside those walls, she'd never emerge alive, she was sure.

"Dakota asked you if Cas Everett was your neighbor and you denied it," Carruthers said sharply. "Nor did you tell me you were meeting him to *say hello*. You're not dealing with a hayseed in me, my dear. Despite all I've done for you, you little ingrate, you intend to run off with Everett."

"Levi, that's just not—*oh*!"

He slapped her again, even harder. Near the window, Hop Sing was pulling gowns out of the Saratoga trunk and feeling every seam. If Carruthers searched her, she realized, in his present mood he'd kill her on the spot for having a dagger.

"Shut your filthy, lying harlot's mouth!" he fumed. "Don't you see who and what I am? They lick my boots in this town, yet you go sneaking off to some worthless bounty hunter who got his entire family killed! Well, it cost me more money, but I settled with Al this afternoon—no more faro dealing for you. From now on you'll be where I can watch you, and I guarantee your 'feminine sensibilities' won't stop me from enjoying what I've purchased lock, stock, and barrel."

Chapter 21

Cas' success in thwarting attacks at the window forced the enemy to new, safer tactics. Just before he and Yancy blew out the candle that night, a bullet shattered the room's only window and sent shards of glass flying in like tiny spears.

More slugs thucked into the inside walls and sent plaster dust spouting. Cas, staying low, grabbed his Spencer and inched to one side of the window until he spotted yellow-orange streaks of muzzle flash about fifty yards out. He returned fire, the light carbine repeatedly kicking into his shoulder. A minute later he heard the rataplan of hoofbeats retreating through the trees above the gulch.

"That'll fetch the widow," Cas fretted, force of habit making him immediately thumb reloads into the carbine. "She's the straight-and-narrow type—we're goin' to lose our digs, and the timing couldn't be worse."

A hesitant knock sounded at the door. Yancy opened it to reveal Mrs. Huckabee, wearing a woolen wrapper and a long nightcap, her mousy gray hair in curl papers.

"Are you two all right?" she inquired, holding up her lantern to peer inside.

Plaster dust still floated in the air, and the stench

of spent powder made her sneeze. Broken glass crumbled underfoot as Cas hastened to put his gun away. He knew they'd get the boot if he told the truth, but he saw no way around it.

"Mrs. Huckabee," Cas said, "I'm awful sorry—"

"You know," she cut him off, "we have a terrible problem with stray bullets from the gulch hitting this house. I'll have the window repaired tomorrow. I have a knife for digging bullets out of the wall."

Cas and Yancy exchanged surprised glances.

"You know, Mr. Everett," the widow added, her voice softening with emotion, "I read through some old newspapers today. And I think I know why you're here. My prayers are with both of you. It's men like you who are going to turn this wicked camp into a decent town fit for families. But *please* be careful—the forces arrayed against you are formidable."

"She's got *that* right," Cas said after she shut the door.

"Yah shoor," Yancy agreed as he stretched out in bed fully clothed except for his brogans. "But it's not both of us takin' on this fight—I been as useless as a duck in the desert, Cas. I don't know beans from buckshot about how to put the quietus on these easy-go killers and ruffians."

"Hogwash," Cas replied. "You're learning. You saved my bacon the first night we got to Deadwood, and you'll do more. I'm glad to have you along. Now quit whining—we've got a hell buster ahead of us, and this is no time to go puny."

Cas, Yancy noticed again, was all business during waking hours and shook off any grief over his family as if it hardly touched him. Just before dawn, however, Yancy woke up with a hankering for some cold cider Mrs. Huckabee had left in the icebox for them. He glanced over at Cas as he sat up, and felt a cold hand squeeze his heart.

Clearly the hurt was on Cas so hard his face had crumpled and his body twitched. His eyes were wide-open, but unseeing, and a patina of sweat glistened on his forehead in the first raw light of day.

"Cas boy?" Yancy said uncertainly. "You all right?"

But though his wide-open eyes stared at something, Cas was seeing deep inside, not without. Yancy wanted to shake him, but in truth he was afraid for both of them. It just might be dangerous. *A man's face, it can't get that way,* Yancy thought—not unless he was hurting so deep it took over all of him, and that could get dangerous in a hurry.

However, when Cas rolled out for the breakfast bell a half-hour later, he seemed rested and focused on present battles.

"Yancy," he announced as he shaved in a little wall mirror above the washstand, "I'm in a trouble-seeking mood today. How 'bout you?"

"Shoo, does a fat baby fart? I'm slightly touched in the head—you know that. But I never have to seek trouble. It sniffs me out like a hunting dog."

"Glad to hear it." Cas rinsed his straight razor and ran it across a leather strop nailed to the wall. He was sick and tired of the petty clichés and devices of frontier bullies. "All these notes, the ambushes, shooting through our window—face it. They're afraid of us. Or else they'd just kick down the door and waltz it to us. So from now on, we start the trouble, and we do what they're afraid to do—face 'em dead on."

"Is Dakota Boggs fast?"

"I'm told he's faster than ever, but don't expect to see him, Ike Bass, and Charlie Deets in the streets. I've still got proof to get, but those three, and Nat Hendry, were the ones who rode down to Sabine County. Kathleen's sure of it, too. They may be the lowest scum of humanity, but they know the wrong of what they did, and they're scared. Dakota Boggs could stare down a grizz, yet he won't meet my eye. They never meant for it to get out, but you can't stifle a thing like that."

"So tell me, Texas Tornado, who do we start trouble with?" Yancy asked.

"Those saloons down there are full of tin stars who like to hot jaw. They work for Dakota. If we're goin' to draw him and his two lick spittles into a showdown, we start by thumping on his men. That way, either he deals with us or his own men rebel and kill him. Case you haven't noticed, parliamentary rules don't apply around here."

"You got the Gem in mind?" Yancy asked.

"Nix on that. Kathleen works there, and I want no connection between me and her. We're Texas boys, so let's start with the Lone Star Saloon."

The two friends ate breakfast and walked to the livery to care for the horses.

"Did you see how the widow heaped our plates?" Yancy asked as they scuttled down the stone face of the gulch. "I get nervous when folks turn kind."

"See there?" Cas replied. "You're definitely learning."

It was still too early for robust saloon business, so they visited a gun shop on Sherman Street. Cas purchased two one hundred count boxes of .44 cartridges and examined a box of .56 shells for his carbine.

"Hand-crimped or machine-pressed?" he asked the clerk.

The man laughed. "Son, you're too young to be

a mountain man. Relax, it's all machine-pressed now."

"I'll take these shells, and much obliged."

Yancy, busy looking at a display of weapons in a glass-top case, tugged on Cas' sleeve. "Why, look here!"

Yancy pointed to a .32 pin-fire gun displayed on a white satin pillow. "The card says it was Wild Bill Hickok's gun! Found on his body after he was killed. And it's only one hundred dollars."

"You muttonhead," Cas muttered, " 'famous' guns are a going concern in gunshops. This is Deadwood, so naturally every greenhorn wants Wild Bill's gun. I'd wager they've sold a hundred by now. C'mon."

They headed back over to Main Street and walked slowly along the boardwalk, watching Deadwood liven up as sunlight slanted into the gulch. Twice Cas had to kick at rooting pigs to clear the way. A gunshot, toward the end of the gulch in Chinatown, was followed by high-pitched voices arguing.

Cas glanced toward the bright white facade of the Crystal Palace, wondering which windows were Kathleen's.

"Nice-looking building like that," he remarked, "fronting on a street like Main—just doesn't seem real somehow. They're using pigs for sewers, yet that hotel's got a marble walk."

An old walnut-wrinkled hag approached them, and Yancy was immediately impressed when she declared herself an "astrological doctor"—she had a cowl over one eye, a milky membrane that marked her as a visionary to superstitious people like him. He paid her four bits to work up his chart while an amused Cas kept close watch over the increasing flow along Main Street.

"Your fate is in the eighth house of the zodiac," she finally told him, starting to move on.

"Say, old gal, for fifty cents that's too far north," he protested. "I don't know the eighth house from the outhouse. The heck does it mean?"

"The eighth house," she informed him reluctantly, "is death's house."

She moved on and Yancy stared at Cas, his eyes suddenly huge. "Did you hear that?"

"Yeah," Cas said, pulling his stunned friend into motion. "She said you're going to die someday. Is that a revelation to you?"

"But she—"

"Will you give *me* four bits if I tell you you've got your shoes on your feet? Swede, you're a caution."

They had reached the batwings of the Lone Star, and Cas slapped them open. The place had a few customers, already being worked by the sporting girls.

"No Regulators yet," Cas observed. "Let's have a drink and see if some show up."

They walked to the long s-shaped bar and Yancy plunked his cash before the bartender. "Whiskey for me," he ordered, "and a barley pop for my little sister here."

A *nymph du pave* stepped inside and eyed both men, but dismissed them when she looked close into Cas' eyes. She wisely decided to stay out of harm's way.

"Say, boys," the friendly bartender said as he polished a glass, "if you're keen for sport and in a wagering mood, there's plenty of action about to start down in the cellar."

"What kind of action?" Yancy demanded.

"We got three champion ratters down there."

Yancy, his curiosity whetted, started to head

toward the cellar door, but Cas stopped him. "Not a good idea for us to split up, old son."

"I just want to see what it is," he complained, for he had spent little time in saloons.

"It's called ratting," Cas explained. "They fill a ring with rats and then turn loose a dog on them. You bet on how many rats it'll kill by such-and-such time."

"Sounds lively," Yancy opined. "Folks'll bet on anything, though."

"There's a version with two-legged rats," Cas remarked, watching the batwings in the back-bar mirror. "And here come the rodents now."

Four tin stars strolled in. One of them, Cas noticed, sported a new bandage around the meaty portion of his right shoulder. He stared malevolently at Cas.

"Bet I know," Yancy muttered, "where your knife landed night before last. And it wasn't in a tree."

"Well, look-a-here, chappies," the bandaged vigilante called out. "It's the nickel chaser and the pig farmer, the pride of Texas. No wonder them Texers lost the Alamo. They're *all* one-horse."

"Cas," Yancy announced so all could hear, "now *that's* what I call stepping in something he can't wipe off, huh? I'm gonna pound that blowhard into pemmican before he crawls outta here."

"Olaf, that's mighty tall talk," the bandaged Regulator snarled, coiling in a threatening manner.

Cas drank deeply and thumped down his mug. "Yep, there's a joker in every deck."

An eyeblink later he spun a quarter turn, jerked his .44, and shot the loudmouth in his right thigh.

Everyone in the place looked stunned, including Yancy and the Regulators. The man Cas shot dropped to the floor, writhing and alternately screaming and cursing. His companions stared defiantly at Cas, stroking their holsters but afraid to pull.

Cas made their job easier by leathering his ivory-gripped Smith & Wesson. "Go ahead, boys. It's three on one. Skin 'em back."

"Everett," snarled a tin star with his greasy hair tied in a knot to hold it back, "who you tryin' to bluff? You don't stand deuce high against Jim Courtwright or Jesse James. I know 'em both."

"The question is, how do I stand against you, mouthpiece? Jerk your gun or show yellow. It's all one to me. I'm through *talking* about killing."

The hardcase lost his sneer as he realized just how close he was to the grave. "Hell, I ain't no draw-shoot killer."

"No, you're not even a man. You're a low-crawling, murdering coward. If you were a Sioux, they'd make you wear a dress for shaming your clan."

All three standing vigilantes were numbed into silence by the depth of the insults. This was not a man interested in posturing or "escalating" the tension by time-honored rituals. His was the behavior of a man with a blood vendetta. None of them dared speak up in the face of such implacable purpose.

"Yancy," Cas said, "take the wounded one's shooter and then toss me your widow maker."

With both of Patsy's sawed-off barrels leveled on the Regulators, Cas announced, "All right, no more playing ring around the rosy, boys. Shuck them irons and pile 'em on one table. Knives and hideout guns, too. Any man who hesitates gets blown to rag tatters."

They complied with alacrity. Cas looked at the bartender. "There's bound to be damage. I'll be picking their pockets to pay the bill. But you might also want to get some wagers going. It's going to be a real fandango, and for your information, the smart money's on that blond clodpole."

The bartender nodded and headed for the cellar to recruit bettors.

"Everett," greasy hair said, still swaggering to hide mounting fear, "you best take the temperature of the water before you rock the boat. Us Regulators *own* this gulch. Bring this to a whoa right now, and you might live to bounce your grandkids on your knee."

Cas said, "Seems I heard such talk from the late Nat Hendry, too. Another tin star who owned the gulch. Yancy!"

"Yo!"

Cas moved into the doorway so no one could escape. "These night-riding yellow bellies been havin' a high old time insulting you. Show 'em what a pig farmer's made of."

Yancy grinned as he stalked toward the trio, rolling his sleeves up past brawny arms shaped like tenpins. "Thought you'd never ask, Caswell. Boys, it's about time somebody read to you from the book, and *I'm* your holy man."

With Cas holding the Wells-Fargo gun on them, Yancy turned loose on the bully boys with a silent, impressive vengeance. The notorious brawler from east Texas shook off their best punches as if they were swats, picking up greasy hair and tossing him through a flockboard wall as if he were a bale of hay. A second, screaming man was swung around several times by the ankles before Yancy sent him through the large front window to land facedown in a half foot of mud and waste on Main Street.

"Watch that last one," Cas warned. "He just slipped brass knucks on."

Yancy grinned wickedly as he bore down on the ashen-faced Regulator. "That's good. I have brass fists. And after I smash out his teeth, I'm going to kick him in the stomach for mumbling."

He proceeded to keep his word, pulping the thug's lips against several broken teeth with a bone-jarring jab. He followed up with a vicious uppercut. The Regulator reeled backward, groaning, and collapsed atop a billiard table, ready for a long sleep.

"That's the show, boys!" chortled the delighted bartender to his circle of bettors. "My Texan won, so pay up."

Yancy cleaned out the pockets of all four men and gave the money to the bartender.

"Damn it all!" groused the wounded man on the floor. "You can't rob us, Everett! We're the *law*!"

"Sure I can," Cas replied cheerfully. "I shot you, didn't I? And the frolic is just beginning, oh *hell* yes. If you boys plan to stay above the ground, you best have a heart-to-heart talk with your boss. It's Dakota Boggs who brought down the thunder by killing my family, and now he's letting the Regulators stand in for him. He could at least split the blood money with you, uh?"

"Killed your family?" the astonished man repeated. "Dakota?"

"Dakota," Cas confirmed. "You think he's hiding because he's shy? He's letting you boys take the arrows for him."

Just as the two Texans emerged from the Lone Star, a familiar voice hailed them. Harney Robinson hurried along the boardwalk to join them, his brass-framed Henry tucked under one arm.

"Bad news," he greeted them. "Levi Carruthers found out Kathleen met with you yesterday, Mr. Everett. She's now a prisoner in his house."

Cas exchanged a troubled glance with Yancy, then asked, "You're sure of this?"

Robinson nodded. "I got it from Ruby, a girl at the Gem who relieves Kathleen at the faro table. One of Al Swearengen's spies told Carruthers. Now Kathleen won't even be allowed to run the faro rig. Carruthers has hired two mean cusses who use to be operatives for Allan Pinkerton. They take turns watching the house. I heard Carruthers can shoot, too."

"Pile on the agony," Cas muttered, recalling that fortresslike house. "Yancy, I told you we had a hell buster ahead of us. Soon as it gets dark, we're gonna chew the fat with Levi Carruthers, see if we can bring him to salvation."

Night had settled over Deadwood Gulch like a dark cloak. Stars burned from deep in the firmament, and a sliver of moon glowed like an ivory scimitar. Dressed in the darkest clothing they had, Cas and Yancy lowered themselves by rope into the raucous flow along Main Street, fully aware that death dogged their heels.

"I still say we should just kill this Levi Carruthers," Yancy argued as they made their way along Main Street, sticking to the shadows and watching everyone. "He has purchased Kathleen into slavery, and you heard Harney tell how Carruthers has stolen claims from prospectors, even killing them. He's overdue for justice."

"You'll get no argument from me. But it's a case of preferring the devil we know. Kathleen has to stay somewhere until we take her out of here. With Carruthers dead, who stakes his claim to her?"

"Why, Dakota Boggs," Yancy supplied.

"Now you're whistlin'. That walled house is actually the safest place for her to be—once we put the fear of God into Carruthers."

Among the problems they faced was that broken glass was embedded along the top of the masonry wall. To counter it, Cas had grabbed a horse blanket from the livery and folded it into a thick pad.

"There's the alley leading to his house," he told Yancy. "Remember, there'll be at least one man outside and prob'ly another inside."

"Can we kill them?"

"Only if we have to. They're just paid jobbers. I'd rather put them out of the fight."

"God forbid we should muss them up," Yancy carped. "The Texas Tornado, mollycoddling low-bred scum. I never seen the like in all my born days."

"Shut your pan and keep your eyes to all sides," Cas ordered, leading the way into the short alley.

The house lay about forty yards straight ahead. Small willow and pine trees lined one side of the alley. Cas leapfrogged from tree to tree, stopping about halfway there.

"What in Sam Hill?" Yancy whispered when Cas sat down to yank his boots off. He hid them behind a tree and opened the blanket to expose a pair of the strangest footgear Yancy had ever seen.

"Made 'em myself out of sponge and leather," Cas explained, slipping his feet into the odd contraptions. "When you sneak up on dangerous killers for a living, you need every advantage. These might look foolish, but they barely leave a track or make a sound. Got the idea from an Army scout."

Despite his nervous fear, Yancy had to stifle a laugh. Cas' feet looked oddly misshapen.

Cas stood up, clutching the refolded blanket and several lengths of rope. "I'll lead the way in. Each time I pump my fist, you move up to my spot. Until you see the signal, you're bolted to the ground, understand? Stay in cover. I'm taking care of the outside guard first."

Cas moved out, shunting from tree to tree. Despite the advantage of nearly soundproof footgear, he waited for the soughing wind to cover his movements. He had already spotted a figure with a rifle in his hands slowly circling the house. Occasionally other shadowy figures turned off Main Street and passed through the alley. Each time, Cas palmed his .44 and pressed closer into the trees.

He waited until the patient sentry rounded into view. He started up the south side of the house, away from the alley. Cas drew his six-gun and moved silently and swiftly behind him, tapping him in the back of the head just hard enough to knock him out cold.

He made quick work of binding and gagging the guard before making a fast turn around the house to make sure the second guard wasn't outside. The iron gate was locked, and Cas didn't want to make noise blasting it open. He returned to the alley and pumped his fist. Yancy trotted up, his clumsy brogans making more noise than a bull in a cane field.

"We're both going over," Cas whispered as he tossed the folded blanket onto the top of the wall. "You first. Land as quiet as you can, and make sure you stay on the blanket. Stand still until I get over. Here, give me Patsy."

Cas propped the express gun against the wall and bent down, forming a stirrup with both hands. It took every last ounce of will and muscle to lift the huge man up so he could gain a purchase and clamber on top the wall.

"Just lay your gun so it pokes over the other

side," Cas said, handing it up. He winced, moments later, when Yancy landed on the other side with a crash and a loud grunt.

Cas took a run, leaped, got his arms onto the blanket and heaved his weight up, the silent shoes no clumsier than high-heeled boots. Before he leaped down, he got a quick glimpse of a stone bench and a flower garden to his right. This was the east side of the house, with the main door on the south.

"Those shoes of yours are threshing machines," Cas whispered. "Stay here until I locate the other guard. I'll be back for you."

Perhaps because of the wall, most of the curtains and drapes were not closed completely. Cas moved silently to a window and peered inside. He spotted a hallway lighted by candles in wall sconces, their flames gleaming in the walnut wainscoting. Spanish fist shields and gleaming sabers dotted the wall. A door in the opposite wall stood open, revealing an impressive library. Tall shelves were lined with the gilt-lettered spines of books.

A real display of culture, Cas thought with scorn as he recalled what Harney Robinson and Kathleen had told him about Carruthers.

Cas moved to the next window and struck pay dirt. It was a bedroom, and Kathleen sat at a vanity, pulling a horn comb through her thick hair. She wore a silk dressing gown. Cas tapped on the windowpane and she started, coming quickly to her feet. He pressed his face close until she recognized him and hurried over to slide the window up.

"Cas! What—"

"Wish this was a social call, pretty lady," he told her. "Where's the inside guard?"

"He's . . . let me see. He's in a small room at the back of the house on your side."

Cas nodded, drinking in those eyes flawless as emeralds. "All right, just stay here. Where's Carruthers?"

A cloud moved across her face. "On the opposite side of the house, if he's in his room. He ordered a meal served to him there before he goes to the theater. We're both going to see *Tristan and Isolt* at the Deadwood Opera House."

"Sorry to ruin it for you," Cas said, "but Levi Carruthers is a dog off his leash, and I intend to step on him hard."

"Oh, *do*," she implored. "But be careful, please. He's wearing a weapon now and has another gun in his right boot."

"He'll not be using them," Cas promised. "Hang on, lady. Things are coming to a head around here."

He slipped back to the rear of the house, passing Yancy on the way and holding a finger to his lips when his neighbor started to speak. The guard's room was dark, but the window was cracked open. Cas inched it up until he could fit through.

Whiskey fumes were strong in the room, and Cas heard rhythmic snoring. A quick tap to the side of the jaw immobilized the guard while Cas bound and gagged him. Then he whistled Yancy inside and they moved out into the hallway.

Halfway down, the same Chinese boy Cas saw carrying Carruthers' camp stool now served as a bootblack, polishing a pair of Hessian boots to a high gloss. The kid watched him from wary eyes until Cas hooked a thumb toward the front door. Then the kid bowed once and left.

To play it safe, Cas ducked into the library to make sure it was unoccupied. Even now, with his muscles steeled for action, he couldn't help a spurt of anger as he took in the leather wing chairs and huge scrollwork desk.

"I guess he papers over the murders with all this highfalutin furniture," Cas whispered to Yancy. "All he deserves is a gallows limb."

His hand filled, Cas led them to a shorter hallway that went to the other side. On the way over, they passed through a parlor with a magnificent circular sofa, a cylinder measuring at least seven feet in diameter with a central column rising from its center as a backrest.

"God's galoshes!" Yancy whispered. "That fancy-fine millstone could seat a town."

They had moved into another long hallway along the west side of the house when the furious ringing of a bell arrested them.

"Hop Sing!" an irritated male voice shouted. "Where the deuce are my dress boots?"

Cas pointed toward a door and each man took up a position to one side of it.

"Hop Sing! You worthless layabout!"

The door banged open to reveal Levi Carruthers, dressed in swallowtails for the theater, a Borchardt-Winchester .38 revolver with walnut grips worn on his left shoulder in a canvas rig. But one look at the hardware aimed at him dissuaded the speculator from reaching for it.

Cas tore the rig from his shoulder and tossed it far down the hallway.

"You two saddle bums are trespassing," Carruthers said with imperial arrogance, drawing himself up. "And if you're smarter than you look, you'll leave now."

Cas pushed him back inside the large bedroom, Yancy following. "Saddle bums?" Cas backhanded him, repeatedly and hard. "You'll keep a civil tongue in your head, prissy, or I'll cut it out."

Carruthers turned choleric with rage. Yancy

moved behind him and grabbed the claw-hammer coat by each tail, ripping it up the back. Just then, however, his nose caught the delicious odors emanating from a serving cart at a nearby table.

Cas felt both astounded and infuriated at the sight of ribs and potatoes and baked salmon, with plenty of French custard ice cream and fruit sherbets for dessert. Evidently, Carruthers had not yet touched dinner—a carafe of coffee and a newspaper marked his spot at the table.

"Cas," Yancy pleaded in the voice of a man with no pride, "I will *never* have the chance to tie into a meal this—"

"Go ahead," Cas told him. "But face the door with Patsy on the table."

"Now see here," Carruthers protested, "this is not a home for bagline bums. Both of you had better—*unh*!"

Carruthers staggered when Cas threw a short right into his soft midsection. Cas followed with a left and then a fast, hard series of slaps that mussed up Carruthers' carefully coifed hair.

"My parlor manners are a mite rusty," Cas admitted as he brought a knee up hard into his enemy's crotch, bringing him to his knees.

"Cas, you *must* taste these ribs," Yancy managed around a mouthful of food.

Cas, however, had other priorities. Kathleen had warned him about a boot gun, and Carruthers was indeed still wearing boots despite hollering for his dress pair. His right hand shot down, and Cas made him deeply regret it when he grabbed the arm and twisted it, jerking it down so hard he dislocated the shoulder.

The scream wrested from Carruthers was high and piercing like a woman's.

"Oh, Jerusalem!" an unperturbed Yancy managed in the midst of ravenous eating noises. "Cas, this fish is good fixens!"

Carruthers squirmed in dire agony on the fancy Persian rug, trying to move his numb and nerveless arm. Cas dropped down over him, bringing his face within inches of the injured man.

"I'm gonna stay on you and Dakota Boggs like ugly on a buzzard, Carruthers. If you doubt I can, ask both of your guards. If you or Boggs touch Kathleen, your life won't be worth a whorehouse token. You have my cast-iron guarantee on that."

It was sheer frustration at Kathleen's plight that made Cas pay this shock visit tonight. He always tried to exhaust every other method before resorting to brute force. But Kathleen was in imminent danger for her life and her dignity—that cloud on her face told him that. So any action was preferable to none, nor was Cas sure the point had been made strongly enough.

Without a word he knelt beside Carruthers' head, cocked his Smith & Wesson, laid it flush alongside Carruthers' skull, and fired it. The bullet thumped harmlessly into the back wall, but Cas had once been the victim of this torture. He knew how the jarring explosion inside the skull pierced the eardrums like sharp needles.

With Carruthers begging in a shrill, hysterical voice, Cas fired again. Muzzle flash scorched Carruthers' scalp.

Again Cas brought his lips a fraction from the sobbing, frightened man's ear. "If *any*body harms Kathleen, you'll pay the price. And don't rely on that lazy coward Boggs to save you. He can count the rest of his life in hours, not days."

Cas stood up, keeping his gun handy. He was sickened by what he had been forced to do tonight, and couldn't stomach the grotesque sounds coming from Carruthers.

"Let's dust, Yancy," he said. "We'll pick up my boots and head back to the room."

Yancy had watched everything unfold with only passing interest, mesmerized by the feast. "Go *now*?" he protested. "But, Cas boy, my coffee's not even saucered and blowed!"

Cas shook his head in wonderment. "What are you jabbering about, you glutton? It's all beer and skittles to you, huh? Well, Carruthers is a church social compared to Dakota Boggs and his scurvy-ridden gunmen. And any way you slice it, that's who we lock horns with next. Now come along or I'll shoot you in your full belly."

Chapter 22

It was still early and pockets of mist floated between the surrounding peaks like gossamer clouds. Under a somber morning sky the color of dirty bathwater, three heavily armed riders trotted their horses toward Spruce Gulch just east of Deadwood.

"Dakota," Ike Bass said in an urgent tone, "going to this meeting is a fool's play, I'm tellin' you! The moment we ride into that clearing, it's a lead bath for us."

Dakota's long teamster's mustache couldn't hide a huge, grape-colored bruise on his chin, legacy of Cas Everett's rope trick yesterday.

"Bottle it," he snapped. "It's a choice between trusting our own men, no matter how riled up they are, or facing Cas Everett alone."

"Well, we sure's hell can't trust the prospectors," put in Charlie Deets, whose Greener lay across his horse's shoulders. "Some of 'em are showing some spine since Everett arrived. There's even talk of a defense committee."

Boggs swore to express his contempt. "Prospectors ain't fighters," he scoffed.

"Neither are farmers," Charlie said, "but that big Swede beat the snot outta *three* of the men yesterday."

Boggs already knew that—it was one reason for this morning's meeting. The other reason would be the most problematic: the rest of the men wanted to know about Cas Everett's family and just who killed them.

"Look, boys," he said, "I will allow that we're up against it. I've even wondered sometimes if the three of us oughta just pull stakes and leave the Dakota Territory. I know all these nasty rumors about Seth Bullock and how he's close to having U.S. marshals sent out. But this is no time to rabbit, not when we're on the verge of takin' over Levi's empire. Besides, running won't save us—Cas Everett is the type to hang on like a tick. If we run, we'll spend the rest of our lives looking over our shoulders. Best to kill him."

After a moment, Ike nodded. "As for Everett, my stick floats the same way as yours. He'll track us to the moon if he has to, so we better blow out his lamp while he's here."

Deets said, "That shines. I can't cipher nor write, like you two, but I know the science of killing."

"Now you two are talking sense," Boggs approved. "Either we roll up our sleeves, and quick, or we'll lose far more than our shirts. And we start by taking control of this meeting."

Boggs was the kind who nursed a grudge for life, and he figured Cas Everett had made a big mistake when that stretched rope sent Boggs chin first into a tree. He brooked such treatment from no man, and it only hardened his resolve to kill Everett and his farmer friend.

The trail was about to emerge in a cathedral-sized clearing often used by the Regulators.

"Keep that crowd gun in clear sight," Boggs told Deets. "Ike, loosen 'em up."

Ike took one hand off the reins to adjust his

Colts in their red sash. He had quit using holsters after seeing how J. B. Hickok wore a sash to gain precious time in the draw.

"All right," Boggs muttered. "Look cocky, not scared."

Boggs knew he was dead the first moment he showed weakness or doubt. So as he broke out into the clearing, his was the confident manner of a man who held the high ground and all the escape trails.

A dozen men stood around smoking and sharing bottles of whiskey. Boggs picked out several who bore marks of yesterday's beating at the Lone Star, including Jimmy Raintree leaning on a hickory cane to ease his wounded thigh.

"All right, boys!" he called out in a hearty voice. "Let's skip the whining speeches and hear your gripes!"

The sullen-faced men shuffled their feet and cast their eyes about, uneasy.

"Here's what we need to know," Raintree finally said. "Cas Everett's family was rubbed out during the same time you three and Nat rode out. Now Everett claims—"

"Sure, we killed his worthless family," Dakota cut him off, his tone boastful. "Stone MacGruder hired me to do it. My only regret now is that I didn't get some use of his sisters before we plugged 'em."

The bold and irreverent brag stunned even these hardened Regulators into jaw-dropping silence, Ike and Charlie included. Dakota knew it was useless to deny the fact and figured the "sin bravely" approach was safest among cutthroats.

"Well, God A'mighty, Dakota!" exploded Linton Krueger. "You killed the women! Maybe the rest of us should send a delegation to parley with

Everett, offer you three up to get him off the rest of us."

A sneer divided Dakota's big, bluff face. "So what if we killed women? What's got into you boys? Religion? Swearengen beats a whore to death at least once a month and tosses her to the hogs. I could name a man or two among you who has knifed or shot a sport."

"These women in Texas wasn't painted cats," Raintree objected.

Boggs burst out laughing. "Listen to my cold killers! Jimmy, Everett *shot* you, and now you take his part. What's next—religious tracts and psalm singing?"

Boggs had some success in thus blunting the men's moral outrage. However, Krueger's next question was the real sticking point.

"What right have you got to cash in big and leave *us* to face the music? Everett is right. You're making us take the arrows meant for you."

Boggs knew the question was coming and he didn't hesitate for the bat of an eyelash. "It's only fair. That's what right I got. A rising tide lifts *all* the boats. I earned that money for all of us."

"Then where's our cut?" a voice rang out.

Boggs waved this off. "It's seed money. We can own the entire Dakota Territory, not just Deadwood. Cattle are already coming in, and the railroads will be next. We can all cash in big without ever breaking a sweat, but it requires plenty of legem pone to grease the palms of the right judges and sheriffs. The money I was paid is set aside as gate money to buy off some pus guts in Yankton."

That was a lie. Boggs had kept ten thousand for himself and let the other three divide up the remaining ten thousand. Some of his men, however, nodded approval.

"Yeah, but you shoulda told us you done for his family," Krueger objected. "Dakota, you picked the wrong man to do the hurt dance on. I saw him cut down Red Johnson in the up country of the Powder. Red had a lightning draw, but he never got off a shot before Everett drilled him in the forehead."

"Nat Hendry lies colder than a wagon tire," a man named Big Bat Jones reminded the others. "Ace McGinnis could shoot a shot glass off the head of a bulldog at forty paces, yet Everett blew him out of his perch. This Cas Everett is a hard man to kill and a top-notch sharpshooter."

"Have you heard about Levi Carruthers?" Krueger added. "Last night Everett taught him the truth about Ruth. Doc Babcock told me Carruthers got so scared he wet his britches. Said he looked like Kiowas worked him over."

In fact Dakota had seen Levi this morning on a business matter. His face was swollen and bruised beyond recognition, his right arm in a sling. He was so nervous he started at every sound.

"Sure, he looks a mite peaked," Dakota replied. "But he's alive, hanh? Boys, *I'm* not letting this strutting Texan run me off like a distempered wolf. Trouble never goes away on its own if you run from it."

"Hell, it's not us Everett came up here to kill," Big Bat said. "What's the payoff for us in standing up to him?"

"Clean your ears or cut your hair. I already told you we're close to our own private empire here. I'm not talkin' about the leavings in Deadwood, neither. Boss Tweed just died, but I figure we can have our own Tammany Hall."

Now Boggs played his ace. "Boys, you know how rich Carruthers is, and I know for a fact he doesn't bank most of his gold. I know where he keeps it, and *every* man loyal to me will get an equal share. But first we have to remove the thorn of Cas Everett from our side."

Boggs was lying about the gold, too, but he had played the only hand he had: an appeal to the average criminal's greed and laziness. They had scant interest in siding with Boggs against Everett unless they stood to gain by keeping their leader alive. Evidently his appeal had worked. Raintree and a few others looked unconvinced, but the rest appeared ready to eat their own guts.

"Let's end it tonight!" Linton Krueger shouted. "A massed attack on the widow Huckabee's place!"

Boggs fought off a smug grin at his ability to haze these men in the direction he wanted them to go. "I thought about that, but a simple siege takes too long. So we'll torch the place and cut 'em down when they flee the flames. Once we ring that house and drive 'em out, no fancy draws and twirls will save their hides."

Cas had remained resolute of purpose since that cruel day in May when he arrived at his burned-out house. However, the ordeal was taking its toll. He had rarely spent time in Wild West hellers, only if a bounty pulled him. Every hour in Deadwood, he told himself, was surely worth a month in hell.

It was midmorning and he and Yancy followed prospector Harney Robinson and his partners up a staircase ledge beside the waterfall Cas had selected as a last bastion. Cool mist dampened his leather vest and low-crowned black hat, and even the steady roar of falling water could not mute Yancy's powerful singing voice.

Buffalo gal, won't you come out tonight,
come out tonight,
come out—

"Stow that," Cas snapped. "The water makes
enough noise. We're not larking about on Fid-
dler's Green."

Yancy looked back at him as his long legs easily
climbed the wide-spaced stones, his weather-beaten
face creasing in a grin. "I can swallow your rebuke
just as easy as I swallowed those victuals last night.
If I die in Deadwood, Cas boy, I'll die well fed."

"Ease off on that dying talk."

"Why? My fate is in the eighth house of the
zodiac," Yancy reminded him. "Death's house.
Take your complaint to the planets and stars."

The staircase led to a sturdy granite shelf just
behind the falling water. The solid curtain of foaming water divided into two separate falls exactly in
the middle of the shelf, leaving a clear gap about
fifteen feet wide for watching and firing on the
gulch below. The major drawback, Cas realized as
he joined the rest on the shelf, was its lack of
depth—only about ten or twelve feet before reaching the solid-rock north face of Deadwood Gulch.

"We'll have no time for breastworks or to dig
rifle pits," Cas told the prospectors. "Our only
siege defenses are natural. The ricochet danger up
here might be the worst thing. So we won't be coming up here unless we can't hold out below."

"They'll be pouring the lead at us," Harney
agreed, removing his broad-brimmed plainsman's
hat and glancing carefully around. "But we have a
good angle of fire to hold them back out of easy
range."

Cas looked at their rifles. Oliver Dunbar carried
a Winchester '76, Justin McKinney a .44 caliber

North & Savage repeating rifle in a buckskin sheath. Two good skirmish weapons.

"That Henry of yours," he told Robinson, "will be useful for its magazine capacity. But the tube magazine will be hard to reload under battle pressure."

"Yeah, I've bent two already."

"Losing time reloading, against the numbers we'll likely face," Cas said, "could get us killed. You boys try to lay in some extra weapons. Back in the room, I got two Colt Navy revolvers one of the tin stars dropped. They're single-action but good short irons—I'll bring 'em up next time."

Ricochet danger . . . Cas told himself he dare not bring Kathleen up here. There was no safe place to hide her, so she was probably safer right where she was. Then again, what in God's name would she do if he and Yancy were killed? Carruthers (or Boggs if he survived) would have free rein over a trapped and beautiful woman. Perhaps it was better if she took her chances up here. His mind surfaced from these gloomy reflections, jarred by Yancy's voice.

"Why, what about food?" the farmer demanded. "No telling how long we'll be up here."

Cas grunted. "Food? Swede, you were just crying about how you'll be killed up here."

"Shoo, why should I die hungry?"

"I've got cornmeal," Dunbar said.

"There you go," Cas told Yancy. "You were in the Army. You know how to make ash pone and ramrod bread."

Cas looked each prospector in the eye. "I won't sugarcoat it, boys. If this scrape goes against us, we'll likely die hard."

Harney nodded. "Yeah, we talked about that. But we druther die than sign over our claims."

"I don't believe we *will* lose the fight," Cas added, letting a little light into this dark situation. "I don't respect the enemy. Sure, the numbers bother me. But outlaws are lazy cowards, at heart, and won't hang tough in the face of a determined foe. I think we can whip them into flight, and if Dakota Boggs isn't killed in the fight, I'm making sure he stays behind to face me. He *will* look me in the eye before I kill him."

He paused to glance below, through the opening between the curtains of plunging water. The horses were still safe in a little bracken of ferns.

"When we looked you fellows up today," Cas reminded Harney, "you said there was a meeting of the tin stars this morning. Did you hear any of it?"

"No, nor see it either. Friend of ours works a claim in Lead. He was riding back from filing papers in Yankton when he seen Dakota Boggs a-horseback in Spruce Gulch—tin stars gathered round him like flies on dung."

"They're tightening the loop, Cas boy," Yancy said.

"Looks like it. And if they made some move on the boardinghouse, the widow or someone else could suffer hard."

"Not to mention," Yancy reminded him, "that me and you could end up trapped between the sap and the bark."

Cas frowned so deeply that the furrow between his brows made them touch. "You're right. We overstayed in the house. We leave later today."

"And go where?" Yancy demanded.

Cas grinned and spread his hands wide.

"Here?"

"Needs must when the devil drives. Besides, it won't be for long," Cas assured him. "Harney, we need a signal for when it's time to rendezvous here. How 'bout two close shots followed by two wider apart?"

"Sounds good, Mr. Everett."

"Harney, just use my front name. Goes for all of you."

Cas knew that plenty remained to be done. Their gear had to be hauled up here and a better hiding place found for the horses.

"All right, boys," he said, starting to head down. "We're burning daylight."

"Mr. Ev—I mean, Cas?"

He turned around to look at Harney. "Yeah?"

"We took the liberty of tying a knotted rope to a tree up on the lip. Nobody can see it. Would you and Yancy have time to ride around topside and meet us after we climb up?"

"Sure, but why?"

"There's somethin' we'd like to show you. It's in a cave about a quarter mile away. Might help us."

"What is it?" Yancy demanded.

"Never mind. We'll find out," Cas told him, leaping from the shelf to the first moss-edged stone step. "Mystery adds a little savor to life."

Chapter 23

Harney Robinson pulled back a stiff canvas tarp. "I don't know what it's called, or even if it works. But the size of it makes it so even a couple of men can move it around. It'd fit real snug up on that granite shelf."

The weapon, smaller than a cannon but bigger than a buffalo gun, was mounted on a big tripod. Cas recognized it from his brief stint with the Army, but it was Yancy who spoke up. "Why, it's a Parrot artillery rifle. I fired one during the war. It shoots as quick as you can drop shells down the muzzle and jerk the lanyard."

"How'd it get here?" Cas asked, squatting to examine the Parrot in the light from a cave entrance. The horses had been taken inside and hobbled out of sight of roving vigilantes.

" 'Bout two years ago," Harney said, "right before Custer and his Seventh were sent to glory, the Army sent a patrol into the Black Hills to scare out bands of Sioux that were attacking surveyors and mail riders."

Cas laughed. "But they had trouble—right?—getting the featherheads to stand still so they could kill 'em with this?"

Harney nodded. "The soldiers got routed and

left the gun along with ten shells—that's them in the leather bag. Me and my brother, Tim— Regulators gunned him down in the Bella Union six months back—saw no point in wasting this. We knew about this cave, so we lugged it inside. I figured it'd be stolen by now."

"Those are just one pounders," Yancy explained, watching Cas heft one of the shells.

"Yeah, so is it worth the time and trouble to haul it?" Cas wondered aloud. "It's been covered, but cold winters can corrode the inner workings. We don't know if it works, and testing it outside the cave would only mark our location before we're ready."

"What if it does work?" Yancy countered. "All we do is drop in a shell and jerk the lanyard. Easy as rolling off a log."

"I've watched the Army use this weapon," Cas said. "A gun that small isn't likely to turn a battle. Those small shells require almost a direct hit to do much damage."

"Yah shoor," Yancy said. "But they make plenty of smoke and noise, and they scare horses *and* men."

Cas said, "That's my point. If we scare the men back, but not off, we'll just prolong the fight. We don't *want* a prolonged fight. The longer we're down in the gulch, or worse, under that waterfall, the lower our chances of winning. Well-aimed bullets will run them off quicker than smoke and noise."

"That barrel is rifled," Harney reminded him. "That means the gun can be aimed better than a cannon."

"And what if Kathleen's up there with us?" Yancy asked. "You said she might be. There's ricochet danger and the Parrot might at least help in keeping the tin stars at longer range so more of their bullets miss."

Cas mulled it and finally nodded. "I'm leaning against the idea of taking Kathleen under the waterfall with us. Matter fact, I don't want *us* up there if we can hold out below. But your point about ricochet danger is a good one. Well, since you've operated one, Yancy, you'll be our gunner."

"Soon's it gets dark," Harney said, "the three of us will lower it down."

Cas nodded, poking his head outside to check for riders. It was only early afternoon, but a vagrant wind gust brought him the sound of revelry from Deadwood Gulch. Hearing it reminded him what had to be done when his shadow began slanting toward the east.

"Just remember," Cas said, "all of you—it'll be superior rifle marksmanship that wins the battle, not smoke and noise. Don't jerk your trigger, don't buck your weapon, and *don't* waste your ammo on toss shots. You don't squeeze that trigger unless you're sure it's for score."

Although gummed envelopes were readily available now, Levi Carruthers enjoyed the regal feeling of sealing his letters with wax. Thanks to Cas Everett, however, he could no longer do it unassisted. Even more galling, that worthless Seth Bullock had refused to arrest Everett even though this house was beyond the deadline.

"You've seen me do it plenty of times," he told the Chinese boy Hop Sing. "Don't spill the wax on my new blotter."

The boy folded the letter and slipped it inside an envelope. Then he pulled a stub of candle out of a drawer and lit the wick with a lucifer. He held a nubbin of sealing wax over the flap of the enve-

lope and touched the candle flame to it until liquid
pooled all over the flap.

"Perfect," Carruthers said, pressing the seal of
his ring into it.

"Who you writing to, *boss*?"

The unexpected voice from the hallway beside
him made an already nerve-frazzled Carruthers
cry out.

Dakota Boggs laughed as he strolled into the library. "Mite jumpy, hey? Judging from your face,
that high-handed Texan whipped you sick and silly.
Sorry I missed it."

Carruthers twisted around in his chair. "Why did
the guards let you in?"

"Why'd they let Everett in?"

Carruthers saw the homicidal malice in his hire-
ling's eyes, and panic froze his features. Boggs
laughed again, enjoying himself immensely, a tiger
taunting its prey.

"You work for me now, Hop Sing," Boggs told
the lad. "Pull foot."

The boy raced out of the big room. Boggs moved
closer to the desk, his breath whistling in his nostrils. "I paid your guards off and sent them packing,
Carruthers. This is my house now, and Kathleen is
my woman. Wha'd'you think of that, you perfumed sissy?"

Carruthers' right arm was supported by a sling,
but the Borchardt-Winchester .38 was tucked into
his waistband near the left hip.

"Stand up," Boggs invited him. "See, I use my
left hand too on account of Everett. Let's see who
uses it better."

Carruthers paled and fought down the urge to
vomit. He knew he was about to be hurled into
eternity, yet even now he was outraged at human
insubordination.

"You're a gunslinger, Dakota," he protested. "I'm a target shooter."

"All right then, I'm a target. So shoot."

Carruthers refused to stand up. Boggs moved closer, palm caressing his holster. "Face it, poncy man, you can't even enjoy a woman without her permission. Jelly spines like you belong back in the States, where law says men have a 'duty to retreat' from danger. 'Cause I'll double-damn guarantee you won't retreat from *this*."

Carruthers never saw the draw, but there was no doubting the cold, unblinking eye of steel now aimed at his head.

"Dakota, *no!*" Carruthers pleaded. "I'll give you anything you want! Please don't—"

"Why push if a thing won't move?" Boggs replied just before the Colt bucked in his fist and a thin scarlet rope of blood spurted out between Levi's bone-chip eyes. He slumped back in the chair, twitched violently, then slid dead over one arm, blood spattering into a pool on the Persian rug.

Boggs tore open the envelope and pulled out a sheet of fancy deckle-edge stationery. His lips lifted off his teeth in a lupine grin: the letter was to Romer Hanchon, a notorious and expensive killer in Chicago. Carruthers probably got the name from Swearengen. It didn't name the intended victim, of course, but Boggs could fill it in.

His next thought was of Kathleen Steele. The shot just now was hardly likely to wake snakes in Deadwood. Still, this house stood above the deadline, and Boggs knew Seth Bullock was allowed to enforce the law here. Bullock had refused to go after Everett for breaking in, but he had been waiting for a chance to catch the leader of the Regulators in a crime up here. It was better not to be here if he showed up. Even more daunting, Everett knew the woman was here, and he could show up at any moment.

Boggs passed Kathleen Steele's locked door, behind which she recoiled in terror, willing herself the strength to use the dagger in her hand if he broke in. She knew it was he—she'd heard his unpleasant voice. Boggs had threatened to kill Carruthers, and now he had. They were both repugnantly evil, but Boggs was also the most brutal man in Deadwood.

When she heard the front door slam, then the grating of the iron gate, her legs went wobbly and she slumped against the wall. Cas was right: things *were* rapidly coming to a head. She had heard the shooting and screaming last night, but still found it difficult to connect that hair-raising visit with calm, contemplative, easygoing Cas Everett.

She glanced at the dagger, grateful that Cas' visit made her miss the opera last night. Had she used the dagger as Swearengen urged, she would only have been doing Al's dirty work. She'd found out from Levi that Al owed him money used for rebuilding the Gem after a fire last fall. Now Boggs had resolved the issue with a bullet.

And he would soon resolve another issue—with her. She knew it must be the threat Cas posed that sidetracked Boggs for now. However, the next time he returned to the house, she feared she wouldn't be so lucky.

"What are you scribbling?" demanded Yancy, who was standing guard near the newly repaired window of their room.

"A note to Boggs," Cas replied.

Yancy stared at him. "Have you been grazing loco weed?"

"Nope. It's just a note to tell him he'll find us in the gulch from now on, not here."

"All right, finish your little joke."

"Nothing funny about it, old son. I like Mrs. Huckabee, and paying for a broken window was nothing. But next time they'll likely resort to fire, and I want to spare her place. I also want to push him and his ragtag militia into a fight. I'd just as soon get it over with."

Yancy pondered this answer and suddenly laughed. "I'm a madman, crazy as a shitepoke, and I like it. Say! Let's send him a rose, too."

Cas grinned before he blew out the candle and stood up.

"Sending it to his room?" Yancy asked.

"Nah. He has to go there eventually, but he's always in the Gem."

The last feeble rays of a bloodred sun streaked the window. Cas drew his .44 and rolled the cylinder, giving a quick puff to clear blow sand from the works.

Both men had packed their meager gear.

"We get our horses now?" Yancy asked. "By the time we saddle up and ride there, Harney and them should have the gun out of the cave."

It was Yancy who had come up with the useful idea of leaving their horses and gear in the same small cave where the Parrot artillery rifle was hidden.

"Not just yet," Cas replied. "First I need you to stand guard while I visit Charlie Wagner's Grand Central. C'mon."

"You're gonna kill Boggs now?"

Cas sent him a pitying glance. "What's the point of that? I want *all* the men who rode to Texas, and the only way I do that is if they side Boggs in a shooting scrape with us. Otherwise they'll scatter."

"Makes sense," Yancy agreed. "But if you don't

mean to pop him over, why risk running into him early?"

"He won't likely be there until late. It's prob'ly just a place to flop, and he's busy right now keeping his men motivated and in fighting fettle—they plan a move on us tonight. I'd bet my horse on it. Else, why the meeting this morning?"

"It was no temperance lecture," Yancy agreed as they left the house by a side door, eyes to all sides and protected by grainy twilight. "But, Caswell, what can you hope to gain from Boggs' room? We know that him, Ike Bass, Charlie Deets and the—ahem!—the *late* Nat Hendry were the ones who killed your family. Hendry as much as said so."

"Oh, I know it certain sure," Cas agreed. "And I don't require any more proof. The thing is, I still don't believe Boggs was the heap big chief who thought it up."

"Me neither, but it don't seem likely a criminal would keep such proof."

"To me and you it doesn't seem likely," Cas agreed. "But the mind of a hardcase is its own wonder. I've taken in murderers with their victims' scalps dangling from their belts. What we call legal proof, they call mementos."

They climbed down into the gulch, where a small fire at the Empire Bakery on Sherman Street was under control thanks to a bucket brigade of prospectors.

"They best haul in more water wagons," Cas remarked. "This wind's picking up somethin' fierce."

Cas hailed a young Chinese man who wore the white armband of a message runner. He agreed to deliver the note for a dollar.

"Think he'll really do it?" Yancy asked.

"He'll do it come hell or high water. They built the railroads at half the pay of white men, and worked twice as hard."

Yancy kept Patsy conspicuous as they moved along the shadows of Main Street. "Yah shoor, but is it smart tellin' Boggs tonight?"

"Why not? They don't know where we'll be in the gulch, and besides, they can't fight us in the dark. They'll check to make sure we've left the widow's place. Then they'll go looking for us tomorrow morning, and by then we'll be ready for the fandango. I've had it with the cat-and-mouse game—it's time for a clash of stags. Otherwise, Boggs and the other two will just scatter to the winds."

They had reached the Grand Central. Cas led the way around to the rear. Lantern light leaked under the edge of the hotel's back door. Following Harney's instructions, Cas moved to the corner of the building and a split-slab door with a rawhide latchstring.

"Place is dark," he whispered, standing aside and thumping the door with the side of his fist.

No one answered and nothing stirred within. Still standing out of the doorframe, Cas lifted up on the string and the door slowly meowed open on its own.

"Stay here in the shadows," he told Yancy.

"What if Boggs returns?"

"Call me out when you see him."

"What if there's no time?"

Cas shook his head in amazement just before he eased inside. "Then shoot him, you idiot. You need permission to defend yourself?"

Cas shut the door behind himself, his face puckering at the pungent stench of rancid food and sweaty clothing. The room's only window looked out on a steep erosion gully in the north wall of the gulch, still visible in the dying light only because it was literally within spitting distance.

Cas struck a match to life with his thumbnail and found a kerosene lantern near the room's only chair. He lifted the chimney and turned up the wick, lighting it. A mouse ran toward a shuck mattress that dangled half off the wooden bedstead, disappearing into a tiny rip. The mattress was probably infested, Cas realized, but Boggs slept on it anyway. Fitting behavior for the vermin who had destroyed his family.

He took a quick look around. There was a rusted hand pump bolted to a wooden sink, and crossed-stick shelves above it bearing nothing but cobwebs. Cockroaches swarmed over some old food on the floor. The gunrack on the back wall caught his interest. He selected the Winchester '76 and a Spencer shotgun, noting both were loaded. He propped them by the door to take with him.

The shrieking of the wind, as it gathered speed roaring up the narrow gulch, rubbed Cas' nerves raw. He cast his eye about the filthy room and saw little that he was even willing to touch—until he spotted a Bible on the floor under the bed.

"Who you kidding, Boggs?" Cas muttered as he crossed to the bed. In fact, he was surprised that such a hell-spawned creature could even *touch* the Bible without getting burned.

He knelt and pulled it out, noting how the leather binding was stained and scarred. A newspaper clipping fell out when he riffled the pages, an account from the *Black Hills Pioneer* about the massacre of the Everett family. Cas felt his face break out in sweat. Given his family's lack of prominence or fame, there was no good reason in the world for Boggs to save this—except, Cas had to reluctantly admit, as a spiteful memento of the man who ruined his cocking thumb.

The door creaked open and Cas filled his hand.

"How much longer?" Yancy complained. "I'm gettin' some dirty looks out here."

"Won't be long," Cas promised. "Get back out there."

"Smells like a bear's den in here," Yancy said by way of parting.

Cas examined the Bible pages more closely and discovered a soiled sheet of old foolscap, folded in thirds. He opened it, feeling a premonitory tingle in his scalp. It was a badly misspelled letter printed in watery black ink that hadn't been blotted:

Dakota,

I no you reed noosepapers so you must no that your old pard is in prizon. Wont be long befor I get the blinfold. I dout if any man can kil the cool basturd who run me in.

But I swar on our frendship that I wil steer you strait toword $20,000 in duble egels if you do for his famly lik we dun to them nesters in New Mex. You always hatted the basturd on acount of how he woonded you. Hers a chans to get reeveng for both of us and for you to get rich. Soon as its dun and I heer of it, you wil get wurd how to fine the gold.

Yur old pard S.M.

"Stone MacGruder," Cas said aloud the moment he read the initials. Just a typical heartless murderer whose other crimes included everything from kidnapping and rape to counterfeiting and train robbery. Obviously, though, he was atypical in his ability to nurse a grudge. Cas had read that he was recently executed in Omaha, small consolation for the loss of a loving family.

He folded the letter and slipped it in his shirt pocket—no telling when proof might be requested of him in the future. The newspaper article, however, he laid atop the Bible in plain view, weighing it down with a bullet to make his point. Let Boggs think about *that.*

Cas grabbed the Winchester and the shotgun and went outside.

"Find anything?" Yancy demanded.

"Found everything we need," Cas assured him. "But I'll show you later. We've got one last stop before we get the horses."

"Kathleen?"

Cas nodded. "That cave gives me an idea. We just can't have Kathleen smack in the middle of a shooting fray. Since our horses will be in the cave, she can wait with 'em. I'll leave Comet saddled. That way, if we don't make it, she can try to ride to Cheyenne or someplace."

Yancy nodded, though reluctantly. "She could make it, all right. There's good men in gold country. And plenty more who will take anything they want."

"I pray God I'm right," Cas said, "but I think she's safer going with us than staying in that house. Even if she isn't, I know her—she'd prefer a bullet to what Boggs and his ilk have planned for her. Best way to find out, I guess, is to ask her."

Chapter 24

Wagner's Grand Central was tall enough to block from view much of the gulch. The moment Cas rounded the corner of the building, however, he noticed a reddish-gold penumbra glowing over Sherman Street. The bakery was engulfed in flames whipped back to life by violent, at times even tornadic gusts.

"Lee Street is next," Cas said, raising his voice above the howling wind. "And look how burning embers are flying in the wind. The grocery at Main and Gold has caught fire."

The earlier fire was back with a vengeance. Suddenly suspicious, Cas glanced up toward the widow's place. But there was no fire up on the brim—not yet, anyway.

"By the lord Harry!" Yancy swore. "Cas, you *said* this place was a tinderbox."

There was a mesmerizing beauty to the sawing and whipping flames, to the lurid yellow-orange glow that bathed the gulch and its striated bands of rock. Momentarily transfixed, Cas was late to notice a figure in the street beside him—he was just suddenly aware the man was aiming a handgun at him.

A moment of stunned immobility passed in a blink, and the strong will to live instinctively asserted itself. Throbbing blood surged into his face, and Cas tucked and rolled just as the attacker's gun spat muzzle flash. Cas rolled up into a crouch with his .44 at the ready, but the man escaped into a fast-moving crowd, and Cas dared not shoot.

"See his face?" Yancy demanded as they broke into a trot in the direction of Main Street.

"It's all one face now," Cas reminded him. "The face of an enemy that means to kill us."

"We're in for six sorts of hell," Yancy lamented. "Starting with that Nancy boy Carruthers—he's had time to hire him some real guards."

To their surprise, however, they found no guards at the walled house. Lacking a blanket to pad the jagged glass, Cas simply shot the lock off the iron gate. A second shot blew open the front door.

Inside, Yancy watched the hallway while Cas knocked on the door of Kathleen's room. "Kath! You all right?"

A bolt lock snicked, and the door flew inward. "Cas, sakes alive! When I heard the gun out front . . . oh, thank God, it's you!"

Both men feasted their eyes on the beauty. She wore a peony-print dress and her hair was down this evening, tumbling in lustrous confusion to the middle of her back.

"Miss Steele," Yancy said, "you were always a sight for sore eyes and still are. Prettiest girl in Sabine County. You remind me of my Kirsten, may she rest in peace."

"Thank you, Yancy." Her eyes fell to all the weapons they were lugging. Besides his belt gun, Cas held his carbine in one hand, a Winchester in the other. Yancy carried two scatterguns, and his big dragoon pistol protruded from his belt.

"Looks like you two expect trouble," she remarked.

"Trouble considers us his favorite boys," Cas admitted. "And we all might have an extra serving, too. You can't see it yet because of the wall around you, but part of the town is burning."

Kathleen's eyes widened. "It must have been dangerous for you to come here."

"Shoo," Yancy said. "It was coffee-cooling detail compared to getting out of the Gem alive."

"Yes, I know exactly what you mean." She linked her arm through Cas' and started down the hallway toward the library door. "There was trouble here today, too."

She threw open the door. Generous light from the hallway washed over the body slumped in the chair.

"Dakota Boggs is carrying out his threat to take over Carruthers' interests," Kathleen said. "He always complained that he did all the . . . work while Levi got rich."

"Neither man," Cas said with cold indifference, "is worth the powder it would take to blow him to hell. But around here it's Boggs who's the biggest bull in the woods."

Yancy strolled across the hardwood floor toward the body. "The more the merrier," he said, seizing the experimental Winchester six-gun. "I meant to take it last night, but a delicious meal sidetracked me."

Kathleen searched Cas' face. "You two are surely compiling an arsenal."

"Yeah, and I need to talk to you about that. Yancy, stand guard in the hallway a minute, wouldja?"

Cas led Kathleen back toward her room, his pulse rate quickening at the touch of her arm on his and the smell of her honeysuckle perfume. Just before they stepped inside, Yancy's deep voice sounded behind them.

"Miss Steele, any gingersnaps in the house?" he called, his tone pleading.

Startled, she turned to look at him. "I don't know, Yancy. I've hardly left my room. There's a Chinese cook, but she left after the killing."

"T'hell with your dang gingersnaps," Cas rebuked him. "Fire is about to gut the gulch, and killers are lookin' to unlimber on us. Stay in the hallway in case Boggs shows up."

Cas shut the door and looked directly into her wing-shaped emerald green eyes. "Kath, I want to get you out of here. But because of what I need to do first, you'll have to face some danger—maybe plenty. Do you want out that bad?"

A rush of emotion closed her throat for a few moments. "How could you even ask me that, Cas?" she finally managed. "Have you lost so much respect for me just because I made a terrible mistake in coming here?"

"Kath, I've lost nothing, and I know you were tricked. But a fellow can't just butt into a gal's life after years of not seeing her and expect everything about her to be the same."

"A fellow could," she corrected him, "if he'd never butted *out* of her life."

Cas flushed. "I asked you to marry me, and you said no."

Her nostrils flared. "Caswell Everett, that's a stretcher and you know it! I said 'not yet.' My father was right when he said you had the 'tormenting itch' for adventure first."

Cas surrendered with a smile. "Well, it's too dead to skin now," he told her. "But not a day's gone by I haven't thought of you. The thing is, I made a solemn promise over the graves of my family, and that promise must be met before anything else. It'll be risky for you, Kath. We could hide you with our horses. That way, if me and Yancy don't make it, leastways you'll have a chance. That's the best I can do for you."

"I'm going back with *you*," she said firmly.

He glanced at her clothing, including the velvet slippers. "Then I'd recommend that you change, especially your shoes."

"I know exactly what I'm going to wear," she said, hurrying toward a Saratoga trunk at the foot of a canopied bed. "The very clothing I wore when I left home to become a schoolteacher."

Cas stepped away from the door to give her some privacy.

"This window's showin' more orange in the sky," Yancy reported from down the hall. "Fire must be worse."

"It won't stop the sinning or our showdown," Cas predicted. "They'll hardly miss a beat even if the place is gutted. The honky-tonks will throw up tents and have new buildings in a few weeks. Some of these boomtowns are rebuilt five or six times."

Yancy loudly crushed a sassafras candy between his teeth, the sound irritating Cas. "Did you kiss her, Cas boy?" he pressed, his "whisper" like a shout in the domed hallway.

"No, he did not," a musical female voice replied, and Yancy choked on his candy. "But he hasn't taken back his proposal yet, so there's still hope."

Kathleen, knowing time was critical, must have set a female record for changing, Cas marveled. She emerged into the hallway wearing a plain white shirtwaist with a blue homespun skirt. Side-lacing ankle shoes had replaced her slippers.

Cas loosed a long whistle of appreciation. "Not

so fancy and showy as your other dresses, but I like you better this way."

"We've got our Texas beauty back," Yancy agreed. "A pretty gal stands out even more when her dress don't play first fiddle."

"I was forced to wear what Carruthers bought for me," Kathleen told them, "but I confess I grew to enjoy wearing the dresses and gowns and shoes. Clothing, for me, was the only *quality* thing I could find. A reminder of beauty."

Cas grinned. "All you required for that was a mirror."

Kathleen smiled at him and hoisted a small clasp bag. "All right if I take a few things?"

Cas nodded. "We best head out now. Earlier, the fire wasn't big enough to draw many tin stars. But now it 'pears to be growing into an inferno, and it should be easier to slip you across town and out of the gulch."

She hesitated. "Cas? I have a friend here. A true friend. Her name is Ginny Lofley. She was lured out here from Illinois the same way I was. She's a singer at the Montana Saloon. We . . . well, we have a pact that we'll leave together. Is that possible?"

Cas didn't welcome the idea of delaying in Deadwood, but Kathleen's pleading tone and eyes were irresistible. Besides, a friend might help Kathleen endure if he and Yancy didn't survive. He looked at Yancy.

"Why not?" the Swede said. "We have two horses."

"Oh, I thank both of you so much! But even if we do all get out of here alive, I'm *not* just running away and forgetting about the place. There are girls here as young as twelve years old who will die before they reach eighteen. Swearengen needs to be tried and executed."

"For my money," Cas said as he led the way to the front door, "you could skip the trial. Let's go find this friend of yours."

As the trio made their way along lower Main, howling winds buffeted them and fanned the flames of destruction all around them. Cas saw Calamity Jane, her hair and clothing singed, standing in the middle of the street, dead drunk and cursing all Creation. The many structures with raw planks and shake roofs were fueling the fire, which burned with a roaring, snapping sound.

"The Gem!" Cas shouted. "It's goin' up like a bonfire! Looks like everybody got out."

Evidently the theater saloon was the victim of windblown embers. Al Swearengen was running around out front in his long handles, shouting orders no one carried out. Suddenly, abrupt as a thunder clap, the entire building collapsed, sending up fountains of hot, brilliant sparks.

Cas estimated that a third of the buildings in the Badlands were on fire. Despite the ferocity of the blaze, however, he figured most people had time to get out of harm's way.

Until, that is, a man came crashing out the second-story window of a Chinese brothel, apparently trying to leap to safety. He had the misfortune, however, to spin a somersault and land just ahead of them on one of Deadwood's many unremoved tree stumps, breaking his spine.

Kathleen screamed and clutched Cas' arm tighter. The man lay grotesquely contorted on the stump, saliva bubbling in his throat as he fought for a breath of the wind that had been knocked out of him. Flames reflected a dull red on his tin star.

Cas looked closer and recognized one of the men who'd tried to jump him on his first night in Deadwood. Just then, however, Kathleen tugged his sleeve urgently.

"Cas! Oh, my stars! That's the Montana in flames just ahead on the left, and Ginny's room is on the top floor!"

The trio of Texans raced across the street, both men holding one of Kathleen's hands as they skidded in the muck.

"Lord no, Ginny's in her window!" Kathleen cried. "She's about to jump! That's Crawley Deacon, a bartender from the Gem, trying to save her!"

A terrified woman in an anchor-print dress was sitting on a windowsill, struggling for breath and on the featheredge of leaping. The jump would not normally have cost her more than a sprained or broken ankle, but Cas saw the problem: a huge pile of building scrap lay just below her, full of broken, jagged-edged boards and other debris. Crawley was valiantly trying to pull the dangerous objects out of her way, but billows of black smoke kept driving him back.

"Why, this is pee doodles!" Yancy announced, grounding the two scatterguns and striding purposefully toward the scrap pile.

Yancy didn't waste time trying to diminish the pile. Instead, he scrambled atop it, adding his six feet five inches to the height of the pile and then extending his tree-branch arms toward Ginny. A short drop and she was clinging to him as Yancy somehow made it off the pile without falling.

In her almost hysterical gratitude, Ginny showered the big man with kisses that, Cas knew, had to be making bashful Yancy blush. Roaring flames showed the singer was tall and willowy, with hair golden as new oats and cornflower blue eyes.

"You're all grit and a yard wide," Cas praised Yancy as the two women hugged. "Still feeling useless?"

Yancy, who swallowed compliments as easily as he did baked salmon, swelled out his impressive chest. "Shoo! There's nothing to this hero business, Texas Tornado. Say, she's mighty easy on the eyes, huh?"

"Speaking of eyes," Cas remarked, glancing around them, "this fire's turning night into day. Let's make tracks."

They hurried to the end of the gulch and the knotted rope that led up to the livery. Both men helped the women up, Cas intensely aware of Kathleen's supple body pressed against him. For the last time, he and Yancy tacked their mounts in Cedric O'Flaherty's livery barn. Looking at the two scared women, Cas again felt guilt lance deep.

"I know we should just leave the gulch now and get both you ladies to safety," he said as he centered his saddle. "But if I do that, I may never have another chance to face down the three men I'm after. They put my entire family in lonely graves, and if I leave now, they could all scatter. The chance to kill me on their terms is the only reason they're still here."

"Of course you're going to keep your promise to your family," Kathleen insisted.

"We're grateful enough," Ginny chimed in, eyes lingering on Yancy, "that you're even willing to help us."

"Cas," Kathleen said, "did you ever find that proof you said you wanted?"

Without a word he slid the note from his pocket and gave it to her. Yancy, too, crowded in to read it by lantern light. All three of them paled at the cold-blooded words.

"Who's S. M.?" Yancy demanded.

"Stone MacGruder. They just hanged him in Nebraska."

"I hope now he's kissing the devil's . . . ah . . . hind end in hell," Yancy edited himself for the sake of the women. "There'll be more joining him."

The women rode postillion behind the men, who balanced the purloined long guns across their thighs. The ride along the north lip of the gulch to the cave was uneventful except for the eerily beautiful sight of the fire below, subsiding a bit as the wind tapered off.

"The Parrot and the shells are gone," reported Yancy, the first one into the moonlit cave. "Harney and them must've lowered it down."

Cas took a stub of candle from a saddlebag, lit it, and led the women inside. "It's mean quarters," he apologized. "You'll find bedrolls under our cantle straps. There's a good chance you're going to hear one humdinger of a gun battle tomorrow, just below this spot in the gulch. If me and Yancy don't come back, take our horses and light a shuck out of here. Head south to Fort Laramie or Cheyenne."

"Cas," Kathleen protested, "we can't—"

"You *will*," he told her firmly. "If Comet gets skittish and starts acting up, don't pull his nose up. Let him smell the ground and he'll settle down."

Both women, realizing the awful danger these men faced, seemed about to cry. Cas forced himself to the hard discipline that had kept him alive so many years on the trail.

"Nix on the waterworks," he snapped. "You'll find food for the ride in our saddlebags. And you might as well hold this, too."

Cas handed Kathleen his chamois money pouch.

"Shoo," penny pincher Yancy said, digging out his tow wallet and making Ginny take it. "Why let Boggs and his jackals have it?"

Despite his tough exterior, emotion pinched Cas' throat closed. Afraid he'd frighten the women even more if he spoke, he got busy bundling all three of his long guns tight with short ropes and hooked one of his bull's-eye canteens onto his belt, leaving the other for the women. Yancy carried both scatterguns and a gunny sack filled with ammo and extra short irons.

Awkwardly, Cas bussed Kathleen's cheek, wished her and Ginny luck, and headed out into the darkness, Yancy following. They couldn't make it down into the gulch on the rope Harney had provided, not this loaded down, but it wouldn't be a long hike until the steep sides rounded enough to let them climb down.

"Cas!"

Kathleen's voice arrested both men. She and Ginny came flying out of the cave and into their arms. When Kathleen spoke, it was the strong, confident, fearless voice of a woman born under the Lone Star and forged in the bloody crucible of the no-surrender era.

"You'll *both* be coming back," she ordered them. "And the four of us will be riding out of here. These cowards you'll be fighting have neither God nor guts on their side, and you two have both. You're better men, and you *will* prevail. Cas Everett," she added, "did you or did you not take back your marriage proposal?"

"I did not, Kath."

"Do you wish to now?"

"I'd sooner take back my baptism."

"Good. Then the future Mrs. Cas Everett will be waiting for you."

"As for you, Mr. Carlson," Ginny said, "we have no marriage proposal binding us and we've only just met. But when you save a girl's life, you become her special hero forever. I'll be waiting, too."

Both women returned to the cave, their shapes

fading quickly in the darkness like retinal after-images.

"That Kathleen is some pumpkins," Yancy praised.

"So's Ginny," Cas retorted. "You oughta toss a loop around that one."

"Hmm. Would you really marry Kathleen?"

Cas grunted. "Would and will. Soon as I kill Dakota Boggs and figure out a safer way to support her than bounty hunter's wages."

Chapter 25

There were nights, Cas had learned the hard way, that belonged to the Wendigo, to the souls in torment, to *odjib,* the things made of smoke that could not be fought, but could frighten a man to death. In fact, his endless night in the gulch made him long for the looming battle, where the only terror was death.

The airy roar of the waterfall should have lulled him to sleep. Instead, like Yancy, he napped and woke, grabbing uneasy sleep in handfuls. A light rain briefly tickled his face now and then, and each time it woke him, he would gauge the time by the height of the dawn star in the east. Both men, damp and stiff, were wide awake when the dawn chorus of thousands of songbirds filled the gulch with a warbling beauty.

"No point waiting," Cas said, sliding his six-gun out. Regretful at shattering the peace and quiet, he gave the signal to summon Harney, Justin, and Ollie—two close-spaced shots followed by two widely spaced. If all went well, Cas expected them in less than an hour.

"Wish I could get outside of some hot grub," Yancy complained.

"The bottomless pit," Cas said. "Even Ma couldn't fill you up."

"At least she tried, God bless her. Why didn't we knock up some grub for the battle?" Yancy demanded bitterly.

"Listen to this jay! No point to it, that's why. This battle will be hard, but it'll be over quick. Now whack the cork—I'm hungry, too."

Yancy opened the breech of the Spencer shotgun and slid the shells out, wiping the dew off them with his shirttail. "Shoo, how can you know the battle will be quick?"

"We're gonna make enough catarumpus to wake snakes," Cas replied. "They'll hear it throughout the gulch. The tin stars don't have free rein—remember, this isn't the Badlands on Main Street. This is Lawrence County, Dakota Territory. Sheriff Bullock can find enough men to arrest all of us."

Yancy grunted, still shivering from the cold and wet ground they slept on. "Your point bein' they'll want it over fast?"

"No, mush head, *we* are gonna end it fast—nobody'll be starving us out—take my drift?"

"Yah shoor. Either we win or we die fighting. What about the shelf behind the falls?"

"We'll fall back there if we have to," Cas replied. "But we won't let the fight drag out—we can't outlast a siege. Every move we make has to be offensive."

Enough weak light had penetrated the gulch to reveal the large limestone outcropping under which both men sat. The wall of the gulch was behind them, much of it a belt of banded rock. Perhaps seventy yards to their left, water foamed and splashed in the pool beneath the waterfall.

Cas watched the main trail to their right but

doubted the hard-drinking, lazy Regulators would mount a sunrise battle.

"Cas boy," Yancy opined, also watching the trail, "maybe the fire last night did change things. Could be that Boggs has other problems, and we've got no battle."

"Could be," Cas admitted, "but I doubt it. Don't forget, I went into his roach pit of a room and left him proof that I *know* what he did. I also sent word he can find us in the gulch. Boggs needs me dead *pronto*."

"Why? He could just run. That's what I'd do if the Texas Tornado was blowin' my way."

Cas said, "Not all bullies are cowards. Boggs is a hard twist, and he has faith in his speed if it comes to a draw shoot. Besides, he's settin' himself up for real gravy here in Deadwood Gulch, and nothing will hand him the keys to the mint like fitting me for a pine box."

Three figures, moving cautiously along the edge of the trail, emerged from the morning mist. Yancy gave a shrill whistle and the trio of prospectors angled toward them, their pockets bulging with ammo and salt meat.

"Glad you could make it, boys," Cas greeted them in a businesslike tone. "The attack could come at any moment now, so let's get the extra guns distributed and go over a couple things."

Cas assigned each man a well-covered position, widely spaced from one another and forming a curve so that the most daring attackers could be hammered from all sides. He also worked out the order for falling back to the ledge one at a time so volume of fire could remain the same while repositioning.

"Remember what we talked about," he told them. "Don't jerk your trigger, buck your gun, or shoot without a target on bead—with one exception. When I yell, 'Cover fire!' bust caps fast and furious to make plenty of noise and confusion.''

"Cas, you think we should avoid killing their horses?'' Ollie Dunbar asked.

Cas shook his head. "In a fair contest, sure. But in a shooting scrape where you're outnumbered by murderers, that's like trying to separate the water from the wet. It's all one.''

Harney Robinson nodded agreement. "Most of the Regulators are left-footed when it comes to sol-dierin' and such. But Boggs is skillful,'' he warned. "Before he chose the owlhoot trail, he scouted for Generals Hancock and Sherman in the Rosebud Territory. He'll likely use some tactics.''

"Well said.'' Cas looked at Yancy. "The Regula-tors will have no idea we plan to use that ledge. Since you can't aim a rifle, and a scattergun is a close-in weapon, we need you up with that Parrot gun. You'll have to operate it by yourself. Can you do that?''

"Shoo, would a cow lick Lot's wife? But we don't even know if that gun works.''

"Yeah, so fire a test shot when you get up there. Just remember, hold your whist, old son, until they're about to overrun one of us. Don't try to score direct hits, or one of us might cop it. But make sure the shell hits close to the horse and spooks it.''

Yancy, exhilarated at the prospect of manning an artillery rifle, threw his head back and howled. "I'm a madman! Boys, we're goin' on a tear!''

The trio of sourdoughs stared at him, wondering if he *was* mad. Cas burst out laughing. "Yancy, you'd drive a saint to poteen. But I like that strong-heart talk. Boys, this old chicken plucker survived four years of bloody war and plenty of battles with

Comanches, the tribe that killed more whites than any other. Don't worry about him."

The prospectors looked scared but determined.

"The three of us fought Shoshonis once," Harney said. "But they tend to run after one or two get killed."

"And there's a whole passel of tin stars," Justin McKinney fretted.

Cas grinned. "We've trimmed their numbers some. Besides, numbers mean very little. Buck up—the will to win will determine the battle. I know for a fact you three have plenty to fight for—including, for Harney, a murdered brother. They're fightin' out of criminal greed, that's all. Sure, it'll be hard slogging for us at first, but they'll rabbit before it's over."

Harney pulled a bottle of Old Taylor and a jolt glass from his old musette bag. "Bourbon County," he said, handing them to Cas. "Get us started with a toast."

Cas poured a shot of the shimmering liquor. "Confusion to our enemies," he proposed.

"To dark bars and fair women," Yancy tacked on.

Each man drank to both. Cas was about to send Yancy up to the Parrot, when he learned the brutally hard way that Harney was right—Dakota Boggs possessed some formidable field skills. With fierce shouts of triumph, as many as twenty riders spurred out of the brush on the far side of the trail. Riding all holler, they charged the stunned men.

"Cover down!" Cas yelled, realizing there was no time to take up their assigned spots in better concealment. "Stay frosty and shoot plumb! *Move!*"

Fear throbbed in his palms, but Cas refused to let it master him. In a chilling reminder of warpath

Comanches, Boggs and his gunnies swooped in from the direction of the sun, making it difficult for the defenders to aim.

So many enemy rifles detonated at once that the barrage sounded like an ice floe breaking apart. Rounds pinged in all around the five trapped men, the close ones humming like blowflies. It was all happening fast, much too fast, as death and hellborn havoc choked the air all around Cas.

"Steady on, boys!" he shouted above the racket, his face fierce as a Viking's. "Let's put at 'em!"

The defenders, too, were pouring lead, but they had the advantage of stable firing positions. Cas emptied his Spencer carbine, shattering an attacker's knee with the last shot, and tossed the weapon aside for the Winchester '76. It kicked into his shoulder and he watched a tin star on a blood bay catch a round in his lights. With death thundering closer, he lowered the sights and brought two horses down, one pinning its screaming rider. Cas tossed a finishing shot into his head.

Boggs, unwilling to risk heavy casualties, had only intended this charge as a softening attack. He wheeled the men around and withdrew out of easy rifle range. Cas immediately made sure his own men were not hit, then sent them to their positions with orders to reload.

"Hey, Everett!" Boggs roared out, his tone clearly gloating. "You couldn't have saved your family even if you'd been home when I came callin'. Why get your friends killed now? Let's make medicine!"

"I'm not one to dicker," Cas called back. He had his brass-framed field glasses out and got a good view of the barrel-chested gunsel astride his blue-gray smoky.

"Harney!" Dakota yelled. "You and your pards

best join us now, or widows *will* be wailing, mark me!"

Cas had etched the faces of Ike Bass and Charlie Deets into his mind for life. Ike was easy to spot because of his bright red sash. Confident Everett was out of likely rifle range, Ike nudged an ugly little paint with powerful haunches up beside Dakota. Cas already had his telescope-equipped Sharps Big Fifty in the grass beside him, hidden from the enemy. He unfolded the bipod mount and lowered one eye to the scope.

"Hey, Everett!" Ike shouted. "Know what? I had a *fine* time torchin' your house! But the best part was when your sisters ran out screaming, and I—"

The Sharps fired with a commanding report, and the top of Ike's head was lifted off like the lid of a cookie jar. Pebbly gobbets of brain matter sprayed Dakota. The shock of it froze the men in place for a few seconds. Then they reined their horses around and disappeared into the brush.

Cas' companions loosed a cheer, but he was having none of it.

"They'll be back," he predicted. "Three men killed won't give 'em icy boots. Yancy, get on that Parrot and test a shell."

Once again, however, Boggs surprised them. Before Yancy even reached the staircase ledge, the Regulators attacked. This time, however, they had wisely hobbled their mounts in cover. Boggs and his minions fanned out on a line, a double arm's length between them, and advanced toward the defenders in short bursts, dropping into the tall grass to cover and shoot.

Outgunned four to one, Cas and the sourdoughs were hard pressed to fire back, which required breaking cover. They were able to hold sections of the advancing line, but others surged closer. The moment enemy fire shifted higher, Cas realized that foolish Yancy was trying to reach the gun.

"Cover fire!" he roared out, and now four long guns barked furiously, sending most of Dakota's men to cover.

Ollie Dunbar was holding Yancy's scatterguns. Although out of effective range, he fired two blasts from the express gun to intimidate the Regulators. Cas glanced at his position and it was a quick, bad dream: massed enfilade fire cut Ollie down before he could duck. He folded forward like so much cloth, blood pluming from his bullet-torn heart.

Cas saw it, but this was do-or-die time and he stopped the flow of his thoughts, attending only to the language of his senses and raw, brutal instinct. He had no idea if Yancy had made it to the ledge and the Parrot, not with a half dozen men almost close enough to kiss him and preventing Cas from looking behind him. Several more had sheltered behind a long spine of rocks on his left, and now bullets hissed in from two directions.

Cas took several deep breaths, rolled hard to his right, and thrust up into a crouch, his .44 spitting flame. Two of the men in front of him went to glory instantly. A third screamed piteously as a slug ripped out his right eye and exposed much of the socket. Cas glimpsed his twelve-gauge Greener and recognized Charlie Deets, killing him with a slug to the forehead.

The Regulators behind the rock spine, however, drove Cas back to cover, one bullet so close he felt wind rip on his nape.

"Cas!" Harney called over, desperation spiking his tone.

He didn't add anything else, but Cas knew what Harney left unsaid: he was out, or almost out, of ammo.

His breathing ragged, his face hard and eyes fierce, Cas thumbed reloads into his .44 and watched a pack of rabid killers close in on him.

"You know the plan!" he told Harney. "On my command!"

However, Cas had little faith in the fallback to the waterfall, not now. With Ollie Dunbar dead, Yancy dead or missing, and ammo almost gone, they would be targets in a shooting gallery. And Cas had no plans to die before Dakota Boggs did.

Three of the swine who killed his family were dead, and Boggs was the last. But was he still here?

Chapter 26

Yancy Carlson knew full well why he had made it to the last bastion: because Cas and the others had expended valuable ammunition to keep him alive. And now they were all about to be slaughtered like Ollie Dunbar.

Yancy dragged the tripod-mounted artillery rifle closer to the front of the ledge, his heart leaping into his throat at the terrible sight below. Harney had joined Justin McKinney, and they were barely holding on—but only because most of the Regulators were waltzing it to Cas.

"Stay frosty and shoot plumb," he muttered, quoting Cas as he pulled the tarp off the gun and quickly aimed it through the twin curtains of falling water into the men about to overrun Cas.

Would the blasted thing work? The Parrot was a crew gun designed for two men, but Yancy hoped his long arms would be crew enough. He dropped a one-pound shell down the muzzle and heard it slide home solidly. He wrapped the lanyard around his left hand, then double-checked his elevation and windage settings.

With a silent prayer, he jerked the lanyard and the rocket wooshed toward its target, pulling a long white trail of smoke. Yancy's weather-beaten face eased into a grin of triumph when a Regulator took a near-direct hit and flew ten feet into the air on a crack-booming explosion.

However, the grin melted in a heartbeat when the smoke cleared and he saw Cas lying prone in the grass—in his hurry, Yancy realized, he had hit too close. There was no time, however, to worry about it. Yancy grabbed another rocket and dropped it through the muzzle.

Below, Cas reeled from concussive shock, his mind playing cat and mouse with awareness. Then memory flexed a muscle, time shifted back to the present, and he woke to pandemonium—the right kind finally.

Cas had placed little faith in the Parrot, either that it would function or that the one-pound shells could have much effect. But Yancy's shell had not only killed one man; several more were shrieking with pain as they fled—the kind of unnerving scream that often went with massive powder burns. A second rocket exploded behind the rock spine. Evidently the hideous screams of the victims tore it for the battered and bruised Regulators—they were retreating now in headlong rout.

"Harney!" Cas shouted. "Do you see Boggs?"

"Ask me, not him!" a belligerent voice replied. "I ain't hard to find, Everett, happens you want to see me!"

Cas rose warily, noticing the last of Boggs' men disappearing into the brush. The bodies of men and horses dotted the floor of the gulch. Boggs stood in plain view near the trail, hip-cocked, obviously waiting for him.

"Harney," Cas said quietly to the exhausted and powder-blacked miners, "you and Justin gather up weapons and ammo from the dead in case this is all a trick and they plan to attack."

"No tricks, Everett," Boggs called out. "I'm just damn sick and tired of hearin' how fast you are. You're about to meet a man who's faster."

Cas walked closer, eyes studying the terrain.

"Don't let that no-account, woman-killing trash slicker you!" Yancy warned, bounding down the rock steps behind them. "If he's so willing to face you, why's he been hidin' the last few days?"

"He's got a fox play planned," Cas agreed. "But I'm ready to kill him, Yancy. This is his day to die, not mine. Say, old son, that was good work up topside."

Dakota Boggs, watching his nemesis advance, felt confused and disoriented, like a man who had gone to bed in one country and woken up in another. Cas Everett possessed a dangerous calm that was obvious—the steady, flawless calm of a man dedicated body and soul to a mission. Facing him now, Boggs felt regret so intense that his legs trembled. Everett fought for duty and love, not merely his own survival, and Boggs hoped like all hell the card up his sleeve would take this hand.

"It's gonna be low in the belly, Boggs," Cas informed him in his businesslike tone. "Two slugs about two inches below the belly button. For hours you'll scream so hard you'll tear your own vocal cords apart. When you finally die and go to hell, it'll seem like relief."

Sweat poured in rivulets down Boggs' face, but his sneer of cold command remained. "You overrate yourself, Everett, and you *under*rate me."

Cas continued moving in. "No, I don't. You're fast. But even now you can't look me square in the eye, uh? What you did in Texas was so monstrous even you can't live with it."

Cas coiled for the draw, his eyes hard and piercing. "Now skin it back, you soulless worm, and never mind your two-bit tricks—nothing will stop me from putting you in a suit with no back."

"Show the smug bastard he's wrong, boys," Boggs said, and instantly gunfire erupted from the brush on both sides of Cas, a deadly cross fire. Yancy had retrieved his double ten and now discharged both barrels into the brush on Cas' right. Harney and Justin opened up on the left. Not, however, before a slug chewed into Cas' left forearm halfway between the wrist and the elbow.

Bullet shock rocked him back, and the pain exploded all the way to his neck and numbed the arm. Not once, however, did he take his eyes off Boggs' left hand. The moment Boggs slapped leather Cas' hand moved in a blur of speed, the .44 leaping twice as he planted the promised slugs.

Boggs collapsed in a writhing heap, his screams startling the insects and birds into silence. Cas kicked the killer's Colt out of reach and watched him squirm, begging for a mercy bullet. Cas heard more shots on both sides of him as Harney and Justin finished off the wounded ambushers hidden in the brush.

"With two .44 pills in his guts, he can't be saved," Cas told the others. "Tie him up and gag him. Then drag him into heavy brush so his pals can't toss a head shot into him later. He'll be hours bleeding out, and I want him to enjoy every minute."

"Still too good for him," Yancy complained, busy tying a folded bandanna around Cas' copiously bleeding wound.

"You're right," Cas agreed, wincing at the sharp stabs of pain. "Strip him buck and lay him facedown on a mound of red ants."

Leaving Harney and Justin at the cave to keep an eye on the women, Yancy and Cas rode into

Deadwood from the west, the only accessible side on horseback. Fully one-third of the town lay in charred ruins, but they found Doc Babcock in his cubbyhole office, listening through the wall with a tubular stethoscope to the activities in the adjoining brothel.

"Just testing it," he muttered, flushing beet red and laying his stethoscope on a shelf.

He bathed Cas' wound with a cloth soaked in camphor and wrapped it in bands of bleached gauze dipped in gentian. The bullet had passed through clean, but Cas had lost plenty of blood. Doc Babcock insisted that Cas drink a "blood restorative," a vile concoction made up of milk, molasses, egg yolk, yeast, and ground calf's liver.

"Far as the pain," Babcock told Cas, "quinine and whiskey are all I have left. The sporting gals steal all my laudanum."

"Quinine makes my head ring," Cas replied as he rolled down his shirtsleeve, "and whiskey puts me to sleep. It hurts a mite, but I'll be happy to bear it."

His eyes met Yancy's, and both men grinned like coconspirators.

"Son," Doc Babcock said, "it's not my policy to ask about gunshot wounds in Dead—"

"Good policy," Cas cut him off, slapping three silver dollars on the desk. "Thanks, Doc."

Word had already swept through Deadwood about the desperate showdown that, within days, would become immortalized in headlines as the "Last Stand at Deadwood Gulch." Levi Carruthers and Dakota Boggs were much of the problem in Deadwood, and now both were dead. True, Cas told himself, Al Swearengen remained and he wouldn't be touched yet—he'd been careful to pay off the right officials in Yankton. But he had to rebuild the Gem. And with the Regulators beaten and leaderless, and the prospectors forming a defense committee run by Harney, Cas knew Swearengen would no longer have a free hand in trapping women.

At the insistence of Harney and Justin, Cas and his companions took over Ollie Dunbar's roomy tent until they were ready to leave the gulch. Cas decided Cheyenne would be their first stop. Located on the Union-Pacific line, it offered Ginny the fastest way home to Illinois.

Rather than let the four ride double, grateful prospectors donated a coal-box buggy pulled by a spike team, two wheelers and a single leader. Before Cas and Yancy threw the harness on the team and hooked up the traces, however, they had a solemn obligation to fulfill.

Despite only one day's notice, Ollie Dunbar's burial, at the same cemetery where Wild Bill lay, drew armed prospectors from every nook and cranny of the Black Hills.

" 'Earth to earth, ashes to ashes, dust to dust,' " intoned a miner who had been a Methodist preacher back in St. Joe. " 'In sure and certain hope of the Resurrection unto eternal life.' "

"Amen," Cas said softly with the rest. When the pine coffin was lowered and the ropes lifted from under it, he misted up for his own dead, and for the everlasting grief of a wandering son who came home too late.

On his first morning in Cheyenne, Cas slept until the sinfully late hour of nine a.m. The click of a key turning in a lock brought him wide-awake.

"What in Sam Hill?" he said, amazed at the gaudy sight filling the hotel doorway.

A proudly grinning Yancy was decked out in

brand-spanking-new dyed buckskin trousers, a frilled rodeo shirt, a bright red bandanna, stitched calfskin boots, and gaudy, star-roweled spurs of Mexican silver.

"I want to blend in with you frontier types," Yancy explained. "I'm tired of sticking out."

"Oh, sure, you don't want to stick out," Cas managed before paroxysms of sputtering laughter forced him to roll out of the bed and crash to the floor, dragging the blankets with him. "Good God! If it ain't the Back Forty Kid!" he managed between howls of mirth. "Old son, you're either a mail-order cowboy or a circus clown."

"Shoo, you're just jealous," Yancy fired back, admiring himself in a full-length mirror on the door. "Would you believe that nowhere in this entire town do they sell gingersnaps?"

"You want a handkerchief, bawl baby?" Cas teased as he started to dress. "Say, it's good to laugh again."

Both men were a long way from their last shave by the time they reached Cheyenne. Cas scraped at his beard while Yancy shook out a copy of the local *Daily Leader*.

"You know," he said, "you were dead wrong, Cas boy, about that Parrot gun. And the Texas Tornado was also dead wrong when he predicted the vigilantes wouldn't fight hard."

"Why stop there?" Cas admitted, trimming a sideburn. "Don't forget they also jumped us by surprise earlier than I thought, more humble pie for me to eat. But we *won*, didn't we?"

"Yah shoor. And according to this write-up, you were right about law coming to Deadwood once Boggs was killed. Not even a week since we left, and Seth Bullock has brought six U.S. marshals to the gulch. He has eliminated the deadline and laws

will be enforced everywhere. The Regulators have
lit a shuck out of there, all facing John Doe warrants. Two buckboards filled with women have already left for Fort Laramie, with more leaving
soon."

Cas smiled at himself in the mirror. "You'd
ought to be proud, Yancy. I'd call you the real
hero, hoe man. Those gals owe their freedom to
you and that Parrot gun you believed in."

"Shoo! I didn't face three guns at once to kill
Boggs. Speaking of that murderin' wretch—
according to this inkslinger, he was found two days
ago, parts of him eaten down to the bones."

Yancy laughed, but the report made Cas reflec-
tive. He knuckled aside the curtain and glanced out
the second-story window into the busy street. A
stagecoach, swaying recklessly on its thorough
braces, rounded the corner near the newspaper office. The driver raised a dust cloud when he reined
in his team of big Cleveland Bays and threw the
brake forward. The coach shuddered to a stop in
front of Longstreet's Mercantile Store—the only
emporium in town boasting the luxury of a green
canvas awning and sturdy duckboards out front for
rainy days. The only passenger to disembark was a
young woman in a black silk traveling dress.

"Killing Boggs doesn't change much for me,"
Cas admitted. "What I lost can't ever be found."
He watched the woman wait for the driver to hand
her bag down—apparently starting her new life in
the West. "But we got Kathleen and Ginny out of
that slime pit, and other women can now leave. I
reckon that's worth plenty."

In the room next door, Ginny Lofley stood before a long cheval glass, frowning slightly. "Kathleen, are my eyes set too close together?"

Kathleen laughed and clapped her hands. "See?

Only five days since we left that horrid place, and you're asking vain questions. Wonderful! We're recovering."

Ginny, too, laughed. Both women had read the news about events in Deadwood and knew full well that Cas and Yancy had set in motion this historic crackdown on the outlaw town. Ginny smoothed her soft cotton chemise, then wiggled into a whalebone corset that laced up the back and hooked in front. Later that morning, she would board an eastbound train to join her family in Illinois.

"Yes, we're recovering," she repeated, leaning forward while Kathleen drew her laces tight for her. "And Yancy has promised to visit me soon. He's terribly shy with women, but I like him."

"He's shy," Kathleen agreed, tying on her own white lace undersleeves. She had set by a small fortune in faro winnings and had gone out this morning to purchase a cut velvet traveling suit for the journey home. "He's a hopeless romantic and loved—loves—his wife with all his heart. But he's taken with you, Ginny, or he wouldn't travel so far to visit you. I *do* hope you and I may be neighbors someday."

"From your lips to God's ears. Will the three of you be leaving today?"

Kathleen shook her head. "We'll be laying over at least one more day. Long enough that I can buy one more dress."

Ginny spun around from the mirror. "A *wedding* dress?"

Despite Kathleen's radiant smile, warm tears of joy brimmed over. "A wedding dress, yes. When Kathleen Steele leaves Cheyenne, she'll be Mrs. Cas Everett."

Epilogue

August 1878
Sabine County, Texas

"There's Morgan's Hill!" a homesick Yancy called out excitedly. "You two slowpokes are on your own now!"

The low, pine-covered mound marked the spot where a sandy lane left County Line Road for the Carlson and Everett farms.

"Remember," Yancy called out as he spurred his sorrel ahead, "your room will be ready as soon as I air it out. And we'll have you a fine new house before you can say Jack Robinson!"

Cas drove the buggy, Comet tied to the back by a lead line.

"Yancy's awfully excited that you've decided to resume farming your place," Kathleen said. "And so am I. But is it really what you want, Cas?"

"It's *our* place, Mrs. Everett," he corrected his new wife. "Knobby Pendergast has wanted to buy it for years, but if I sell it, I'll have to move my family to new graves in dirt they never owned or worked. Besides, farming was good enough for Pa. No glory in it, either, and I've had my fill of this 'touch you for luck' hogwash."

Cas reined the spike team off the lane when they reached the pine windbreak, easing through the cool, dark shade to the burned-out house. He jumped out, went around to help Kathleen light down, and opened a saddlebag.

"I'll be right back," he promised his wife. "There's something I been waiting to do."

Cas made his solitary walk to the wind-polished knoll. All five crosses remained in place. The sixth cross, of hammered silver and gold, he pulled from its drawstring pouch. The St. Louis jewelers had attached mounting brackets. Cas had never intended it for his mother's grave, but he knelt before her wooden marker and used his shoeing hammer to nail the small cross to the larger one, perfectly centered.

When he'd finished he stood up. "Your labor is not in vain in the Lord," he said softly—one of his mother's favorite sayings.

Cas knew he would carry the pain he felt now to the grave, but since that fateful battle and showdown in Deadwood Gulch, he had signed a private treaty with his Maker. A glorious sun blazed behind distant hills. Cas gazed out on that glory and vowed to make his family proud and their farm flourish.

When he turned, unshed tears filming his eyes, he saw Kathleen waiting for him, her skirt wind wrapped around her legs. Heart swelling, he walked down the hill and returned to the woman who had given his life new meaning—and whose love for him would populate Texas with the next generation of Everetts.

SIGNET

MAX McCOY

THE EARLY DAYS
BEFORE THE LEGEND

A BREED APART
A NOVEL OF
WILD BILL HICKOK

0-451-21987-2

History remembers him as Wild Bill, but he was
born James Butler Hickok, a young man who forged
his future as a scout on the plains, and as a Union
spy during the Civil War. But it was on one
afternoon in Springfield, Missouri, that Hickok
found his calling—with a revolver in his hand.

Available wherever books are sold or at
penguin.com